HEL'S EIGHT

PRAISE FOR *HEL'S EIGHT*

"A real brutal tour de force, pulse pounding action
and eye-opening ideas."
ADRIAN TCHAIKOVSKY, AWARD-WINNING AUTHOR
OF CHILDREN OF TIME, DOGS OF WAR AND MANY MORE

"Sharp, addictive, tightly-paced, with every word in the right
place. I've loved this author since Nunslinger, but they just get
better and better"
JOANNE HARRIS, BEST-SELLING AUTHOR OF CHOCOLAT,
THE GOSPEL OF LOKI AND MANY MORE

"A gritty, transgressive cyberwestern adventure that feels like
Sergio Leone crossed with Mad Max. Glorious!"
PAUL CORNELL, AUTHOR OF THE SHADOW POLICE AND WITCHES
OF LYCHFORD SERIES

"With scalpel-sharp prose, Holborn carves beauty out of a
brutal world where possibilities are both a blessing and a
weapon. For all the sand-blasted action and brawls against
an unknowable terror, it's ultimately the tale of a main
character—a double-sided coin of grace and gruffness—on a
journey for redemption. Holds all the grit of Mad Max: Fury
Road with a smoky mezcal chaser that lingers long after the
final page."
NATHAN TAVARES, AUTHOR OF A FRACTURED INFINITY

PRAISE FOR *TEN LOW*

"Holborn shows what a rich imagination she has."
THE TIMES

"Packed with wildly memorable female characters, the pacey prose keeps things whip-cracking along."
SFX

"Stark Holborn continues to impress. Great characters and a blistering pace."
GARETH POWELL, AUTHOR OF THE EMBERS OF WAR SERIES

"Ten Low showed me the most vibrant desert world since Dune. *[It] leaves the old guard masters in the dust."*
ALEX WHITE, AUTHOR OF THE SALVAGERS TRILOGY

"Stark Holborn's writing is clever, original and thrilling."
R. J. BARKER, AUTHOR OF THE BONE SHIPS AND AGE OF ASSASSINS

"An action-packed SF adventure with an intriguing majority female cast? OH, HELL YES!"
STINA LEICHT, AUTHOR OF PERSEPHONE STATION

"I loved this from beginning to end. Stark Holborn grabs you by the throat on page one and never lets you go!"
CAVAN SCOTT, BESTSELLING AND AWARD-WINNING AUTHOR

By Stark Holborn and available from Titan Books

Ten Low

HEL'S EIGHT

STARK HOLBORN

TITAN BOOKS

Hel's Eight
Print edition ISBN: 9781803362298
Ebook edition ISBN: 9781803362304

Published by Titan Books
A division of Titan Publishing Group Ltd.
144 Southwark Street, London SE1 0UP
www.titanbooks.com

First Titan edition: March 2023

10 9 8 7 6 5 4 3 2 1

A CIP catalogue record for this title is available from the British Library.

Printed and bound by CPI Group (UK) Ltd, Croydon, CR0 4YY.

For Nick

*Lay the coin on my tongue and I will sing
of what the others never set eyes on.*

"DESERT FLOWERS", KEITH DOUGLAS

PROLOGUE

THE TRADE POST stands alone, a dying ember in a hearth too vast for warmth. Not that any trade happens here; when someone will only part with your salvation on credit, it's theft, whichever way you look at it.

The winds crash in vast swells against the walls, as if they want to bear the building away, sweep it from the edge of the moon into the Void. Inside, three mercenaries sit at a table and don't speak.

All have been corroded by the system, pinballing their way between conflicts across the stars, before guttering here, at the bad edge of the system. Lunar Body XB11A, otherwise known as Factus.

One of the mercs has greying hair and a pair of blue fibreglass teeth that don't sit right. The other is younger, marked out as a former terraform rigger by his radiation-damaged face and his hands, swelled to twice the usual size. The third has a shock of blonde hair, shaved on one side to show off a tattoo of allegiance: a silver infinity symbol with her name beneath it. *Gris*. She reaches into the pocket of her grimy yellow uniform and takes out a canister of oxygen, snuffing air from the spigot.

The younger merc looks on, resentfully. A bottle recently full of lurid pink liquid stands on the table before him. Throat Paint, people call it. About the only thing it is good for, swilling grit from a gullet, making you forget your dry mouth and chafed flesh for half a night. He pours the last measure sloppily, splashing his hand, and winces. His knuckles are raw from giving out a beating.

'You,' he slurs. 'Another.'

Across the room the bartend swallows and decants cloudy liquid into a second bottle.

The oldest mercenary watches the younger suck spilled liquor off his hand.

'Clean yourself for love's sake, Matchet,' he says. 'You don't know where they've been.'

'Sure, Vas.'

Matchet downs the last inch of liquor from the bottle and spits a fine spray across his outstretched fingers. The liquid spatters the walls, but most lands on a fourth figure who slumps in the corner, shackled to the stove pipe. One blue eye looks out through tangled, oxide-red hair. The other is swollen shut.

'At least spit it into my mouth,' they croak.

'Shut up, rat,' Vas says.

The figure lets their head fall back, revealing two telltale scabs on their throat from a recently removed prison collar. 'I told you, it's Weasel.'

'Gotta pay for this, Mx,' the bartend says, placing the second bottle down on the table.

Gris shows her teeth and throws a silver token at him. 'Lutho-Plex are paying.'

The bartend turns the silver in his fingers. 'Don't take scrip,' he mutters.

Vas stops pouring and gives him a look; the threat so simple it doesn't need speaking.

The prisoner watches the bartend scuttle away. 'Is this how you plan to find the Seekers?' they ask. 'By drinking rotgut and staring at the walls?'

'Told you to shut up,' Vas growls.

'If you're the best hunters Delos has to offer—'

Matchet tips out of his chair and drives a crusted boot into the prisoner's side, once, twice, three times, his face growing pink with exertion in the tinny air.

'Enough,' Gris barks. 'Don't bust any organs. Lutho-Plex'll cough a hundred if they're alive, dead's only fifty.'

Matchet drops back, agleam with violence, as if all the wrong done to him is bundled in the person at the end of his boot.

The prisoner retches and spits a precious gobbet of fluid, their jumpsuit stained by pale boot prints.

'Water,' they croak.

Gris jerks her head at the bartend, who unlocks a tap with a key from his belt, and dribbles two inches of water into a cup. She takes it and contemplates for a moment before spitting into the liquid. 'All yours, shackleworm.'

The prisoner snatches the offered cup and drinks it down while the mercs roar with laughter.

As if in answer, a gust of wind wracks the building, dampening their amusement.

'What was that?' Vas asks.

'The wind.'

'No.' He raises his head like a cat sniffing air. 'That.'

There's another sound outside, a harsh, throttling cough. The bartend squeaks open the shutter.

'A light,' he murmurs.

Gris strides to the window. 'Seekers?'

'No. Looks like a mule. Someone alone.'

Jaw tight, she takes out her charge gun and arms it. The others do the same. The sound of the engine grows louder until it wheezes and stops somewhere near the stable. Silence stretches, like fabric pulled taut, before a fist bangs on the door. Once, twice, three times.

At Gris's nod, the bartend shoots the bolt and the door flies back, wind screaming in as if it has been waiting outside all this time, furious. It batters the place, sends faded posters flapping, the mercenaries swearing as grit gets in their eyes. Finally, leaning bodily on the door, the bartend is able to shove it closed.

A stranger stands among the settling dust. No one saw them step inside. They look like the Barrens made flesh: every item of clothing sun-bleached, from the cape of ancient thermal blankets to the old flight helmet, bearing a large dent in the back. A shiver lifts the fine hairs of the prisoner's neck before the stranger reaches up to remove the helmet, dust cascading from their shoulders. The hair beneath is grey, frizzed and flattened.

'Bad night,' a rough voice says.

The prisoner stares. The stranger is a woman, perhaps in her sixties, older than anyone they've seen on Factus. Her face has been toasted by the elements, the lines at the edges of her eyes deep and deliberate, as if etched by an artist's hand.

She looks around, sees the prisoner and the guns and raises heavy brows in surprise. Gris smiles slow, spelling out every thought as she takes in the old woman's clothes, her well-laden pack. 'Easy, grandma. We're all friends here.'

'What a storm,' the woman says nervously. 'Thought it'd have my skin clean off and carry it away.'

'Most like,' Vas agrees. 'Nothing to do but sit tight and wait it out.'

Cautiously, the woman pulls out the only free chair and sits down with the three mercenaries and their guns. 'Can't tell you how glad I am to find shelter,' she says, 'travelling gets harder every cycle.' She smiles at the bartend, a real smile, not a threat. He looks almost taken aback by it. 'Do you have pálinka?'

He grunts. 'Throat Paint or brine. Or syrup.'

'Oh, Paint's fine,' the woman says, shaking her wiry hair, sending dust flying.

Matchet is still staring, as if she has fallen from the sky. 'What you doing out here?' he demands.

'Right now, asking myself the same thing.' She shrugs out of the overcape, revealing a heavily stained jumpsuit below. 'I'm on the way to Redemption, to visit a friend. She's a working girl there, just had a child. Made her the toast of the settlement, that. Never thought I'd live to see children on Factus. Poor thing picked the wrong moon to be born on.'

She searches her pack as she speaks. It's stuffed full with water bottles, a canister of oxygen, even the gleam of an airtight. Oranges. Vas licks his stolen teeth.

'Ah,' the woman says, and pulls a packet free. 'Here we are.' She untwists it to reveal a pile of grubs, still greasy with frying oil. 'Care for one?' she asks. Gris inclines her head and picks one out. Matchet shakes his head, disgusted, looking from the woman to his boss.

'Does that offer extend to me?' the prisoner croaks.

The woman hesitates. 'What's the crime?'

'Weasel Monroe here tried to escape a work camp. As you can see, they didn't get far.' Gris leans back, satisfied. 'We'll be escorting them back to justice.'

Weasel gives her a withering glance. 'Can I have a grub?'

She picks one from the table. 'Catch.'

The fat grub tumbles to the floor an arm's length away from Weasel. They stare at it for a long moment before worming onto their side, trying to scrape it towards them with shackled ankles across the filthy floor while the mercs jeer.

'You're working for Lutho-Plex?' the woman asks, once the laughter has subsided. 'I didn't think they patrolled this far out.'

'We're freelance.' Vas smirks. 'On a special detail.'

He reaches into his jacket and takes something out. A much-handled bulletin sheet.

WANTED
BY ORDER OF LUTHO-PLEX

ANY MEMBER OF THE FUGITIVE GANG KNOWN AS
THE SEEKERS

ALSO THEIR LEADER
HEL THE CONVERTER

A SUBSTANTIAL REWARD FOR HER APPREHENSION

The stranger frowns at the words. 'I thought Hel was just a folk tale.'

'Bounty on her's real enough.'

Anxiously, the bartend slides a cup before the stranger.

'Thank you,' she tells him. 'I'll settle up when the evening's done.' She raises the cup to the room, meeting each eye, even the prisoner's as they chew sullenly. 'Egészségedre.'

'Eggy what?' Vas barks.

The woman winces at the taste of the raw liquor. 'An old saying, where I came from on Earth.'

She has their attention. Even Matchet's hostility flickers, a sliver of the boy he must have been showing through, as he learned his planets from the murals on the walls of satellite rest-stops. 'Earth?' His hand rests on the gun he knows he'll use before the night is out. 'Real Earth? Then what are you doing *here*?'

'What's anyone?' She sighs. 'I needed work, went where I could find it. Bounced all the way to this end of the system.'

'Bounced all the way to the hulks,' the prisoner mutters. 'That a collar scar on your neck?'

'Is Weasel a warden-name?' she retorts.

'What's *your* name?' Matchet demands.

The woman looks over her cup. 'Me? Oh, everyone just calls me Pec.'

'Pec.' Gris squashes a grub's head with her thumbnail. 'Aren't you afraid to travel alone?'

'Afraid of what?'

'Lots of bad people in the Barrens. It's a hungry place.'

'Lots of bad,' Vas agrees. 'What with the Seekers waiting to rip you open and take your liver, and then there's those… *things*.'

'You believe in the Ifs?' Pec raises a brow.

'Heard the stories.'

'Yeah and that's what *they* are, tap-licking, air-starved babble.' Gris snorts into her glass. 'Invisible luck demons.' She laughs again. 'The only *things* out there are escaped convicts and lunatics.'

Pec only shakes her head. 'I'm not sure. You hear such terrible tales. Like that beetle hawker and her family, near Nozhovka, shot all to pieces for a few miserable gallons of fuel. Tragic.'

Matchet jerks, as if stung. Gris tilts her head at him to stay silent. Unsaid words fill the room like smoke. Even Weasel goes still, aware of the tension, of every breath being taken.

'To think we might be stuck here all night.' Pec sighs.

Gris's fingers inch towards her gun, only to stop dead when something clatters onto the table. A heavy silver coin, etched with a crude representation of a snake eating its own tail. The stranger flips it over to reveal an infinity symbol. In the fitful glow of the sodium lamps, the loops look dark as scabs.

'Anyone for a game?' she asks.

'Where the hell did you get that?' Vas asks, frowning at the coin. It looks just like the scrip in his own pocket, but older, un-refined. 'You work for Lutho-Plex too?'

Pec laughs. 'Lux, no. Someone gave it to me. So how about it?'

'No.' Vas draws back from the table. 'It's dangerous.'

'To play at chance?' She toys with the coin, sending it dancing over her scarred, worn fingers. 'What could happen?'

Vas stares ahead fixedly. 'It's banned in the camps.'

She smiles and sends the coin spinning through the air. They all flinch – but the coin simply clatters to a stop, resting on the snake.

'Snake eats all. I'd win, if we were playing for anything.' She nods to Gris. 'How about your jacket?'

Gris squints. 'In exchange for what?'

Pec reaches into her pocket and brings out a leather sheath. Inside, is an old, worn scalpel. 'This is quite precious. An heirloom.'

'Why not.'

With a nod, Pec goes to ask the bartend for a rag to clean the spilled liquor. Immediately, Vas lurches from his chair.

'Gris,' he hisses. 'Don't do it. Those *things*—'

'You saw. She tossed. Nothing happened.'

'I don't like it. Don't like her.'

Matchet shifts so that his gun is in easy reach. 'You don't need to much longer.'

'Let's do it now, then. I swear I seen her face somewhere before. And she knew about Nozhovka—'

Gris pats Vas's cheek hard and shoves him away as the woman returns. 'Let's play.'

'Best of three?'

Pec sends the coin spinning above the table. It lands on infinity.

'Eight,' she murmurs.

Gris shakes the coin like someone in supplication before thumbing it skyward.

Eight.

Weasel watches as the stranger reaches for the coin. For a moment her fingers look red, as if slick with blood.

Eight.

Gris bares her teeth in anticipated triumph as she grabs the coin. For an instant, her hand is that of a corpse, the knuckles scraped to dull white nubs, tossed into a bucket with a hundred others.

Eight.

She scowls. Outside, something tumbles in the wind. Vas looks up, jumpy, but his boss is focused, her pupils pipped as the stranger prepares to throw. The bartend wrenches at the shuttered window, peering out nervously.

The coin spins and sparks, clattering to the table.

'Snake,' Pec says.

It happens instantly, so fast the prisoner doesn't even have a chance to scream. Their awareness is ripped from their skull as the world turns inside out, as *things*, numberless, vast beyond imagining, rush upon them. The mercenaries are screaming, firing wildly at the air. Only the stranger stands untouched, her eyes dark and inhuman as the mouth of a gun. The world is splitting apart, realities tangling in seething mass, but she moves through them all, sharp and deliberate – a needle threading worlds.

As Gris spins to shoot her, the woman's arm flies, metal flashing in her left hand to slash the mercenary's throat before she can cry out. Matchet fires, but the stranger simply pushes Gris's convulsing body into the path of the bullets, seizing up her fallen gun and blowing Matchet backwards against the wall a second later. Vas writhes on the ground, holding his head and shrieking in agony.

In terror the prisoner looks up, into the stranger's eyes.

A silver bird crashes into dark sand. War machines stamped with infinity roll over the bones of the dead. A snake eats its own tail. One life, many. A tally…

The prisoner heaves in a breath, choking. Their ears are ringing, their head pounding but they are alive. Through streaming eyes, they look up at the trade post. It is just that, a small dismal shack, filled with sounds of the dying and the smell of blood, and the stranger is just a woman, cold-eyed and bloody but human. Whatever was here has gone.

A pounding at the door. The woman strides to answer.

Seekers step into the place, six of them, seven, carrying the desert on their ragged clothes. Any relief the prisoner feels vanishes when they see the belts, hung with scalpels, hatchets, saws... The Seekers' boots are blood-stained, their hands cracked with chemicals, their eyes sad and raw from running roads between worlds.

'Done, Pec?' asks one, a huge woman with slicked-back red hair.

The stranger jerks her chin at the bartend. 'These were the mercs who killed the family at Nozhovka?'

The bartend gives a silent nod, pressed against the wall.

With a choke, Vas lurches to his feet and bolts for the back room, sending crates toppling.

'Alive?' the Seeker asks, weighing a knife in her hand.

Pec shakes her head coldly. 'They killed five. Three adults. Two children.'

The Seeker nods. 'Then he owes.'

Calmly, she follows the oldest mercenary into the back room. There's the sound of a brief struggle, then a choked-off scream.

In horror, Weasel tries to scramble backwards. They've heard the stories. Seekers leave no survivors.

A shadow falls across them. The stranger. She kneels and takes their chin in her fingers, studying the bruises, the collar scars. Weasel feels the tackiness of the blood, smells its overpowering iron tang.

'You escaped a Lutho-Plex compound?'

Weasel nods frantically. 'I couldn't stay there. Inmates kept disappearing, dying...'

The stranger's grip tightens. '*They* need lives. Do you understand?'

'Yes,' Weasel whispers, although they don't.

Seekers come forwards to release the shackles and haul them to their feet. Upright, they tower over the woman, but there's nothing they can do to stop her as she unsheathes the scalpel and lowers it to the back of their hand, scoring a symbol into flesh: two sloping lines and one across. Done, she wipes the blade on a piece of rag. 'So we know you.'

Weasel stands, stunned, as one of the Seekers drops a medical kit onto the table beside them. The trade post has become a scene of slaughter, blood in great pools across the floor, the stench of sundered flesh in the air. But Seekers work fast, and already they are packing the cryo-crates with flesh and blood, carrying the organs away from the mercenaries' plundered corpses, ready to be sped to the desperate and the damned on this and other moons.

'Leave the remains outside for the wind to bury,' the woman instructs the cowering bartend. 'Show what happens to people who take what belongs to *them*.'

'Wait,' Weasel croaks as she steps towards the door. 'Are you her? Are you Hel?'

The woman looks back. The wind plucks at her tattered clothes and for an instant her face seems to slip, blurring into another. Her worn lips twitch into a smile.

'We are all Hel,' she says.

ONE

THE
BOOK
OF
THE
DOCTOR

THIRTY YEARS LATER

THE SAND IS blood-hot with noon, grey as emptied flesh. It eddies against my boots, settles there in small drifts like a creature seeking shelter from the sky. I nudge it away, staring at the prints that lead away from my heels and out into the wastes, towards the Edge.

Did I walk from there? My skin feels chalky, dust an unwelcome passenger in the seams of my clothes. Maybe I walked from there. Maybe I was dreaming again, following ghosts of my other selves through the walls of worlds.

I blink hard. Too long out here. Too long alone. Sometimes I forget my own face and have to study what looks back at me from the cloudy tin mirror. I'm not sure, these days, which version of me my mind's eye holds as true – the pilgrim in her coarse woven clothes, the medic in her uniform, the collared-convict, the dead woman of blood and sand… The face I see is none of them. Lean as a century trunk, skin wind-scoured, brown hair hanging in ropes to my chin. But it's the eyes that are most different. Some days, I feel like I could reach into the void of my pupil and pull myself through, into another self, into another reality where I never made the choices that brought me here.

A faint breeze eddies, stirring the trinkets that hang from the leafless century trunk beside the shack. Wishbones and defaced playing cards, dice with their pips chiselled off, vulture feathers, long-desiccated snakes and rats. A tree of dead luck. Once I would have frowned and called it heresy. Later, I might have scoffed and called it superstition. Now, I know it for what it is: protection.

Everything is still. Rowdy sits silently on the front step, taking the sun's heat into his battered old body, his one remaining ear swivelled towards me. Nothing for kliks. So why do I feel like something is coming?

A dangerous thought. I shake it from my head and go to fetch my hat. There's work to be done.

I place a hand on Rowdy's warm back, waking him from his doze. His eyes flash weakly as he recognises me.

Doc, he barks through metal jaws.

I smile back at him, this collection of circuit boards and cobbled together parts who has been my old friend for so long. Both of us leftover from the war, still existing, far beyond the purpose we were built or trained for.

When I walk, he sways after me on bandy legs. I let him. It's too hot to move fast, anyway, the sun sliding off my hat and onto my shoulders like molten metal as I follow the fuel line that runs from my shack out into the wastes, connecting my generator to a makeshift shelter, half a klik out.

The cryo-cooler sits there in a tiny square of shade. Even a decade old it is one of the most valuable things I own, advanced tech by U Zone standards. There's only one reason thieves or Road Agents haven't stolen it: the Seekers' symbol, emblazoned on the side in crimson paint. Two sloping lines and one across. The twin of the scar on my chest.

Slowly, I kneel and open the lid. Dry ice billows out, vaporising instantly in the day's heat. The cooler is full of blood. Twelve bags of it, glinting dark and secret red. There are other offerings too, sterile and sealed. By rights, I should be in this box, every useful part of me separated into a Seekers' harvest. If it weren't for *them*, I would be.

I close the lid, unhook the chest and lift those stolen lives into my arms.

By the time we make it back to the shack, Rowdy's gait has become even more erratic and I am gasping from the heat and the weak oxygen, feeling every hard year lived on this moon. How long now, since I first stumbled, bleeding and delirious from the wrecked escape craft, since I shed the name they gave me on the hulk? Seven years? Eight? Years passed not in time but in hunger and bloody sunsets and the heart-breaking beauty of desert dawns, riding the limits, never staying longer than a night for fear that *they* will appear at my heels and undo the work I've done, the lives wrenched back from death.

Re-hooking the chest to the generator, I wipe the sweat from my face and shake a couple of breath beads from the tin.

Be content, I tell my body as the plastic shatters between my teeth and the dex-amphetamine dissolves, mimicking a rush of oxygen I have not felt in so long. I wash the shards down with a dipper of treated water from the drum, pungent from whatever chemicals the local water baron mixed in to keep it good.

It sloshes against the walls of my belly, reminding me that humans must eat. There are a few unlabelled airtights left; a gift from a patient. I hack the lid from one. Silkworm grubs, I see, far past the expiry date given them on some distant planet.

Rowdy sways in the shade, his grey-brown body clicking as it cools and I drop to the stoop beside him to work the rich, greasy flesh between my teeth. The grubs are full of memories; the face of a child who was not a child wrinkled in disgust, a feast among friends in another life. Recollections that are almost worth the ache of loneliness after I have swallowed.

Just as I scoop a second grub, something sets my nerves to thrumming. These days I can feel the land like a second skin. Licking oil from my fingers, I reach up for the pair of cracked binoculars.

Far off, I see it: a dust cloud, rolling towards me across the flats. It is too high for a mule or a mare. A buzzard of some kind, then. I squint for detail but find none. Road Agents ride buzzards – no one else can afford the fuel.

Tro-uble, Rowdy growls, one of the only words he has left in his bank. *Trou-ble*.

I lay a hand on his sensor to tell him I've heard. He's right. We have few options. Run and the buzzard would overtake the mule and shoot us down before we got far. Lock the door and risk being burned alive.

And what if it's a patient or a penitent?

Then I'll be ready.

First the long, threadbare scarf that wraps my neck from collarbone to earlobe, hiding the brutal scar around my throat but leaving the one on my chest exposed. Second, the scalpel. My only weapon.

The buzzard wallows to the ground some distance off, its engine cackling into the stillness. The rider dismounts and for a time, just stares at me through smoked glass goggles. I stare back from the darkness of the doorway.

There is a reason I live out here, a handful of kliks from the Edge, where compasses and navigation systems no longer work. The point where reason frays, fear takes over and the dead loiter at the edges of the firelight. The border of reality. Walk in and never walk out. It is more than enough to deter all but the most desperate of patients, the most wracked of penitents.

This person does not look like either. Nor do they look like a Road Agent, in their long black duster that could be real leather and their broad-brimmed hat and dazzle scarf. They look more like a bounty hunter. A red light winks at their hip, reflecting in grease-black body armour: a charge gun, primed and ready to fire.

Warned, Rowdy barks, eyes flashing. *Warned*.

'You the Leech?' a voice calls across the distance. 'The Blood Doctor?'

Whoever's speaking sounds young, too young to die. I grip the scalpel. 'I am. Are you a patient? Do you wish to heal your future?'

A low laugh drifts across the dust. 'Can't heal a dead girl.'

The laugh is familiar, so familiar that it bypasses my brain to stab straight into the crumbling remains of the woman I once was, threatening to drag her out into the light.

Rowdy whines as I take a step forwards. I am wrong. I have to be wrong. It is a trick of the Edge, a phantom from another world, a dream summoned by loneliness.

'General?' I whisper.

The stranger tugs the dazzle scarf from her face, and smiles. 'Hello, traitor.'

∞

'How did you find me?'

My hands move across the shelves like a machine's, taking down cups as my brain whirls in confusion.

The young woman leans in the doorway. 'Wasn't easy. You buried yourself deep, Low.'

That name is a hook, dragging up the past. 'No one calls me that, anymore.'

She looks around at the shelves that hold medical supplies and dried herbs, the ant farm and spider house. 'So I see.'

Warned, Rowdy persists, clumping in after the girl. *Warned*.

Rolling her eyes, she bends down in the doorway, removing her hat and scarf to show Rowdy her face, so he can memorise it.

As his brain whirrs, I see her clearly for the first time, this young woman who once fell from the sky into my life, who once died in the desert beside me.

If Rowdy were a newer model, connected to some wire receiver,

34

he would record her face, run a query through the Accord's systems to ask who she was and receive an impossible answer:

Name: Former General Gabriella Ortiz, Implacabilis, Hero of the Battle of Kin

Rank: Commander of the Western Air Fleet of the Accorded Nations

Company: Minority Force (defunct)

Age: Thirteen Years

Status: Deceased (five years, three months)

But Rowdy's only a battered old guard dog who barely works anymore, and so his eyes just flash uselessly while he whirrs. As if she knows the problem, the young woman puts him out of his misery.

'Ortiz,' she tells him clearly.

Ortzzzz, he repeats.

'Close enough.' She snorts and stands to look me in the eye.

Five years have wrought many changes. The child with the mind of a battle-hardened war veteran and a body and brain pumped full of enhancements is gone. Now I am looking at a young woman. Her once-full cheeks are lean, the premature lines between her brows and around her mouth have deepened, and at some point over the years her nose has been broken. Her black hair is tightly scraped back, shaved on the sides in G'hal fashion and I see that the tattoo of rank that once marked her temple has been removed, not burned away clumsily with a hot iron – deserter-style – like mine, but by a professional, leaving nothing but discoloured flesh.

'You are alive,' I say uselessly.

Her smile is a challenge. 'So are you.'

I turn away, back to the cups, not knowing whether to laugh and grab her into an embrace or shove her out of the door. Her boots clang as she stalks around the shack. Rowdy follows her creakily, as if trying to remember a question.

'*This* is what you left us for? I know you're used to roughing it but you could at least live in a proper building.'

The guilt that rises in me belongs to another woman, I remind myself, and take a breath.

'I am glad you're well.'

She raises a dark brow. 'I'd say the same but I'm not sure living in the arsehole of the U Zone as some kind of witch doctor counts as "well".'

I shove down a flicker of annoyance. 'I am just a medic.'

She looks pointedly at the cryo-cooler. 'Don't know many medics who deal in blood and tell fortunes.'

'If I can save a life, I will.'

She looks at my hands and an expression crosses her face; distaste and almost pity as she takes in the two hundred and thirty-eight scars that cover the backs of my hands from wrist to fingertip. Some of them are old and pale, others new and scabbed. The tally.

'You're still trying to make amends.'

She makes it sound so futile. Something within me shivers, threatening to sunder.

'What are you doing here, Gabi?'

Her lips twist. 'You've been gone so long you've forgotten the rules.' Before I can stop her, she seizes up the bottle of liquor and sloshes some into the cups. 'Drink first, questions later.' She raises one to me. 'Egészségedre.'

Once I would have told her that she was too young to drink, she who had commanded armies before her eleventh birthday. Now, I take a cup, knowing it contains trouble.

I meet her eyes. 'Egészségedre.'

The liquor is not much more than rectified alcohol and flavourings, but she doesn't complain, only winces at the taste. She glances up and beneath the brash exterior I see weariness, not just from the long nights and perilous days spent in the saddle to find me.

She swallows. 'I'm here to bring you back.'

Nerves sour my gut. 'To where?'

'The land of the living.'

I'm not dead, I almost say, but swallow it back. According to all records, I'm as dead as she is. 'This is living. I treat people here. I'm the only free medic for a thousand kliks.'

'This isn't living. It's hiding.'

I grip the cup and say the words I have mouthed to myself so often, every time I wipe the blood from my hands. 'I am at peace.'

She – creature of war – tells me what I already know. 'There is no such thing.' She sits back in the chair, watching me. 'You

37

don't know what's been happening out there, do you? Beyond the U Zone?'

'No wires here.'

'Then you won't know that we lost Landfall Five.'

Landfall Five, the name drags images from the past; an Accord base exploding with gunfire, Malady Falco's bar filled with G'hals and smugglers and black-market dealers from across the moon… with people I once called friends.

'Lost it how? Is Falco—'

'*Now* she's concerned. Now she cares. Falco's alive. Peg too. But we lost five G'hals. Rat, Linny, Vainglorious, Toad and Olia.'

'The Accord?'

She lets out a noise of disgust. 'You think a handful of grunts who can't even hold a gun properly could take us? We *owned* that base. Until the Accord sold it from under us.'

Before I can ask she reaches into her jacket, takes something out and tosses it onto the table. A coin. It fills my eyes with silver as it spins, and in the silver are images – *blood on sand, machines of war stamped with infinity, mirrored eyes reflecting death* – I drag myself away from that endless tide and reach down cautiously to pick it up. One face of the coin shows an ouroboros, a snake devouring its own tail. On the other is a figure of eight on its side. Eternity and infinity. No choice at all. The whispers at the back of my head grow stronger, *their* presence rising. I let it fall back to the table with a clatter.

'What is that?'

'Xoon coin. Scrip. Worth eighty on Delos.'

I have seen it before, I'm sure of it, but I cannot think where. 'Xoon,' I murmur, trying to dredge the name from the sludge of the past.

'Lutho Xoon. The Nickel King himself.' Gabi jerks her chin at the coin. 'He's buying up Factus one settlement at a time. And the Accord are selling, whether the residents agree or not.' Her smile is hard. 'Accord have been losing ground to the gangs for years. They don't like how much power Xoon has, but they're hoping this way they can save face.'

I stare at that glimmering silver. 'Why does Xoon want Factus? There's nothing to be had, here.'

'Nothing but control. He already owns Delos, unofficially. If he controls Factus too, he has most of the Border Moons in his pocket. He's building an empire, Low. And the Accord are stretched too thin to stop it.' She sloshes more liquor into her cup. 'Xoon has an army of private mercs. They took Landfall in hours. No smaller settlement will stand a chance. They have better weapons, better vehicles, better armour…'

Realisation creeps like ice into my belly. 'This has nothing to do with me.'

'You think they won't come here too? They're here already. What the Accord won't sell, Xoon is taking. He's got the Alcaides deputising any bit of meat with eyes that can hold a gun.'

I push myself away from the table but she is faster, as she always was.

'We need you, Low. We are fighting back but there aren't enough of us.'

'I can't do anything. I'm just a medic.'

'No, you're not. You're a traitor and a killer, and by your own words, you owe.' She grabs for one of my hands, scarred with the tally. 'You want to save thousands of lives to make up for ones you took? Well this is how you do it. Come back with me. Help us make a bargain with the Seekers.'

My heart is beating faster than it should, my head spinning from her presence. She is like a flame, burning away possibilities, illuminating the past I keep hidden in shadow, for fear it will drive me mad, as it did once before as I sat in a cell on the hulks. *Eight thousand four hundred and forty-seven.*

I snatch my hand away. 'I can't take life.'

'But you'll watch it taken.' She shakes her head. 'Still a hypocrite. Still a typical Limiter, even after all these years.'

I stand there beneath her gaze that pierces flesh, her more-than-human mind trying to solve the problem of me. In the quiet, the ants chitter in their farm, the spiders creep noiselessly and Rowdy's insides clunk and hum through his unfathomable programming.

'We once fought together, Low, despite everything. I don't believe you'll turn your back on us now.'

It wasn't me who fought, I want to say, but it was: the part of me I've been trying to drown in dust for five long years. When I don't answer she just turns away and takes up her hat.

'If you find your guts, we gather at the Barebones, in Sagacity.' She stops in the doorway, her head half-turned. 'Don't let the past burn up your future.'

I wait until the sounds of her footsteps fade and the buzzard's engine cackles into life before opening my eyes. Then, as Rowdy lets out a confused whirr, I take up the bottle of liquor, and drink.

The Personal Notes of Pec "Eight" Esterházy
Lunar Body XB11A – now "Factus"
Lutho-Plex Outpost

Start from the beginning, Yussef says. I'm not sure which beginning he's talking about. My beginning? No. I'm an old woman and the living ink in this screen would run out before I got halfway. Although, who's to say all of this didn't start long ago, with a single choice. Which choice? The day I chose to leave old Earth? The day I decided to run for the Western System? Maybe not one choice, but a million. Too complicated for me to understand.

Fine, then. I'll begin on the day my life changed direction. The day I was summoned to the warden's office on the Intra–System Penal Vessel *Nordstrom*. I had no idea of what was to come, as I stood on the soft carpet, listening to Lester Sixofus on the radio, his voice like honey to my ears after two years among the screaming metal of the hulks.

'Name?' someone asked.

I didn't open my eyes. 'Esterházy.'

'Eight,' came the correction.

I had to look then. Warden Delacey didn't look back. He never did. Guess he found it easier to let our faces blur into meat that way.

'What do you want?' I asked him.

The guard who escorted me raised her stun-stick, but backed off at a sign from him. That made me smile. Words had power, even on the hulks, and Delacey was scared of what might come spilling from my lips. Like the details in the ledger I kept aboard my old ship, the *Heavenly Rest*.

Name: Francis Stefan Delacey
Drink: Pálinka with a cherry. No ice.
Company: Female. No tattoos. Prefers brunettes.
Note: Let an inmate suffocate in an airlock during his first
     tour. Haunted by it.
Works for the penitentiary system. Pays well and on time.

If I talked, my words would drip through the gantries of the hulk and there'd be no stuffing them back in again. Delacey knew that. Hated me for it.

'Eight,' he said, not looking. 'You put in a request to be considered for work-release.'

Everyone did, if they weren't already insane. 'So?'

'We've received a request for labourers. We're sending a cohort.'

'On-world?'

'On-moon. Factus.'

Factus. I tried to picture the star chart that used to hang on my parlour wall and the far-off specks of the Border Moons.

'They finished terraforming?'

His lips twisted. 'Good enough for rudimentary habitation.'

A barb. I let him think it landed.

'The company is Lutho-Plex, a mining concern,' he continued, jabbing at the screen. 'They need workers. The offer is a one-year reduction in sentence, the remainder of which shall be served as hard labour under their supervision.' He was already filling in my details. 'Once you are released, you will be required to remain officially domiciled on Factus for a period of five years. Do you understand?'

The stamp was already in his hand, ready to press down and pack me away. A year off my sentence, free of the hulks... Lester Sixofus whispered from the radio, reminding me that all across the system, people were living their lives in sweetness and sickness. I raised my head.

'No.'

'No?'

'I mean, no, I don't understand. Why would a mining company want me? Young blood's better suited to hard labour.'

He smiled coldly. 'They're not fussy.'

Of course. Once I was deployed off-site, there'd be no easy way to send me back. He'd be rid of me. He could rest, knowing I was far away, being worked to death. His sin, absolved.

He returned to the form. 'You'll need a sentence name.'

'I'll keep the Eight.'

'They don't like numbers in the mines. Too many of you.' He took a book out of his desk drawer, a prison-issue thesaurus with a grey cover and sticky cellulose pages. He thumbed through it, the vein in his temple ticking away, marking the seconds until I was out of his sight. 'What would suit you?' he murmured. '"Taint"? "Sleaze"? "Venal"? Have we had a "Venal" yet?'

Gave him my sweet smile. 'What about "Choke"?'

He froze.

'"Peccable",' he finally said.

Capable of sinning. It was true, and as warden-names went, I'd heard a lot worse. I shrugged and he jabbed the new name into the screen like a starving bird at dry earth.

Tap, his finger went, *tap, tap, tap*.

My vision blurred, and the tapping was the sound of metal, not flesh: *a scalpel clanging against a belt, a silver coin rapped against a table, darkness and whirling sand and a woman's face, with wide brown eyes and a scar on her throat...*

'Approved.' I was back in his office, filled with the stench of his relief. 'Take her away.'

WAKE ABRUPTLY, AS if someone has yelled in my ear.

Motionless, I listen. The night is quiet, save for the clink and clatter of the trinkets on the tree, the flap of the tarpaulin that covers the mule, the distant roar of the Edge. There are no boots scuffling in the dust, no propellant on the air, no clacks or creaks of an ambush. Rowdy stands silently with his head against the wall, oblivious to any presence. And yet I know on the other side of the door, someone is watching.

Slowly, I push back the ex-army blanket. No telling what time it is. The fire in the stove is almost out, just embers in thick coats of ash. I shake them awake, force the last feeble beats from their red hearts.

The wind gives a moan, works its fingers through a gap in the walls to trace my throat. I take up the scalpel, and – inch by inch – push open the door.

At the light's limit she waits, her grey hair caught like wool on the wind of another time and place. Perhaps even the wind that buried her body.

'Esterházy?' I whisper.

The dead woman looks at me with eyes that first opened on old Earth. She is not alone. *They* are with her; I can feel *their* attention on me. Not eyes. *They* don't have eyes. I try to stay calm, to keep my hands from trembling even as every nerve in my body screams for me to slam the door and bury my head in the blanket.

'What is it?' I ask.

Esterházy opens her mouth to speak, but all that emerges is dark sand, pouring past her teeth. I know that sand; I've walked endless dunes of it, through the Edge. Through hell.

She opens her mouth wider and the trickle becomes a rush, revealing something silver on her tongue.

A coin.

At the sight of it, *their* presence grows stronger, turning my stomach inside out. Esterházy spits the coin onto her palm and holds it up in fingers of wind-scoured bone.

Snake on one side, eight on the other. The same as the coin on my table. Eternity and infinity, no choice at all.

In horror I realise what's about to happen. *Heads or tails?* her smile says.

Don't! I try to shout, too late.

She throws the coin into the air and *they* surge around me, battering my mind with images, clawing through the web of my being, searching for something but I cannot ask *them* what or why because *they* are beyond such things, *they* are beyond all meaning…

A choke escapes me, into silence. Shaking hard, I open my eyes. The night is empty. No dead woman, no beings beyond comprehension, just the whistling wind.

I sink down onto the step. There's a *clunk* from behind me as Rowdy waddles forwards to lean his metal chin on my shoulder.

I reach up and hold his head, wondering how this creature of old circuit boards and bad welding knows when I need comfort, or whether his sensors are just broken.

Doc, he wheezes and I close my burning eyes, wishing he were right and that I am what I appear to be: a poor, mad medic with a mind full of nightmares and an aching brain from too much mezcal.

But of course, I am not. Because when I swipe my eyes and lead Rowdy back inside, the two-faced coin is still there on the table, and so is the future.

∞

My imagined peace holds for another day; until I have no choice but to let what is in the cryo-chest spoil, or make the journey into the U Zone. Into danger.

I wait until dusk. Even mad folk know to fear the dark, and most tend to stay within the confines of a settlement or dug-in once the light starts to fail. I stash the cryo-chest on the back of the mule and lift Rowdy onto the seat beside me, securing his legs so he won't fall over, setting his collar to blink red. It's all for show. He can't open fire, or do anything to prevent an attack except wheeze his confused warnings, but sometimes his presence is enough to make mule-thieves think twice.

I check my pockets for breath, only to touch cold metal. The coin – the silver, two-faced Xoon coin – is in my pocket. I don't remember putting it there. Stuffing it away, I tug goggles onto my face and set out for Paranoia.

It is the closest thing to a town, out here; a ragged collection of habs and shacks scattered within suspicious-glancing distance of each other. Once called Neue Freiheit by its founders – a group of Limiter radicals whose dreams of liberty far overshot the beliefs of the Free Limits – it did not end well. But the people who found the carnage and decided to settle down among it must have known its name, because at some point Neue became Noia became Paranoia.

I rev the mule up onto the ridge that runs like a broken spine through this part of the U Zone. From up here, it looks beautiful. The pale dust glows and dusk bathes the sky with lilac-pink-falling-blue, colours too soft to exist in the scorching daylight. A handful of ships wink through the terraform, orbiting in bitter cycles. To the west, Factus's sister moon Delos rolls in her oily shimmer, our planet Brovos rises, pale and stained pink, like the milk it produces marred by blood. And beyond it all…

The Void. Pure darkness. Pure possibility. Like staring into the shining black of a raptor's eye and seeing something raw and wordless.

A red flicker drags my gaze away. Rowdy's head is twisted to one side, his collar flashing as he barks his warning.

A second later I hear people slithering away down the steep sides of the ridge into the ravine. I lay a hand on Rowdy's back to quiet him. We have no trouble with the Barranca Boys. They know my mule is worthless. They know too who treats them when a trap springs wrong, when there are bones to be mended, burns to heal.

I wait as one of them reels in the garrotte that stretches across the trail in double-quick time, as another disarms the trap that would have sent me tumbling down the slope into their canyon. Then, I roll the mule onwards.

Eventually, the track begins to descend, plunging through rocks into the shallow valley of Paranoia. The trail looks empty of carnage, no signs that the Road Agents have been around, but still I drive carefully. The U Zone never stays the same. There are always new gangs springing up, turf wars, newcomers who don't know how things are done or don't care, who are ready to die stupidly or violently and take as many people as they can with them.

As the mule wallows down onto the plain, its headlights catch on a rusted post. The tribute station, set away from the town. Tonight, the manacles welded to it are empty, the dirt stained but dry. But I have seen it occupied by people who have taken lives and await the judgement of the Seekers, to find out if they will be set free, taken, or cut open as tribute for Hel the Converter.

I look away. I do what I can.

Paranoia is filled with the usual activity in a place where there are no authorities to interfere, no supplies save what the smugglers bring, no hospitals or infrastructure beyond what's cobbled together by those mad enough to try and make a life here. Screams of laughter from the Token House, a waft of music breaking through static of the transmitter, like the sun through cloud, gone before it can soothe. Pungent smoke spirals into the air; I pass a bonfire in an abandoned lot, the flames dancing puce and turquoise and purple from whatever is being burned, silhouettes flailing and staggering. Somewhere, a man cries a name over and over. Making for the brightest lights, I roll the mule to a stop alongside the mares and burros and buzzards outside of Lazar's place.

Alacránía, the sign says. *Sting Parlour. Klinika.*

As the engine dies away, I listen, but all seems quiet enough, the dried scorpions outside the door twisting in the night wind, a faint green scent of ghost agave and prickly pears rising from the dusty garden, drinking what blood-tainted water Lazar throws them from the surgery.

Like me, Lazar treats all-comers. Snakebites and plough accidents, charge burns and stab wounds, wire cuts, yellowrot and the slow, wracking diseases that have no name except loneliness and exhaustion. Unlike me, he charges a price to save a life. Those who cannot pay have one of two destinations: Seeker tribute, or the maggot farm.

'Rowdy,' I say softly. 'Stay.'

He yaps silently, metal jaws creaking.

'Good boy.'

Hefting the chest in my arms, I push my way inside.

Immediately the smell hits me, stale sweat and sweet liquor and chemicals. Like the sign says, Lazar's is many things to many people. Part sting parlour, part bar, part clinic and hospital. Four Zoners in various states of intoxication sit slumped in old pilots' chairs beneath the scorpion cages, some semi-conscious, their eyes rolled back in venom-bliss, others clutching freshly stung arms or hands, willing on the toxic high. A skinny individual with century-stained lips makes a gesture over their ears and eyes when they see me, muttering to themselves in what sounds like Russian. *May my thoughts be clear.* A man in a tatted Accord army jacket – AWOL by the look of him – raises his bandaged head miserably from his arm, where a catheter feeds, siphoning his blood into a canister behind the bar. His fee for Lazar's doctoring.

The inner door squeaks open and Lazar appears, sloughing his hands with hygiene powder. He smiles when he sees me.

'Doc.'

I nod back. 'Doctor.'

He smirks at our little joke, the extra syllable an acknowledgement of the truth between us: that he was a professionally trained surgeon and I a bare-bones army medic. That he once worked with clean, lab-grown synthesised flesh in the great warehouse city of Asclepius on Jericho, rather than with what I bring him now in my battered cryo-box.

I have never said so aloud, but Lazar is one of the reasons I chose this place to settle near, when – after four years – the wandering became too much for my bones. I have no idea how he ended up here. Don't ask, the unspoken rule of the U Zone. Despite his warden-sounding name, there are no prison scars on his neck to suggest time served. And his tattoos of rank – those of a Surgeon-Major in the Accord Medical Corps – are still clear on the deep brown skin of his temple. I sometimes catch him glancing at the pink burn scars on my own temples, perhaps wondering which side

I fought for, whether we ever served in the same field hospital, or if I worked across the divide, patching up the Limiters his Accord soldiers blew apart. I wonder what he would do if I told him *both*. Likely, he wouldn't care. He might even smile and say, *same*.

He jerks his head. 'What do you have for me?'

The eyes of the drinkers follow us through the doorway into the surgery, where Lazar's own cryo-unit thrums.

'Twelve pints, three different types. Flesh. And eyes.'

'Thank Lux. I was almost out.'

He works quickly, stacking the bags of blood among the few others, carefully storing the caskets of flesh.

'Someone came looking for you, the other day,' he says to the blood. 'Hunter, by the looks of her.'

His voice is casual, but it doesn't do to forget how sharp Lazar is, beneath the rust of this place. A born speculator. He doesn't know who I was, I am certain of that. But he might take a chance on betraying me if the payout was high enough.

'That so.'

He pushes himself to his feet. 'She was on her own, so I figured the Road Agents would get her long before she found you. Looks like I was right.' I smile back, a bare muscle movement, keeping the past from my face. 'Drink?'

'Of course.'

I follow Lazar through the fizzing blue UV light, back into the bar where he takes down a bottle of liquor and sets the ersatz coffee to brew. A poster is pinned to the wall, the word "BANNED" in a dozen languages, followed by pictures of dice, playing cards, sticks, coins, all with crosses through them. No chance. No luck. No hazard. Nothing that might call to *them*.

Deathbringer, the dead voices on the wind seem to whisper as I take a seat. *Troublecrow*.

The man paying with blood had passed out on his own arm. While Lazar's back is turned I lean over, and twist off the catheter. The stranger with the century-stained lips watches me with bugging eyes.

'Alla nostra,' Lazar says, setting a glass of scorpion whiskey and a cup of acrid black coffee down before me.

I raise my glass to his and drink. The whiskey stings my cracked lips and dry throat like it's supposed to. But it washes away some of the road dust, helps me remember that I am human after all, not just a wandering Leech.

I chase it down with a sip of coffee. Eye-watering, but with a ghost of sweet cactus syrup. Lazar must be feeling generous.

Glancing at the strung-out Zoners, I reach into my pocket for the coin.

'Ever seen one of these?' I pull the coin from my pocket. The snake seems to writhe in the dim blue light.

He has, I can tell from the way his head twitches, but he only shrugs. 'Delos coin, isn't it? Where'd you get it?'

Two questions to my one. Nothing is free in the U Zone.

'Someone gave it to me.'

'A patient?'

'A penitent.' I turn it in my fingers. 'What do you know about Xoon?'

Lazar's eyes narrow for the barest second. 'What's there to know? Made his fortune on material in the war. Buying up land all over the place, so people say. Beats me why but business is rarely simple. Why?' He picks at the skin on his dry fingers, but I can tell he's studying my reaction, waiting for me to drop some clue about why I am asking. No telling what he'd do with that information.

I clear my throat and drain the coffee in a gulp. 'Just wondering. Do you have any for me?'

Lazar waves a careless hand. 'A few in the shed. One of them lost so much juice I couldn't even raise a vein. Stingy mucksnipe—'

'I'll be back.' I shoulder my medkit.

'Doc.' Lazar's voice follows me out. 'They're not worth the medicine!'

∞

The night wind frisks around me as I push my way outside. The scent of burning trash and hot sand, human excrement and spilled propellant reminds me of where I am. I stride through Lazar's yard to the lopsided metal shed that stands alone some distance away. Warning signs are hammered into the ground around it, covered in yellow skull and crossbones: the system-wide shorthand for yellowrot contamination. Ignoring them, I push my way inside.

It's dark, filled with the unmistakable smell of decay and blood and sickness. I can hear bodies shifting and someone taking laboured, wheezing breaths, but cannot see where. Lazar lets the

55

innocent sick who can't pay die here, but light costs extra. Pulling the lantern from the side of my kit I wind it up and flick it on.

The cold white beam illuminates two people; one unconscious, the other huddled in a corner in a crumpled blanket.

'No use trying to take their blood,' the blanket figure croaks. 'Doctor already tried. They're out. Drier than a Seeker's eye.'

'I'm not here for that.'

I kneel by the unconscious stranger and hold their wrist. They're a landloper, sinewy as wire used too many times. An almost empty pack lies near their head, nothing but a heel of jerky and a dented canteen inside.

'Took their blanket,' the other says. 'Didn't reckon they'd need it anymore.'

The landloper's pulse is faltering and faint. Lazar's right, they've lost so much blood they are barely alive. I shine the torch down their body, and see why.

One of their legs is missing, just a stump of grimy bandage above the knee. Spraying my hands with disinfectant, I reach down and peel back the stiff layers. What I had thought to be dark fabric is pale, but blood-soaked. It comes away to reveal a brutal wound, the skin ragged, the bone splintered.

'Road Agents,' the blanket figure supplies. 'Reckon they gnawed right through the bone. God knows how this one pulled themselves here across the flats.'

For a heartbeat, horror threatens to overwhelm me, but then my body does what it remembers, what it was trained to do on battlefields, surrounded by the dead and the dying. Stop the bleeding. Close the wound. Let the surgeon do the rest.

Opening the kit I take out my precious box of spider silk. The strands adhere to the oozing wound and disappear, but the more I apply, the stickier the wound gets until when I spray it with sealant, it doesn't immediately dissolve. I close the remaining skin with sutures, quick and dirty, like I was taught. The only bandage I have is ex-military, like so many things on this moon. I rip it open, bind the wound with sticky fingers and check the pulse again.

Not enough. They've lost too much blood.

Nothing for it. Shucking off my stained duster, I roll up my sleeve and find a vein. Working a catheter one-handed gets easier after years of practice, and within seconds I clip the adaptor into place and feel a tug as my blood slides down the tube, and into the arm of the landloper.

'What are you doing?' the blanket figure asks after a while, almost horrified.

I close my eyes. 'Saving a life. I hope.'

'But your blood—'

'It's alright. I've got an adaptor.'

'A converter.' The stranger's voice has lost its cocky edge. 'You're that Blood Doctor. The Leech.' They shift and I look up to find blue eyes staring out at me from a mass of yellowrot cankers. 'Can you heal me?' they ask desperately. 'Can you tell me a future where I'll live?'

Before I can reply, there's a loud *bang* from outside, voices shouting… Hurriedly, I unhook the catheter from my arm; I'll have to come back.

'Here,' I say, tossing an ampule of painkiller at the yellowrot victim.

They catch it with crusted hands. 'Wait,' they beg. 'Wait!'

The street outside Lazar's is chaotic. A mule stands askew in the dust, people staring down at something, someone else screaming. Several of the parked mules have already disappeared, but mine remains with Rowdy in the seat, his head swivelling this way and that as he tries to track the noises. I push my way forwards.

One person lies in the dust, holding their guts with blood-soaked hands. Another kneels by their head, screaming for Lazar's help. I know them, I realise with a jolt. Doleful and Quint Meeks. Snake dealers from the next settlement over.

'What happened?' I demand, dropping to my knees.

'They burned our place, he tried to stop them but they slashed him as they rode – help him!' Quint screams at Lazar, who stands, looking down appraisingly. 'Please, before they get here!'

'They?' I grab Quint's muscular arm. 'Who did this? Road Agents?'

She shakes her head, face slicked with tears and dust and blood. 'Metaldogs. They torched our ranch, the water tower, everything. Poured prop on the snakes and set them alight in their cages.'

Lazar snorts. 'She's mad. Those body mod freaks wouldn't dare, even if they did have the firepower.'

'They did!' Quint shrieks. 'They did have it! And not just them, they were with others, all of them silver.' She flails for me. 'We ran, took the back trail here but they're following. They'll be here any minute. Call the Seekers, Doc. Call them so they can rip those bastards apart—'

An alarm explodes over her words; the sound of a warning platform, triggered further up the trail. The wind howls, bringing with it the sound of engines, guttural yells, clanging metal.

Trou-ble, Rowdy barks. *Trou-ble*.

I look up into Lazar's eyes.

'Deathbringer,' he accuses. 'What have you done?'

∞

The Metaldogs roar into Paranoia on their modified colts and sleds, baying, hooting, snarling, streaks of steel and violence in the desert darkness. I stagger to my feet. Lazar is right, before now the Metaldogs were just another two-bit gang with a taste for body mods, not even enough firepower to take on their rivals, let alone entire settlements. But now – they rip through the night like blades, their vehicles guzzling karburant from extra canisters, charging down anything that moves with spiked bull bars and rotating blades mounted on hubcaps, exhausts belching flame and sparks into the faces of those who try to run.

Others with them, Quint said, and she's right. Among the badly-cured snakeskin and sun-bleached cellulose I see silver body armour and high-tech augmentations – the kind only available in the chop shops of Delos – flashing blue beneath the skin. Flashing with infinity. Fear sweeps cold through my body.

Xoon's got the Alcaides deputising any bit of meat with eyes that can hold a gun.

'Get him inside,' I shout, bending to seize Doleful's legs.

Quint grabs her partner's shoulders, babbling to him to hold on. Lazar is already sprinting for the bar, stained white coat flying. Others are scrabbling to get through the doors. Behind me I hear a barrage of curses as one of the Paranoia residents starts to hurl homemade firebombs onto the riders from the roof of her house. Grit rains down on us as a spiked colt explodes into flames, the rider hurled ten feet in the air to land with a sickening crunch.

We tumble inside before Lazar slams the doors closed and shoots home the bolt.

Doleful is pleading and moaning with pain, the sting junkies are stirring dazedly from their blissed-out states, the stranger with century-stained lips pressed into a corner, a knife between their teeth and a pistol in their hand.

'It won't hold them long,' Lazar yells, taking a shotgun down from above the door.

No use asking what the Metaldogs want, the answer could be nothing but the thrill of inflicting pain, the violent rush of seeing their existence in a dying person's eyes, in a burned-out house. *I am real. I changed this world.*

On the floor, I rip open the medkit, pull out the injector gun and shoot a dose of sedative into Doleful's neck. If we are overrun, if Metaldogs get in here, it will be a kindness if he never wakes up.

'Help me,' I tell Quint, ripping open Doleful's sodden shirt.

'The hell are you doing?' Lazar almost shrieks. I ignore him as I swab away the blood as best I can, looking for the edges of the wound. I spray it with disinfectant, try to thread a needle but my hands are too slick with blood. It runs down my wrists like gloves of crimson silk…

A woman with eyes like the Void turns my way. In her hand is a blade.

A blast shakes the building, sending the scorpions scuttling madly, the solar lights flickering. Something shatters on the roof and falls. Lazar swears. Glancing up at the scratched window, I see why.

A group of a dozen Metaldogs have gathered in the street outside, flames catching on their modifications. Some wear respirators painted to look like muzzles, welded with steel teeth. Others have injected implants into their shoulders, giving them the stocky shape of attack dogs. All of them are armed with weapons too modern to be from Factus; blasters, charge pistols, flamethrowers, factory-new, taking their first lives. One Metaldog who seems to be the leader waves the others forwards. She has patchy brown and black cropped hair, her lower lip replaced by one made from serrated steel, like the undershot jaw of a bullhound.

'You ticks are trespassing,' she roars, spittle shining on her lip. 'This is private land, property of Xoon Futures.'

Xoon. My stomach turns sour. *You think they won't come here too?* Gabi told me. I should have known Paranoia would be a target. The people here aren't gang members or hardline liberty seekers or cannibals or wild zealots like some in the U Zone. For the most part they're tumbleweeds; ex-soldiers and killers with too many dead on other planets, confinement-mad former convicts and even a few desperate hopefuls like the Meeks who just want to be left alone to live.

'We'll give you a chance,' the Metaldog bellows, armed pistol in her grip. 'You getting this, Muck?'

A silver-clad merc with an augmented eye nods. 'I'm getting it.'

Grinning, the Metaldog holds something up. A silver coin. Fear swoops through me.

'Snake,' she calls, 'or eight?'

'Go to hell,' Lazar yells.

'Wrong answer.' She waves her gang on. Lazar arms the shotgun as they encircle towards the house, baying and hooting. That's when I remember: Rowdy. I stagger to my feet, make it to the window just in time to see a shirtless figure with a silver prosthetic hand drive a boot into Rowdy's side. My scream is lost to the sounds of destruction as the youth uses their metal hand to crush Rowdy's neck, until the collar light fizzes off and his barks of *warned, warned* stop.

'Alright,' Lazar calls over his shoulder, his face grey. 'When they come in, give them three blasts and then run for the surgery. Aim for the faces.'

I look through the bloodied print I have left on the window, dazed. Death, wherever I walk. Lives snuffed out, realities ending. A deep shiver runs through me, the feeling of vertigo that always precedes *their* arrival. I try to fight it but *Lazar's chest explodes from a blaster shot, Quint hurls a bottle and is gunned down to die beside her partner, her hands twitching desperately towards his, the junkies are ridden down as they try to flee, ten dead, twenty as the Metaldogs blaze across the U Zone…*

Something cuts into my other hand, dragging me back from that mess of possible futures. The coin. I am gripping it so hard it has left an imprint of eternity on my flesh. I look over at Lazar as he aims his gun.

'Let me out,' I hear myself say.

'Are you crazy?'

Before he can stop me, I run forwards, drag the bolt and step outside.

'Medic,' I cry, raising a hand, shouting the words that have saved my life more times than I can count. 'No harm. Nenhum dano. Wú hài.'

A Metaldog lunges for me, but the leader with the serrated jaw casually shoots them in the leg.

'Medic?' she asks over their shrieks, her eyes glossy with violence. 'We could use a sawbones.' She motions and the Metaldog who killed Rowdy comes forwards, holding a collar on a chain.

Blue sparks in my vision and I realise that the merc with the augmented eye is scanning my face. They stare at me blankly, iris winking and who knows what that augmentation can do, whether it is linked to a data bank on their ship, whether it will find an old wanted poster with my likeness, or worse, a news article from the war, beneath my name, my sentence…

'Leave.' My voice comes from somewhere else, raw as the wind.

The Metaldog with the serrated lip snorts. 'Or what, dustrat?'

'Or you'll die.' With every second they remain, a chance of them living winks out. 'Leave.'

'Ratto,' someone calls. 'The mark on her chest. That's her, that's—'

'Shut up,' the Metaldog snarls. 'Collar her.'

Cold anger steadies my voice. 'You want to play?' I open my hand to reveal the blood-smeared coin. For a heartbeat, the Metaldogs falter. 'Then let's play.'

I send the coin spinning into the air.

They crash into my awareness, ripping my mind from its moorings as reality fragments into a hundred, thousand branching paths. *Metal-Jaw fires, the bullet ricochets into the neck of one of her own – the youth throws themselves at me with a snarl – the silver-clad merc batters the door down, sending Lazar flying back in a spray of blood, another slashes at me with a razor claw, opening the flesh of my neck – a charge bullet melts my spine – the place goes up in flames…* It is too much, and *they* are everywhere, numberless, nameless, glutting on chance, gorging themselves on the vast potential energy of all those possible futures. I am bacterium, I am nothing and I feel my mind start to shred.

I reach for my belt and pull the scalpel free. Not mine. *Hers*. I cling to the woman who wears my face – my only anchor to reality – and let her into my skin.

As the Metaldog fires I sidestep the charge and take two rapid steps towards her, plunging the scalpel's blade into her jaw and twisting until the modified lip tears free. A mercenary leaps; I pull out the blade and slash their throat before they can fire. One of the fallen Metaldogs has a gun. I pick it up and use it as it should be used, red searing the darkness, aiming for arms, legs so as not to damage organs, so that they might repay their debts. Dimly I am aware of gunfire coming from Lazar's house, and bodies falling around me.

Something flashes in the corner of my eye and I spin, catching a metal wrist in my bloodied grip. It is the youth who killed Rowdy. As I drive the blade towards their chest, I see myself reflected in their wide, yellow eyes; my own as dark as a raptor's, as inhuman as the Void…

Something in me breaks and I jerk the scalpel away, opening a ragged cut across the youth's chest rather than a killing blow. They stagger back, clutching at their skin and the blade falls from my hand with a clatter.

She is gone, the woman who wore my skin, who dealt out death, and so are *they*.

The Personal Notes of Pec "Eight" Esterházy
Lunar Body XB11A – now "Factus"
Lutho-Plex Outpost

You might ask why I agreed to go to Factus. And I'd answer you now as I would have answered then – I didn't think I had a choice.

I let them assign me to the place like a crate of cargo. The only way to get out of it would have been to maim myself so badly they considered me damaged goods. Anyway, I thought then that nothing could be worse than the hulks.

So I set my feet on the road that led me here and found myself standing in front of a corporate recruiter's desk.

'Peccable Esterházy,' they droned. 'Crime?'

'Keeping a brothel in an unregulated sector. Causing, inciting and controlling prostitution for gain. Flying an unregistered abode. Docking an unregistered abode. Keeping a drinking establishment without authorisation. *Docking* a drinking establishment without authorisation—'

'Alright, alright. Violence?'

I smiled. 'None on record.'

'Teeth?'

'Real. One gunmetal.'

'Radiation?'

'Residual from the *Decader* journey from Earth. Nothing so bad.'

'Age?'

'Fifty-one.'

The recruiter grunted and looked up at me, seeing the face attached to the dull yellow jumpsuit for the first time.

'Mirl,' they yelled.

Their colleague was busy re-programming each prison collar with a slapdash series of jabs, nodding to music that sounded like a signal jammer.

'What?' he yelled back. I watched his jittering fingers. One wrong coordinate and those collars would trigger and start to squeeze and we'd suffocate before the transport was even a metre from the docking platform.

'Her.'

The collar-programmer glanced at me, at the creases around my mouth, the deep lines across my forehead. He had the glue-eyed look of someone who had never set foot planetside.

He shrugged. 'Getting rid of ballast. Always a few like that in the batch.'

'Lutho-Plex won't like it. She won't last more than a month.'

He turned his music up. 'Lutho-Plex won't care. Let's go, let's go.'

Ballast.

The word stayed with me as the recruiter finished the registration. Is that all we were? The weights that kept this system steady, cut loose once our jobs were done? I'd heard that in the past, ocean sailing ships on Earth used sacks of seeds as ballast, which – tossed aside –

would wash up on the mud of some distant place and grow there, thousands of miles from the plants that made them. Delacey didn't care if I grew or rotted, as long as I was gone. Neither, I sensed, did Lutho-Plex, for all the caveats that we stayed on once our sentences were served to make a go of it on this newly habitable moon.

I was shunted into the transport capsule, my collar tethered to the overhead rail like freight. The small space was crowded, twenty-one of twenty-five inmates already knee to knee on the benches, talking, grunting, even laughing as if this were some overgrown school outing. I glanced at the faces, at shaved heads and rebelliously grown rat-tails, scalps dyed red or verdigris or with whatever pigments could be scraped up off the workshop floors.

The only person I knew by name was Lon the Bigmouth, her eyebrows dyed blue to match the stubble on her scalp. She avoided my gaze, as she had done ever since she made the mistake of trying to push an "old woman" around during my first week on the hulks. Hardly a friendly connection.

The tether snagged and I dropped into a seat next to a barrel-chested man I vaguely recognised from the repair team. He had the spark-marked hands of a welder, his prison jumpsuit a testament to his favoured status, studded with rivets down the seams and in swirling patterns over the knees and elbows. What had he done wrong, I wondered, to fall from the warden's grace? His newly engraved collar gave a hint: Filch Bosak. He trembled, eyes tightly closed.

Another inmate stumbled onto the seat next to mine, his sharp hipbone digging into my thigh. Every inch of him was covered in living ink tattoos, sucked from bulletin tabs and injected through fine tubes beneath the skin. I watched a snake crawl down the back of his hand and wind around his middle finger. Nice work, if you could stand that sort of thing.

'Don't get it,' he muttered nervously when he caught me looking. A teardrop ran down his face and re-formed. 'Don't get why we're here. Lutho-Plex are big boys, aren't they? There are thousands of mad, air-starved bastards from the Terraform Rigs desperate for work. Why do they need us?'

He had a point. Corps as rich as Lutho-Plex rarely had to babysit convicts in order to get labour. What he did not have was a choice. None of us did. The recruiter banged a stun-stick against the wall.

'Listen up, Cohort Two. That's your new designation. Next stop Factus. Keep your hands where I can see them and your necks free of the tethers, we're gassing down in ten, nine...' They continued counting as they backed away through the crew airlock, until the doors slid shut and all I could see was their mouth, forming the words: six, five, four...

Off the hulks. Away from Delacey. A brand-new moon. Perhaps this was a fresh start.

'If we're Cohort Two,' the nervy man muttered, 'who the hell are Cohort One?'

Any answer I might have given was lost in the hiss of gas that cascaded over my face like water, sending me under.

ALL AROUND, METALDOGS and mercenaries are dead and dying, those who can stand fleeing back into the desert. Some killed by Lazar and the people of Paranoia, some by my own hand. The tally on my skin burns beneath the blood. *Deathbringer*, they call me. *Troublecrow*. They are right.

Faces stare at me from inside Lazar's house. People who have seen what horrors this star system has to offer, looking on me now in fear. The stranger with the stained lips crosses themselves and covers their eyes.

'Hel,' they mutter.

I turn away.

In the carnage around my mule, I find Rowdy, or the pieces of him. His head has been severed, his eye dull. When I touch his ear he tries to bark his words, but all that emerges from his muzzle is a dull *clunk*. With trembling hands, I reach into the exposed workings, find the largest cable and gently pull it free. He whirrs to silence.

I stand, empty, to see a scuffle happening on Lazar's porch. They have caught the remaining mercenary, the youth with the metal hand. I watch as Quint drives her boot into their bleeding chest, as one of the junkies uses the Metaldogs' own chain to shackle them. Before night is done, they will be tied to the Seekers' tribute post to await judgement.

Lazar walks over and hands me the scalpel. In his other hand is a box of blood bags and a cannula. 'We should take tribute,' he mutters. 'Before they go stale.'

I nod dully. There is work to be done.

It is gruesome and brutal and more than once grief threatens to overwhelm me. But Lazar, for all his cold avarice, is right. What sense is there in leaving the blood to dry in these bodies when it could save the life of a mother in labour, in some far-flung U Zone settlement? What use in leaving the flesh to rot when Lazar could use it to save a limb? The Home Planets might have synthesised flesh, lab-grown organs, but out here, we are alone. There is a thread of simplicity in it, the Seekers' way, almost peace: those who take must repay. *They* feed on potential and the more people live on these moons, the greater the store of possibilities and the stronger *they* become.

Finally, it is done. Together, we drag the bodies to one side of the dusty street. Someone will take them for a maggot farm, but for now, I lay them out shoulder to shoulder on a low rise where the wind can stream over them.

In the faint solar light, I see a tattoo on a mercenary's temple. An arrow, encircled by two clasped hands. The symbol of the Free Limits. I touch it gently, remembering the conviction that once rose in me when I saw that symbol, the *truth* I knew I was fighting for – stars and moons owned by no one and everyone. And where had that fight led?

Eight thousand four hundred and forty-seven.

When I lift my fingers from the mercenary's tattoo, my own bloodied prints remain.

By the time I walk back to Lazar's bar, night is waning. Among the carnage, something of a celebration has broken out; coffee is being passed around, a bowl of candied crickets and lumps of precious jaggery to wash away the shock with sugar. This is the U Zone, after all. One of the scorpion junkies has even found a battered steel ukulele and is making up a song about dead dogs and Hel. They stop when they see me.

Only Lazar steps towards me. For all the destruction, he has profited. His cooler is full of enough tribute to supply the Seekers for months, not to mention his own customers. It looks as if he has even agreed to treat Doleful; through the open surgery door, I see the wounded man on the gurney, hooked to a drip, Quint holding his hand.

'Thanks, Doc,' Lazar says, pressing something into my palm. 'Hope you find what you're looking for.'

Wires tangle around my fingers and I look down. Resting on my palm is the Delos mercenary's steel eye, its lights dead now that it has been cut free. On the back, branded into the metal, is an infinity symbol. I resist the urge to hurl it across the room. Tech like this is costly and I know why Lazar has parted with it. When I look into his brown-grey eyes I see the message, as clearly as if it had been spoken.

Take it and go.

Gathering up my medkit and the pieces of Rowdy, I climb onto the mule and ride away.

On Paranoia's outskirts, beneath the washed-black sky, I see the young mercenary with the metal hand, slumped unconscious, chained to the tribute post. Stopping the mule, I go to kneel beside them. The flashing red light above illuminates the scars of a hard life; a split eyebrow, pockmarks on the cheeks. One of their front teeth is dull gunmetal. And the hand. I have never seen one quite like it. The workmanship is fine, elegant. It can only have come from the metal smiths of Delos. I lean closer and see a stamp, where steel meets skin, just like on the steel eye. An infinity symbol and beneath it four words: *property of Xoon Futures.*

The sound of footsteps, crunching in the night-cold dirt, makes me look up.

The Seekers stand at the limit of the red light. I didn't hear their ships, so they must have been watching me for some time. Among them, I see a few familiar faces, glimpsed from the door of my shack, or across a campfire when I roamed the Barrens. They are of all ages: some with straggling hair and gnarled hands and old, old prison scars. Others look younger, their flesh bearing smaller tallies. Who knows how they came to join what some people call a gang and others a cult, what deal they made when the Seekers found them in the wastes.

One Seeker steps out in front of the others. An older person, I think, with white hair and a skinny frame. Their sun-bleached clothes once belonged to a corpse, the bullet holes and knife cuts darned with medical thread. Every one of my nerves prickles as I stare back. We have met before, the night I sat up with Pec

Esterházy's body – the night I made a promise that I have not yet fulfilled.

Their face is covered in small marks, some unfathomable tally of their own. I once asked their name and they only smiled and asked me, *which one*. This close I can smell their scent: old blood, the chemical sting of antiseptic, fabric dried crisp in the fierce sun, and always something else, like ozone, like burning sand. The smell of the Edge.

'Alive?' they ask.

I nod. 'Alive.'

Their brown eyes are bright with fervour and sorrow. Instinct makes me pull the double-faced coin from my pocket. 'Esterházy showed me.'

The Seeker nods. 'So.'

'What does it mean?'

'What do you think? It means a choice.' They shift their gaze to the metal-handed youth. 'This one owes.'

'So do I.'

They regard me and in that moment I know – with absolute clarity – that if it weren't for the symbol on my chest, they would cut the heart from my body without a word. They would judge me and find my debt too large for my flesh and blood to answer.

Instead they jerk their head. 'Will you come with us?'

To stay is to put myself in danger, into the path of the future. But to go will be to step into a place from which there is no return.

'Not yet,' I whisper.

In the shadows cast by the tribute light, the Seeker nods. 'Hel wants to wear your name,' they remind me.

I look beyond the U Zone, to the horizon. 'Hel can wait.'

∞

In a hollow off the trail, I sit in the scant shade cast by the mule, and watch the unconscious stranger's bruised face. Their pale brown skin is beginning to redden from the sun, their metal hand shining. From what I can see, they have never been in prison. But that means little. I take another sip of treated water and reach out to pat Rowdy, only to remember. My hand falls limp to the burning sand.

So kill them, a voice hisses. *Or cut them loose and leave them to die. Who would know?*

From the packs I take a hunk of snake jerky and tear off a mouthful. It's dark and pungent but it makes me work my teeth, gives me time to try and push thoughts into the right order. We are safe enough for a few hours, concealed by a sand-coloured tarp at high noon. Road Agents don't usually venture out in heat like this. I swallow the mouthful down and reach for my scalpel. Disinfect the blade. Sit with it poised above the tally.

Lazar, I want to score. *Quint. The sting junkies. The landloper in the shed.* But every time I lower the blade, a flash of violence returns: the face of a Metaldog or a mercenary as I cut them down. Deaths added to my debt, cancelling out the lives I've saved. But this one – I stare down at the stranger. This one is alive. Carefully, only wincing a little, I make a single incision. When it's done,

I reach for the phial of stinkbug ichor and wave it beneath the stranger's nose.

They come to immediately with a choke, retching at the foul stench that I know will fill their nostrils for hours to come. Wheezing, they try to push themselves up, only to discover the chain about their ankles and wrists, tied to the mule's fender. When they see me, their face drops into terror.

'Please,' they choke, licking the dried blood on their lip. 'Please, don't cut me up, I didn't mean it, I swear. They made me—'

The words dissolve into coughs. I let them suffer a while before tossing over the canteen, which they catch with shackled hands. 'Small sips. Or you'll vomit.'

One eye is swollen, but the other is pinched and guarded as they sniff at the canteen before taking a gulp, then another. They watch me over the rim, trying to work out how to escape this situation.

They kick me in head and steal the mule, they throttle me with the chain, they get the scalpel and—

'None of that will work.'

They freeze, before lowering the canteen. 'Who are you?'

'Just a medic.'

'You're not. You're a Seeker. You killed them all.'

'If I'm a Seeker why are you still breathing?' I nod to their chest, bandaged and dressed. 'I treated you. I saved your life.'

'Why?'

Because there was too much death. Slowly, I take the coin from my pocket. 'You know what this is?'

76

'Xoon coin,' they say suspiciously. 'Scrip.'

'Who paid you to attack the town? Lutho Xoon?'

They wipe their nose with shackled hands. 'The Alcaide paid us.'

'Which Alcaide?'

A slow smile stretches their cracked lips. They've caught up. First rule of conflict; don't kill people with valuable information. 'Let me go and I'll tell.'

'Tell and I'll let you go.'

'Sagacity,' they say reluctantly.

I almost laugh. Of course. I bend to unlock the chain from the mule's fender. The second it drops free, the youth leaps, throwing themselves towards my back. Spinning, I pull out the scalpel and hold it level with their jugular. They stop.

'That's three times now I have stopped short of killing you,' I tell them. 'You hurt my friends, you killed my dog. You made me take lives. If you come with me to Sagacity, and tell my contact there everything you know about Xoon, I might let you live.'

Their gaze flicks to the tally lines that score my hands, and they nod rapidly, the blade scraping against the faint stubble of their neck.

Stowing the scalpel I retreat to the mule's shadow, my brain banging a drum inside my skull. Fumbling for the breath beads, I slide one between my lips and crunch it down. Inch by inch, the stranger lowers themselves to the very edge of the shade. Their bare chest glistens with sweat.

'You have a name?' I ask, without looking.

They nod. 'Rouf. Rouf Cinque.'

'Get some rest, Rouf.' I settle back, pulling the hat over my face. 'We ride at sundown.'

Later, I open my eyes to silence. I stay still, waiting for the wind to stir again, for the mule to click in the heat. When it doesn't, I open my eyes.

Rouf lies curled beside the mule, their silver hand resting next to their face. Dusk has fallen, turning everything hazy, until even my boots seem to melt at the edges.

I push my hat back and see the figures, watching.

There are ten of them, indistinct silhouettes in the twilight, for all they can only be a few paces away. Slowly, I reach for the scalpel.

'Saw the mule,' a voice says uncertainly. 'Saw it from a long way out.'

They sway forwards and I realise it is Metal-Jaw, her augmented lip hanging off, her throat a mess of charred flesh from where a charge bullet blew it open. Behind her, the merc who once bore the steel eye stares with a blank socket, hand twitching as if pulling a trigger.

Metal-Jaw lowers herself to the sand, worrying at her ruined lip. 'What a job, huh?' she says. 'Sounded like a good deal when they first told us. New weapons, new colts, tear up a few towns for Uncle Xoon. Why he wants anything to do with this shithole place…' Swallowing wetly, she peers at me. 'Are you one of those mercs from Delos?'

'No,' I say softly. 'I'm a medic.'

She groans. 'Thank Lux. Think there's something wrong with my throat. Got this pain that won't go away—'

She opens her mouth wide, like a kid saying *aaahh* but no sound comes out, just dark sand, pouring through her ruined gullet.

'I'm sorry,' I whisper, my eyes burning.

'Who are you talking to?' Rouf asks groggily, peering through one good eye.

When I look back, the dead Metaldogs are gone, back to the desert.

'No one.' I push myself to my feet. 'Let's move.'

∞

The mule struggles through the sands, unaccustomed to carrying two. Rouf crowds the seat beside me, wincing at the rough ground.

'My head aches,' they mutter. 'You got any more of those beads?'

'Not for you.'

They grunt, squinting out at the endless, cracked dust that passes in the mule's beams. Despite the smeared kohl around their eyes, the whites are already bloodshot from the day's light. They tug a bit of sacking further over their tangled gold hair and shiver. 'How do you live out here?'

'A day at a time.'

'It's worse than the antimony mines on Delos. You ever been there?'

I glance at the symbol etched onto that elegant hand. Delos. Factus's twin, as unlike each other as shine to rust, commotion to desolation, thanks to the minerals beneath her skin. Once I stood on a plateau and watched Accord dropships destroy the fields of metalworks. Once I sheltered in the vast and silent belly of a stopped factory, treating Delosian partisans and Free Limiters alike, their cries ringing back from the distant ceiling...

I shake my head. 'Not for a long time.'

'That's where this happened.' Rouf opens and closes their metal fingers. 'Explosion.'

They lapse into silence, and I do not question them further, just focus on the trail ahead, watching for traps and pits, garrotte wire and foxholes.

'Where are we going now?' they ask at last.

'Sagacity.'

'Sa... that'll take *days* on this crawler! Why the hell didn't you take one of our buzzards? Garrity had one, factory green, with an air purifier and—'

'And it would have got us all of fifty kliks before it died. Or have you seen many prop stations around here?'

Rouf slumps in the seat. 'Backward-ass moon.'

We haven't made it much further when I spot something, a faint glow up ahead like marsh-fire. I slow the mule to an idle and take up the binoculars.

A large vehicle, maybe a droger's ox, smoulders in the night, the flames already dancing themselves out to the hissing winds. The hairs on the back of my neck rise as I reach down and kill the mule's headlights, plunging us into darkness.

'What is it?' Rouf has the sense not to raise their voice.

'Road Agents.'

Releasing the brake, I let the mule roll towards the scree-covered slope beside the trail. 'Hold on. We're going off-road.'

'Who the fuck are they?' Rouf hisses as the mule bumps downhill. 'Another cult?'

'Cannibals.'

'What?!'

'People say they used to collect taxes for the water barons. Until they went mad, riding the roads.'

Like you, a voice hisses.

The mule wallows down onto a rocky canyon floor. I rev the engine, just a little so that we creep into the darkness.

'Do you even know where you're going?'

'Roughly.'

It is true, more or less. Even though I have never ventured off the trail in these parts, I can *feel* it, the pull of the Edge, like magnetic current linked to my nerves.

After what feels like hours, the rocky ground changes beneath the mule's wheels, turning smoother. I stop, looking around. I can just make out the slope of a low hill in the darkness, and beyond that, the tug of the Edge. But there is something else here – like a barely audible whisper. I peer into the darkness and realise what I am seeing.

Walls. Metal walls that stretch ahead, and nearer to something that glows silver in the night. A sign? I stop, the dust hissing around us.

'What is that?' Rouf croaks. 'Have you led us to their goddam base?'

'Road Agents don't have bases,' I murmur back. 'And I don't know, I've never been here before.' After a moment's hesitation I climb down stiffly.

'What are you *doing*?' Rouf demands.

'Going to look.'

Taking out the torch, I wind it up and point the beam at the sign.

OUTPOST 11
PROPERTY OF LUTHO-PLEX
∞

The sign looks ancient, battered and scoured by the elements. A strange rush of anger goes through me as I stare at the infinity symbol, that it could have been here for so long – like a virus in the blood – waiting to spread across this moon. I creep forwards.

Three pre-fabricated habitats are arranged in a U-shape around a dirt yard, a handful of sheds and shacks straggling towards once-solid gates. The winds have feasted on them over the decades, knocked them askew and worn holes in the metal with rough tongues. But apart from that, it all seems strangely untouched. Little wonder. No one in their right mind would take such a backwater route to Sagacity, and even the truly desperate would be afraid to venture this far off the trail to scavenge.

'Hello?' I whisper.

No one answers, not even the dead. Even the best ambushes are never silent, and I listen, ears straining for the telltale noises of rapid breath whistling through nostrils, armour shifting, charge guns whining, but there's nothing.

I walk across the yard towards an open door in one of the buildings. The corridor beyond is dark, sand piled in great drifts in the corners. Slowly, I creep past an echoing empty mess hall, the tables shoved against the walls, then a former medical room, plundered of every useful item, the instruments gone, the machines borne away, no doubt by the Seekers. Down the corridor, I find what might have once been an office. Paper crinkles as I shunt the door open far enough to step inside. The floor is covered with old bulletin sheets, thin and yellow as a snake's shed skin. The wire itself is long gone, only dangling cables remaining.

I pick up a bulletin sheet.

REQUEST IMMEDIATE EXTRACTION

It is dated forty years ago. I let the paper fall. Above a caved-in desk, brownish stains spatter the plastic wall, reaching as high as the ceiling. Evidence of someone's fate. But beneath the stains… I shine the torch at a faded poster. A map of Factus. I have never seen one so old. Among the cities and settlements I know are places I have never even heard of, that were already long gone by the time I crash-landed here, or only ever existed in the minds of bureaucrats and wet-eyed spin doctors back on the Home Planets. *Landfall Eight, Arenilla Rica, Sandistadt…*

On this map, the U Zone doesn't exist. But I run my fingers over the chalky surface until I reach a tiny square, far out in the wastes, labelled *Outpost 11*. All around it, someone has drawn dozens of tiny crosses. Deaths, I realise with a sweep of horror. I count twenty of them, thirty, many in a cluster at the edge of a hashed area labelled *meteorological disturbance*. The Accord's name for the Edge. What the hell were Lutho-Plex doing here?

I am about to search the papers on the floor when there's a squeal of metal, a crash. Heart racing to my throat I dart from the room, back through the mess hall and out into the yard. In the faint Delos moonlight, I see Rouf staring into the open doors of what might once have been a stable.

'What are you doing?' I hiss, striding across the dust, the torchlight bouncing.

They don't reply. It's only then I notice how rapidly they are breathing, in a way that has nothing to do with the thin air. 'You know you said that Road Agents don't have bases…?'

I spin, flashing the torch into the stable. It's a slaughterhouse, drying flesh hanging from nails, bones tossed into the sand, plunder piled up in the corners among bedrolls.

Fear floods my eyes. Before I can turn back to Rouf and tell them to run, I hear the sound of engines.

The Personal Notes of Pec "Eight" Esterházy
Lunar Body XB11A - now "Factus"
Lutho-Plex Outpost

Hard to remember now what I dreamed of during the long, gassed-out flight to Factus. An inmate's dreams, I think. Horizons that turn out to be nothing but paint on metal walls, vast spaces that are as much of a prison as a cell. But among them, other images. A blue-painted breeze-block house. The taste of pálinka and the smell of engine fuel. A mark carved above a doorway – two sloping lines and one slashed across. A woman who wore death's face...

There were more, but they vanished as I woke, shoved aside by the thumping in my head, louder and more insistent than a rotgut hangover. When I opened my eyes, the coarse yellow cellulose of the prison jumpsuit swam in my vision.

All around inmates coughed and spat as we surfaced from the hours of gas. The oxygen in the compartment was running low and the capsule smelled like old piss and stale breath.

But all of that evaporated when I looked out the scratched porthole and saw stars. My first glimpse of the outside world for more than two years had me straining against the tether. A moon rolled below us, a pale ball of dust shoved into the corner of space. Factus: last speck of human habitation in this sector. A bare handful of satellites shivered in orbit around it, and beyond them...

The edge of the known system. No stars, just a nothingness that yawned in space, swallowing light. The Void, riggers had named it. They used to stagger through my doors from their union satellites with air-starved brains and compressed bones at the end of their ten-year contracts, desperate for softness and oblivion, wearing blinkered glasses to keep out the visions that dogged the corners of their eyes. Not many who made it back from the Border Moons lived long, and those that did came dragging tales of places where the light never changed, cursed space and accidents that were more than bad luck.

I knew all that, but still I looked into the Void and found I couldn't tear my eyes away. It was pure and perfect, it was deepest water, whispering of what it might feel like to jump and I saw myself do just that: break free of the tether, wrestle open the airlock door and spill our bodies out across the stars...

'The fuck is that?' someone swore.

I tore my eyes from the fathomless dark. My hands were shaking. Too much gas, I told myself, then. Other inmates were craning to look through the porthole at the moon's surface, where a patch of air seemed to swell and ripple.

'Sand storm, I guess,' someone said.

'Some storm. Must be a hundred kliks wide.'

'Brace up, Cohort,' the recruiter's voice came over the tannoy. 'We're going down.'

'Yeah, to hell,' someone joked, and I laughed, not knowing then that they were right.

W E FLEE, STAGGERING through the broken gates of the compound back towards the mule. Too late to be furtive now; the engines are close; so close that I can smell them on their air, the acrid reek of propellant and karburant and mosca fuel all mixed together by people who don't care that their vehicles won't last more than a single ride.

Steps away from the mule, something tangles in my legs and sends me sprawling. I splutter out dust to see Rouf backing away, one hand pressed to their ribs.

'Sorry, Doc,' they call. 'I figure you'll keep them busy...'

Stop! I try to yell as they leap onto the mule and slam their boot to the pedal, sending it shooting forwards in a spray of grit.

Choking, I stumble to my feet and run after it, even though I know it is useless. Sure enough, within seconds the mule lurches, sputters and comes to a dead halt.

'Come on!' Rouf shrieks, slamming the pedals.

Heaving in a breath, I lunge at them, slamming my fist into their sternum, sending them doubling over. A shove and they fall onto the passenger seat, wheezing and retching.

With shaking hands I reach under the controls to re-set the ignition sequence that Rouf got wrong, praying that they haven't flooded the engine. Desperately I stomp the pedal but it just coughs uselessly. Before I can reach down to try again, headlights slide over the lip of the slope. There is nothing I can do as the Road Agents race down towards us, a wild cavalcade of stolen mares and mules and broncos, even a dray. There must be ten of them, but it's hard to tell, the way they weave and slalom through the dirt, churning it into a blinding cloud.

Heart kicking against my ribs, I draw the scalpel's blade in one hand and take up the coin in the other. Are *they* here? I cannot feel *them* through the fear and even if I could *they* are not gods, *they* only show me potential worlds and in this moment, survival seems impossible.

'In the medkit,' I hear myself say. 'There's anaesthetic. Enough for an overdose.'

Rouf doesn't move, squinting in the headlights as a Road Agent stops, right before us.

I stare at the figure that dismounts. Their coat is stiff with old stains, but it still bears the emblem of the Freight Insurer's Union. How long ago did this person arrive here, with a job and a name and a pay packet that might have earned them enough money to go back to the Home Planets? When did they lose their way in the Zone?

They peer at me through dark goggles and smile. Their teeth are gone. Instead they wear fibreglass dentures, chipped and chiselled into points.

Other figures emerge through the dust clouds, one of them dragging a headless torso along by a rope. Rouf retches beside me as others close in; I see ragged uniforms, blood-smeared metal teeth and rusted knives. Some carry bags that drip onto the sand.

'Zahlen eller dø,' the leader says in Delos cant. 'Pay the tax or die.'

'Chaahate hain?' Rouf's voice shakes. 'What is the tax? We'll pay it.'

I close my eyes as they start to laugh because I know the answer before it comes. 'The tax is life.'

There's only one possible way out of this; one gang the Road Agents fear. I reach for the scarf that covers my chest and pull the fabric free.

The lead Road Agent stops laughing, peers and recoils at once. 'Unclean,' they mutter in disgust.

'What?' Another raises a bloody chin to look.

'Has *their* mark.'

'Unclean,' another agrees, disappointed.

'Too empty. Too hungry. Too full of Void.'

'Metal one isn't.'

The lead Road Agent looks at me as if I were spoiled meat. 'Get out, Seeker. Go back to *them*.'

Experimentally, I swing one leg from the mule, expecting them to lunge. But they don't. Only turn their nose away from me to focus on Rouf.

'Metal can pay with the other hand first.'

Rouf twists in the seat, teeth bared, face bloodless. 'Get the fuck away.' They look at me, pleading. 'Doc!'

Something in my chest gives a tug, like one magnet straining towards another. 'Wait,' I tell the Road Agent. 'Let me cut off their metal hand. I'll take it as tribute.'

The Road Agent sneers. 'Get away, sawbones.'

I hold up the coin, balancing it on my thumb. 'Shall I call to *them*?'

Several of the Road Agents shift. One glares murderously. I am overplaying my hand. *Silver flashes, clouds roll…* Without waiting for permission I turn and clasp Rouf's wrist, squeezing tight where the flesh meets metal, hoping that they understand…

Their yellow eyes meet mine and I spin, driving the scalpel into the nearest Road Agent's cheek, sending them staggering as the others laugh. Rouf is ready, booting another Road Agent backwards as I drop into the seat, wrench the accelerator and pump the pedal, once, twice…

'Go!' Rouf screams.

I slam my foot down and the mule roars into life, sending us skidding forwards just as a Road Agent leaps for the back of the mule. I try to speed away but they're like an anchor, kicking and flailing in the sand, threatening to topple us.

'Get them off!'

Frantic, Rouf grabs the only thing they can see – my torch – and leans back to pummel the Road Agent's fingers again and again until bone cracks and they finally let go.

We shoot away, wheels spinning as we race up the ridge.

'Lean!' I order. They hurl themselves forwards, tipping the

weight until – with a whine – the mule makes it over the lip.

Relief is short-lived. The cackles of engines batter my ears and I look back to see Road Agents hurtling out of the valley, their tyres eating up the ground in the way the mule can't. With every minute they are gaining on us.

'Check the compass,' I yell over the wind that roars out of the darkness from the wasteland beyond.

'What?'

'Do it! What does it say?'

Rouf leans over the panel, metal hand skittering. 'Nothing, it's broken, it's going haywire—' They let out a yelp as what looks like a throwing knife whistles over their head.

A Road Agent is speeding up behind us on a bronco, another knife in their hand.

Holding the mule steady with one hand, I reach under the seat, scrabbling until greasy plastic meets my fingers. The only gun I allow myself to carry. I rip it free, turn and fire it into the face of the approaching rider.

Blue smoke explodes in the darkness, blinding, sending the Road Agent veering away wildly. As the mule bucks and wobbles, I shove the flare gun at Rouf.

Swearing, they load it and turn in the seat, ready to fire. Twice more we are almost caught, before blue smoke buys us a few seconds of life – *blue for medic* – but the Road Agents are gaining, and when Rouf tries to fire again, the flare gun just clicks, empty.

'Fuck!' they shriek, throwing themselves down in the seat as an old-style bullet whistles over their head. 'We're dead!'

I don't answer, staring into the night before us. The compass on the mule spins madly, the wind howls and at last I see it in the distance: a vast wall of churning sand, lightning forking through it like veins beneath skin. A storm, *the* storm that rages at the limit of the Edge. A shudder runs the length of my body and the tugging in my chest increases. What I am about to do is considered suicide.

'We're dead,' Rouf repeats, rocking the mule as if that will make it go faster. 'We're dead!'

'Not yet,' I mutter and rev the mule, straight towards the claws of the storm.

The Road Agents are at our heels but another minute is all I need, another thirty seconds, another ten…

'Hold on,' I yell.

Rouf's cry is cut off as sand slams into us like broken glass, snatching my breath, raking my skin from my bones. But the storm is *theirs* and so am I and so I hang onto the mule for our lives, riding straight into terror.

Engines roar over the shrieking wind and I risk a glance back to see the first Road Agents hurtle into the storm behind us. I wrench the mule to one side and they try to follow, only for a billow of dust to swallow them whole. Everywhere in the sand are shadows, vehicles, flashes and flickers of other worlds that imprint themselves on my retinas without being seen. Another Road Agent slaloms straight past us into the heart of the storm chasing something I cannot even see.

Metal fingers seize my arm and I look up just in time to see a vast wave of dark sand rushing towards us. I throw my arms over my head and manage one breath before the storm smashes into us with unimaginable violence and everything goes dark.

∞

I open my eyes to light as thick and yellow as amber. There is no sky, no wind. No breath, even. My chest is still, my lungs heavy and silent as bags of salt.

I know this place. I died here.

This is the Edge.

Slowly, I push myself to sitting. Dark sand cascades from my body.

'About time,' a voice says.

The dead woman stands behind me, looking amused as she leans on her stick.

'Esterházy?'

I rise to my feet. There was death and pursuit and violence but the memory is hazy, as if it happened long ago. Wasn't there someone with me? The sands are empty and endless, no footsteps or tyre tracks to suggest how I could have arrived.

'Am I dead?' I ask.

'Of course you are. Somewhere.'

She looks just as she did the day she died; with her tangled grey hair and the faded crescent moon tattoo around her eye crinkling as she smiles. Her dress and the loose leather vest she wears are wet with blood from the gunshots that killed her, and when she turns around I see the devastating exit wounds, sundered flesh beneath torn fabric. Beads of blood drip to the sand and burrow like little red snakes.

'Come,' she says, untroubled.

I follow her as she stumps away, leaning on the stick that is also a rifle. We might as well be standing still, for all the landscape changes. Sweat runs down my face, the plasma-yellow light stinging my eyes as if someone has flung salt into them.

No use in asking where we are going. I have been here before; this is the Suplicio. Part of the Edge that has no beginning, no end and no borders save for the ones that exist inside my own head.

'Is this hell?' I realise I have spoken aloud.

She shrugs, and blood spatters the ground, gathered up by grey fingers that worm out of the sand. 'It might be yours.'

We walk on. Esterházy moves faster than me, perhaps because she cannot see the dead. But I can. They wait for me, all eight thousand four hundred and forty-seven of them. They crawl from their mass graves towards me, begging for their lives back, and the walls I have constructed from the lines of the tally crumble like powder beneath their reaching fingers.

'I'm sorry,' I choke, as a teenage cadet in the uniform of an Accord private reaches for me, her face sunken, blood from the virus that killed her still staining her lips. 'I'm sorry, I didn't know.'

Another dead cadet catches my boots and I stagger, crashing face first into the sand. Immediately, fingers take hold of my trousers, the hem of my coat, pulling me down. Part of me wants to give up, to lie still and let my dead claim me, but then how would I pay my debt? How will I save enough lives?

It doesn't work that way, traitor.

Gabi's voice echoes through my mind. As the sand reaches my chin, I look up. In the endless yellow light, there is a spark of silver.

Not yet, a voice says. My own.

With a cry I start to struggle free of the dead, but there are so many of them. I push, feeling cold flesh give beneath my fingers and am finally able to rise from the sand and lurch away, towards that scratch of silver on the horizon, gleaming like a beacon. I keep my eyes fixed upon it, not looking at the dead, and finally I make out the silhouette of a woman standing on a sand dune, holding something mirror-bright in her hand. A silver coin.

'Esterházy?' I gasp, scrambling on all fours to the top of the dune only to find her gone.

Instead, I look down onto horror.

A battlefield stretches endlessly into the distance. Great swathes of burned sand, scorched to black glass, craters torn from the land like deep nail gouges in flesh. And everywhere, the dead. A thousand bodies, ten thousand, blown apart or run down, shot or burned up. A choke escapes me and I plunge down the side of the dune, already reaching for my medkit… but it isn't here, and even if it were, it would be useless. These lives have been ended;

the threads that once linked them to this and a thousand other realities cut, innumerable possible worlds snuffed out.

A scrap of colour catches my eye and I lean down to roll one of the corpses over. A G'hal – I'd recognise the brightly dyed military surplus anywhere – stares up at me accusingly through one eye, half of her head blown open. I take a step back and see others, not just G'hals but other Factan gangs in their colours, and among them ordinary folk; agregados and ranchers, landlopers and roughnecks and vigilantes wearing mismatched body armour, cobbled together from whatever could be found. All are caught in endless death, in the coils of infinity.

The wrongness and utter loss of it hits me in the guts, just as it did that day above Tamane when I heard the result of my successful mission – how I had struck a blow for the Free Limits by murdering eight thousand cadets with one little stolen virus. No matter that the Accord let me steal it, to end the war. The result was the same.

People don't care about your reasons for killing them when they're dead.

I stagger on, through thin air poisoned further by toxic smoke, towards what looks like a burning settlement in the distance, looking for an answer. I find it in the charred husks of silver birds, stamped with the emblem of Xoon Futures, I find it in the corpses of silver-clad mercenaries, sent here to fight, in the fallen weapons and stamped crates and armoured vehicles – all the rattling, scattered toys of war.

War. That is what I am seeing. Stranded by the tide of one conflict I never considered that another could be rushing up behind me, turning the materiel that had spread across the system towards a new and bloody purpose. And Esterházy is right: this is my hell, everything that I have been running from.

Silver catches in my tear-stung eyes and I turn towards it desperately. Across the violence-stained sands I see what looks like an elevator with glass doors, standing alone, unattached to any building. My stumbling steps take me towards it.

Inside, two figures lie, slumped in death. One wears a leather duster, blood-clogged black curls hanging over their face and even before I bend down, I know who it will be.

Gabi's eyes are blank in death, a pistol still clutched in her hand. Her chest is riddled with bullet wounds that have torn through the skin and the sub-dermal membrane beneath – implanted by the Accord when she was just a child – to sunder organs and bone. I touch the glass and whisper her name but it is already too late. Shaking, I turn towards the second figure and find myself staring at my own corpse.

I have been shot, eight bullet holes glistening across my chest, my face a mess of blood and mica dust. But this is the Edge and even as I watch, my corpse's mouth drifts open and dark sand begins to pour through the grey lips.

'No,' I beg, staggering backwards, but the sand becomes a rush, a silver coin clinking against my teeth to fall to the ground.

I turn away to run, and find myself face to face with Esterházy.

'What is this?' I choke. 'Will this happen?'

She holds the coin, just as she did the night outside my shack. Snake or eight, eternity or infinity. Heads or tails.

Her eyes – as featureless as the Void – meet mine.

'Choose.'

∞

Sand fills my throat and I choke, flailing upwards. It is everywhere, in my nose, my eyes, and for a long time I can only wheeze and retch and spit, sucking in air a ragged gasp at a time. Slowly, my body comes back to me, piece by piece. Eyes burning with grit. Swimming head, aching lungs. One arm gives a sharp stab of pain as I raise it to my face. My hat is gone, and one ear feels clogged; I touch it and my fingers come away red, the skin throbbing and swollen. But pain is for the living, and I was dead. I was surrounded by war. Through blurred vision, I look up.

Ordinary hard white daylight sears my face, rather than the undying light of the Suplicio. Ordinary grey sand and no sign that the dead roll beneath. Wherever I am, I am back.

I manage to get myself to my knees. Nearby, the mule lies on its back, undercarriage baking in the sun. Flotsam scatters the ground around it. Something half-buried catches my eye; battered white with a red star. My medkit. Painfully, I crawl towards it only for something to snag my coat. For a terrible moment I think I am wrong, that the dead have followed me here, until I realise that the fingers that clutch my hem are not grey, but silver.

Rouf.

Turning, I push at the sand, unearthing an arm, then tangled gold-brown hair, then a swollen, battered face. At first I think they are dead but when I brush awkwardly at their lips, bending to blow the sand away from their nostrils, they stir and convulse before heaving in a breath. I try to get a good look at them. Their back is scraped raw, a huge bruise spreading over one shoulder, but apart from that, they look uninjured.

While they vomit up sand, I crawl over to the mule and drag the spare canteen from its holster. The water inside is hot and acrid but in that moment it is the best thing I have ever tasted, like liquid life, washing the sand from my throat and flowing straight to my brain. That done, I sink into the sand beside the medkit and look to my fraying body.

'What happened?' Rouf croaks. 'Where are they?'

The Road Agents. It returns to me in a rush. I squint around, but the flats are empty, just bone-grey sand stretching in every direction.

'Gone.' I slot an ampule of painkiller into the injector gun and shoot it straight into my neck, crunching a breath bead up between my teeth.

'Gone?'

'Gone with the Edge. It moves, you know.'

They sway, frowning at me through swollen eyes. 'Then why aren't we?'

'What?'

'Gone.'

I stop, the old familiar fear creeping across my aching neck. No one walks out of the Edge alive, people always say. I was dead there. How do I know I'm not dead here too?

You don't.

I meet Rouf's eyes. 'You would be, if you weren't with me.'

They swallow dryly, and I know they're picturing the moment they left me to be torn to pieces. 'Look, back there, I didn't mean—'

'You did.' I load another ampule into the gun, and toss it to them.

They catch it clumsily, staring down at the scratched plastic. 'What's this?'

'Painkiller.'

'How do I know? You could be trying to kill me.'

'Then why didn't I leave you for the Road Agents?'

They look at me, their eyes tight from the sun and the pain. 'Why didn't you?'

'I told you. I'm a medic.'

Cautiously, they lower the gun to their arm and pull the trigger. 'You probably shouldn't have bothered,' they mutter, handing it back. 'Odds are I'm not going to live much longer.'

They seem so strong, flexing the metal fingers experimentally, checking for any damage. 'Why?'

'I'm nineteen. Average life expectancy for scrip workers is thirty-three on Delos, and that's if I go back to the metalworks. Probably only got a few years before someone offs me if I stay out here.' They try to smile, their gunmetal tooth shining behind a twitching lip.

And in that moment I'm reminded of Gabi as she was when I met her, proud and heartbroken and war-scarred at thirteen years old, living furiously even as she chased down death…

'Come on,' I say, pushing myself to my feet.

With the painkillers and the dex-amphetamine coursing through me, I have enough strength to salvage what I can from the mule. My pack, the breath beads miraculously unbroken, the tarpaulin, and – sadness washes through me – the bag that contains Rowdy. From the corner of my eye I see Rouf peer inside it speculatively, only to look away, their throat bobbing. Finally, together we roll the mule onto its wheels and stand back, chests heaving, to see the damage.

'Well, shit,' Rouf gasps.

The mule is wrecked. The front is crushed like a discarded airtight, and even if it weren't propellant oozes green from the tank, disappearing uselessly into the sand.

'At least your hat survived,' they say, picking its squashed form out of the wreckage.

Really? I want to ask the Ifs, but if *they* can hear me, *they* have no answer to give.

The sun beats down, and weak as I feel, every minute we stay is another minute closer to dying from thirst. Using the scalpel I lever the compass from the mule's panel and tear it free. It works, more or less, shivering like a frightened animal before reluctantly gesturing north. I squint out across the dust and shoulder the medkit and the canteen, my muscles threatening to give.

'Pick that up,' I tell Rouf, nodding to Rowdy's bag. 'And cover yourself with the tarp, unless you want to fry.'

'We're walking?' they croak. 'We're *walking* and you want me to carry trash?'

The look I give them must be persuasive, because within seconds they are wearing the tarpaulin like a cape, Rowdy's bag clutched in their metal fingers.

I settle the hat on my head and turn east, towards Sagacity.

'Let's go.'

Hot air blasted my face as I stepped from the transport, real air, and I closed my eyes in relief. Until I tried to take a breath. That was when I discovered what Delacey had meant by "rudimentary" habitation. The air was so thin that after a few steps my knees trembled and I had to lean on the rail. Beside me, a large woman who was all muscle helped a thinner person along.

'Breathe shallow,' she said when she saw me gripping that railing. 'Body'll get used in time.'

I blinked away sun shadows and forced myself to look at her properly. Allies were thin on the ground, and she could be a good one. 'Eight.' I held out a hand slimy with sweat. 'Or Peccable.'

The woman frowned at my face, mostly at the crescent moon tattoo around my eye. 'Heard of you. I'm Fifteen.' Her brows knit and she tried to peer at her own prison collar, like a cat washing its chest. 'Harri-something. I forget.'

'Harridan.' The thin inmate looked over at me, and attempted a smile. Though they looked no more than twenty-five, their hair was straggly and white, their frame so skinny the prison collar rattled on the pins that kept it fixed in flesh. 'I'm Mollusc, according to Warden Thesaurus.'

I nodded in greeting, wondering what they did to land in Delacey's bad graces.

'Already said we'll call you Moll,' the large woman reminded.

'Whatever you say, Harri.'

'And I'll call you Pec,' Harri told me. 'Need something short. Can't keep all these fancy wardeny names in my head.'

Who was I to argue with that? As we neared the end of the ramp, I got a first glimpse of our new home. A small pre-fab compound within a sheet-metal fence, a field of sickly-looking ghost agave in the ochre-coloured dust.

I let go of the railing and took my first step onto Factus.

A predator snapped their eyes to stare my way, hungry, inhuman, mouth gaping wide. Silver spun. Footsteps led into hell. A blade gleamed. Dark sand and eternity...

Someone caught me before I hit the ground. Hands covered fingertip to wrist in blood.

'I told you, breathe shallow.'

Harri's solid, pock-scarred face was back. I looked around, heart thundering, but there was nothing. Just the dust and the other air-sick inmates and the joke of a compound.

'Keep moving, grunts,' one of the recruiters yelled, banging the rail with a stun-stick.

We were corralled like wobbly, gravity-born cattle through the main gate onto a parade ground. Back on the hulk I'd pictured a hectic, grimy, mining camp, filled with activity and work and opportunities for those who were creative enough to find them. But here were dark-windowed buildings and a few empty sheds. The Lutho-Plex flag – grey infinity on a blue background – couldn't even muster itself to greet us.

Three people stepped from a doorway. One I guessed was the Commander. From a distance he looked the part; large and broad, filling his Lutho-Plex uniform to the seams. But up close, his face sagged at the edges, like it had been stretched too far out of shape. The second man, by contrast, was taut as wire, his long, black hair tied in a ponytail at his neck. A woman with white blonde hair and eyes hidden behind smoked lenses was the third. She held a semi-automatic charge gun like someone would try to take it from her. I didn't need to look at her for long to know we'd have a problem.

The recruiters clanged the gates closed behind us, and made for their ship at a half-run.

'Welcome to Landfall Five,' the big man's voice rang from the metal walls. 'I am Personnel Commander MacOboy, this is Deputy Song and Warden Santagata. Yes, we are the only official L-Plex personnel planetside. Yes, that means you outnumber us. And before you think of rioting, revolting or staging a coup, yes, we are authorised to neutralise you whenever we deem fit.' He looked us over expressionlessly. 'We could set every single collar to throttle and no one would do so much as stamp a form. But we won't do that, because out here we have to rely on each other, as pioneers, charged with creating life, a noble task for which our names will be remembered...' He trailed off, worrying at the silver pistol at his waist before coming back to himself. 'Rules. No drinking, no drug-taking, no interpersonal relationships, and absolutely no gambling or gaming of any kind. Is that understood?'

I waited for the jeers, the muttered insults and threats, but the inmates were glue-lipped, except one who was vomiting into the sand. As MacOboy turned away, a voice broke the silence.

'Where are Cohort One?'

It was the nervy, tattooed man who'd sat beside me on the transport. Braver than he looked, then. The Commander stopped walking, as if he'd reached a wall.

'Cohort One were reallocated to another site, off-moon,' Deputy Song answered smoothly. 'Inconvenient for all involved. We don't wish to repeat it.'

Without a word, MacOboy stalked away into one of the buildings. Was it a trick of the shifting dust, or were his hands shaking like a drunk's?

'Alright,' Song clapped, some of his steel-like tension loosening. 'I'm Doctor Yussef Song, and I may be the deputy but I'm also the medic, so any injuries or illnesses, come to me before they start to fester please?'

A few snorts of laughter. We were used to prison medicine: sterilising spray, skin staples, a cauterising iron and not much else.

Doctor Song smiled bleakly. 'I see some of you already feel like the wrong end of a disposal unit. This is terraforming for the budget-conscious. Your haemoglobin levels will adjust in time. But until then you might experience weakness, nausea, headaches, even some auditory or visual disturbances. Perfectly normal. A booster will be issued with your evening rations. Now, follow the warden, she'll show you the bunk rooms.'

As he turned away I caught his gaze, and for a second the eyes were not his at all but orbs of pure darkness, endless as the Void. Bile flooded my throat, but soon as it came, the vision was gone and he was just a man, and I was just another air-starved prisoner.

All the same, as I walked away I couldn't shake the feeling that *something* was watching me go.

TWO

THE
BOOK
OF
THE
TRAITOR

W E WALK THROUGH noon, shadows squirming beneath our boots. After hours, I have seen nothing and no one and eventually, I realise why. These are the alkaline flats that mark the edge of the U Zone, so merciless that even gangs can't be bothered to try and make a living so far from the pickings of the settlements. With each step, the ground cracks beneath my feet, sending up dust until it is like trying to breathe chalk. It curdles with the sweat on my face and forms a paste that dries and flakes from my skin like plaster.

Rouf staggers behind me, complaints long lost to gasping. Perhaps they are more injured than I thought. Or perhaps their Delos-bred body is still adjusting to Factus's thin air and searing heat.

There is no shade to be found, but when I hear Rouf's steps start to falter, I call a stop and collapse down onto the cracked dirt.

They drink greedily from the one canteen. 'Enough,' I croak, every word painful. 'Or we'll run out before we get there.'

They look dreadful, their eyes swollen, hair matted with sweat, dust and blood. 'This trade post you remember… what if it's not there? We'll be dead.'

My lips crack as I smile. 'We're already dead.'

'You're insane.'

I screw the cap back onto the canteen and lift my scarf to wipe the sweat-paste from my face, wincing at the sting of fabric on sunburned flesh. Rouf's reddened eyes fix on the ugly scar that encircles my neck, earlobe to earlobe.

'Hell happened to you?' they wheeze.

I let the scarf fall. 'Long time ago.'

'Prison collar scar?' They sway as they sit in the dust. 'What you do? Cut it off?'

My ears are ringing, head full of pounding drums. I am too tired to lie. 'Yes.'

'You a murderer?'

Too close to the truth. 'Told you. Army medic.'

'Bet you were a Limiter. You got that look. Like someone just spat in your grits. Am I right?'

'How did you know?'

Rouf snorts. 'Winners don't usually have to cut their own throats. Glad I didn't fight.'

I swallow painfully, trying not to remember the feel of sundered flesh beneath my fingers. 'You were too young?'

'Please. Got my first job in the War Shops when I was ten. How I lost the hand.' They flex their shining fingers. 'Had this six years and I'm still paying it off. Will be until I'm dead, I reckon. Unless I miss a payment and Xoon Futures come to take it back. Was it worth it?'

'What?'

'The war. Was it worth it?'

They can't know how dangerous that question is; how it once drove me to madness in my own cell. I push myself to my feet and shoulder the canister. 'Shouldn't waste breath. Come on.'

It is almost dusk, my strength gone and we've barely a few swallows of water left when I see a shape on the horizon. I wave for Rouf to stop, praying it isn't a Fata Morgana, and pull the binoculars from around my neck. Through the cracked lenses I see a vehicle trundling its way across the flats, leaving a vast dust cloud behind it. I squint to make out the bright pink words painted on its side.

> ! BARROW-TRAM-A-RAWBONE !
> TCHOTCHKES & KNICK-KNACKS
> CURIOS AND COMPONENTS.
> TEETH ON VALUATION!!!

'Milestone-monger,' I rasp, letting the binoculars fall. 'Quick, your hand.'

Weakly, Rouf hefts their metal hand into the air, twisting it this way and that to catch the light.

Come on, I will the truck, praying it has seen us. Finally, it falters and grinds to a halt. I grab Rouf's arm and we stagger across the crusted ground towards it.

As we get closer I see that it is some kind of ex-army ox, Accord-yellow paint chipped away to the under-skin. A floral tarp covers its rear, the cab hung with trinkets and oddities of all kinds.

Ten paces away, I stop and pull the scarf from my nose and mouth. 'Unarmed,' I call, tasting the rawness of my throat.

No one answers. Waving Rouf to stay alert, I sway towards it, hearing nothing but the click of metal as it cools. Rounding the back, I reach out to push the tarpaulin aside.

'Ha!'

A bolt streaks past me, missing my neck by an inch. Even exhausted, my body reacts, snatching the scalpel from my belt and jamming it against the figure on the other side of the tarp.

'Drop it.'

A crossbow clatters to the ground and I find myself looking through the fabric into the wrinkled face of an old woman. She raises rag-wrapped hands and grimaces. 'Take what you want, but don't hurt the Barrow-Tram.'

Whether she means herself or the truck I am not sure, but I jerk my head for her to climb out. Up close, I can smell her: grease and hygiene powder on unwashed flesh, a lingering funk of century smoke. She wears huge dark goggles, false neon-yellow teeth bared in a fear-grin.

'We are not going to hurt you.'

She pushes the goggles onto her forehead and squints. 'No? What are you, then? Lost or mad? You look like bacon.'

'Feel like bacon,' Rouf croaks miserably.

'Our mule broke down.' I nod. 'You've come from the south?'

'You've come from the Zone?'

I manage a smile, knowing neither of us are going to answer, knowing the negotiation began the moment I didn't kill her. One look at the state we're in will tell her she has the upper hand.

'We are trying to get to Sagacity,' I say.

'Sagacity, Sagacity, everyone wants to get to Sagacity all a sudden.'

'We would be grateful for a ride.'

'Forget it.' She clucks her tongue. 'Can't take up every gaberlunzie stops me in the wastes. This is the Barrow-Tram not a charabanc.'

She starts to stump away towards the cab. All part of the performance.

'What are you doing?' Rouf complains. 'Just shank the old crow and —'

I wrench myself free from their grip. 'What happened last time you tried to steal a vehicle? We can pay,' I call after her.

She stops near the cab. 'With what?'

In my pocket, the mercenary's steel eye rolls. The tech inside it would buy our way there and more. Only, who knows what data it holds, what secrets it is storing. Perhaps even an image of my face in its former owner's final moments… I push the thought away and hold up the kit. 'I'm a medic, I can treat you.'

'Hoo hoo!' she crows, showing her neon teeth. 'Physician heal thyself! I'm healthful as a fat snake.' She runs her eyes over Rouf. 'But if you walked outta the Zone you must be strong. Good strong off-moon blood, eh? Full of oxygen, eh?'

I swallow. 'How much?'

'Two pints. Each.'

'No way. One.'

115

'Hey!' Rouf breaks in.

'Done.' The woman grabs a mummified rat that hangs around her neck and shakes it, before holding out her palm.

'Welcome to the Barrow-Tram, bacons.'

∞

The Milestone-monger jolts along. The woman – whose name I can only assume is Barrow-Tram – sits goggled and gloved in the driver's seat, bellowing a song out over the graunching of the engine. Rouf winces at every bump and jostle, holding their ribs.

We are both a mess. There is no better way to put it, no kinder medical definition. A night and a morning spent in the comparative luxury of the Barrow-Tram has not helped much. We won't die of dehydration, but my throat still cries out for liquid. Even Rouf did not complain about a scant supper of boiled mealworms, sucking down every last drop of grainy, salty broth before collapsing face first onto a rolled-up tarp.

'How do we know you won't shiv us in our sleep?' they slurred to the old woman, eyes already shut.

She grinned, wreathed in century smoke. 'Got no use for spoiled bacon, bacon.'

Whether that is true or not, we wake un-shivved, the truck already rolling over the ground.

Now, I check my warped reflection in the side of a chrome component. No medic, no soldier, instead a desert rat looks back at me, her lips shrivelled and cracked, eyes swollen, muscles sprained, flesh bruised. I reach up and feel my hair, hanging in

116

crusted ropes about my chin. No chance of washing it in the inch of water and the dusting of hygiene powder Barrow-Tram gave each of us to "clean up" with. A cannula squats in the crook of my elbow, draining away blood I can barely afford to give.

I let my head fall back, nauseous and dizzy, and look up at the ox's tarpaulin ceiling, hung with pegs and grenade pins, plastic jewellery and worn-out components, before closing my eyes. For the first time since I set out for Paranoia, what feels like weeks ago, my brain begins to slow, making room for thoughts of something besides *survive*. I try to make sense of what I am doing, and of what I saw there in the Edge, but I am only human, with a mind like a little box. *Choose*, Esterházy said. Between what? Life and death? Fighting and running? I clamp down on the uncertainty. Even to think such things might be enough to call to *them*. If I had just gone with Gabi when she had shown up at my door, none of this—

What? a voice asks. *The Metaldogs still would have come. People would have died. Only you wouldn't have been there to see it.*

And what about the war?

What about it? What does it have to do with you?

I reach for the tally marks on the back of my hand, tracing their lines, counting the lives saved to answer my debt.

She is right. I could help them fight.

What, you're a hypocrite as well as a lunatic? You said you wouldn't take lives.

I would be saving them.

Isn't that what you told yourself about Tamane?

'Shut up.'

'I didn't say anything,' Rouf protests, before nodding sullenly. 'Your bag's full.'

Wincing, I pull the cannula from my arm and twist the valves, sealing the bag closed. Taking it gingerly in my bad hand, I crawl from the back into the cab. Barrow-Tram sees me coming and reaches back to take the blood, stowing it in a cooler beneath her seat.

'Where are we?' I wince in the blinding light, fatigue and blood loss making my head spin.

'Your lucky day, bacon. We're coming up on Sagacity.'

Through the scratched and dusty windshield, I see the shapes of craggy foothills rising from the plain below. A steady stream of vehicles – buzzards, hawks, mules, mares – fly or wallow up the steep slope to the mouth of the mine, like the contents of a grubhawker's wagon dumped out to fight among themselves. From somewhere in the heart of the place, a plume of shimmering dust rises.

'What's going on?'

'Told you, everyone wants to get to Sagacity.' Barrow-Tram clacks her neon teeth. 'Thank Uncle Xoon for that. He's paying out pistareens and you can bet folk are spilling them. They'll want what's on the Barrow-Tram, believe me, bacon.'

I peer at the settlement before me. Sagacity has always been a lively place, mostly thanks to its position in No-Man's Land –

neither fully U Zone nor entirely in the Accord-controlled Barrens – which is how it earned the nickname Saga City. Hawker fights over black-market freight disbursements, vendettas between rival smuggling crews, water barons periodically droughting the place out in their attempt to control more territory, lopers and catchpennies making a living on scraps of conflict. Always something going down.

But now… building work is taking place. A huge scaffold tower is being erected from plain to ridge, brand-new docking platforms on the ancient rusted skeleton already occupied by ships and birds from across Factus. The camp itself has burst like a ripe fruit, scattering itself over the plain and down the slopes in a jumble of tents and tarpaulins and makeshift habs. Whistling, Barrow-Tram rolls her wagon towards the line of vehicles jostling for space on the trail. At the top, the settlement waits.

Are you here? I ask silently, hoping I am not too late.

'You remember our deal?' I murmur to Rouf, who has appeared beside me with their full blood-bag. 'Or do I have to cuff you?'

'Yeah, yeah. I remember.'

'It's a good deal. All she will want is information.'

They shoot me a look which clearly says *Do you think I'm stupid?*

'Remember why you're alive,' I murmur, and turn away.

Barrow-Tram is peering owlishly at the vehicles we pass. 'Xoon town or not, this looks like good trading, bacons. Lots of needing folk. Move it, dogbosses!'

But I am not listening, because high above, mounted on two vast stilts is a sign, a slap of silver in the hard light.

SAGACITY MINING CAMP
PROPERTY OF XOON FUTURES
∞

Bile rises in my throat at the sight of that symbol, the one I saw spreading across Factus on a tide of war… I drag my gaze away.

On either side of the sign are checkpoints, steel and mesh raptor nests where silver-clad guards hold high-tech looking weapons. I drag Rouf beneath the tarpaulin as we pass by, making sure my hat is low, my neck well wrapped. At last, we break free of the crowding vehicles and drive into Sagacity proper.

Shade slides over the Barrow-Tram as we inch down a dirt street that winds between towering walls of stained white rock, its striations like ancient faces. The mine workings stretch away on either side, some yawning caverns wide enough to drive an ox through, others no bigger than a series of crawl spaces in the crusted earth, like cankers in flesh. The air is hazy, thick with smoke and fumes and the shimmering mica dust that sticks to everything. As the crowds press around the vehicle, my head starts to spin. It is too much. After years in the U Zone there are too many people here, too much breath. Accents from across the system, snatches of languages I know and don't, blasts of music and shrieking wire dramas, hissing grills, hacking coughs, voices raised in discord…

Too much life. Chance is everywhere, possibilities tangling around every haggle, every loaded question and every poor decision. Outside a food vendor, a person in a droger's overalls decides between two steaks and *one makes them sick, they miss their flight, abandoned on this moon,* a woman with bright orange paint about her eyes smiles at a man selling glitterworms and *if she speaks to him their child will be a soldier…*

I sit back and press my fingers to my eyes. What have *they* done to me?

Moments later, the truck jolts to a stop.

'Far as you go, bacons!' Barrow-tram bellows, climbing into the back. 'Shift your stumps, I got business to do.'

Gathering up my few belongings, I climb stiffly down into the dust, trying not to breathe too hard, trying not to feel *them*.

'Thank you,' I tell Barrow-Tram, as she shrugs into a sort of towering back-frame hung with trinkets. 'May your thoughts be clear.'

'Better luck, bacon.' She grins. 'Give my regards to Hel the Converter.'

I look at her sharply, wondering if I've misheard, but she's already gone, stumping away, clattering open the sides of the Barrow-Tram and bellowing out her wares.

'Mad old pod,' Rouf mutters, rubbing at their head. 'Hey, give me one of those breath beads and I swear I won't try to run. For at least an hour.'

'If you try to run…'

'Yeah, the Seekers will find and kill me, I know. Please?' They grimace. 'I feel like I got maggots in my brain.'

With a sigh, I dig out the last bead and drop it onto their grimy palm.

'Green,' they say, crunching loudly. 'So where's this contact of yours?'

I wish my mind were clearer, wish I'd had more time to try and get my thoughts straight. I rub at my forehead. 'Do you know a place called the Barebones?'

'Ugh. Yes.' They heft Rowdy's sack. 'This way.'

I follow them towards one of the larger mining tunnels, where a crowd thickens beside an Accord checkpoint. For a heartbeat, I falter, causing a leatherneck to tread on my heel and curse me out. Too late to turn back. Stomach souring at the sight of those double yellow triangles, I walk on, keeping my head lowered, trying to pretend I am what I look like: some destitute desert-dweller fallen on bad times. Plenty of those on Factus, enough that our filthy appearance doesn't raise much more than a sneer from a trader beside me. Rouf wisely keeps their silver hand hidden beneath the tarpaulin cape. Even so, as we draw level with the Accord checkpoint the soldier looks me in the eye and frowns. My hand slips towards my belt, ready to pull out the scalpel, but after a moment she just reaches down into a refrigerated box at her side to pull out something blue and dripping. An ice slug, I realise. Usually found in the ice caps of Prosper, exported here by grubhawkers at great cost. She drapes it around her neck, closing her eyes as it oozes cooling slime down her collar, and waves us on.

A bad sign, when even lowly corporals can afford ice slugs. How far has Xoon's money spread?

We walk deeper into the tunnel, where the daylight fades and the mica in the rock takes over, reflecting back solar and prop lamps like a brilliant ceiling of stars. Stores and emporiums are crammed into every conceivable space; we pass Delos metal shops and doggeries selling spider wine, sting parlours like Lazar's and live contraband shops. Even a doxological stop, its walls a catalogue of various inter-system faiths, accessible by the minute. But the more I see, the more my unease grows. Most people are too afraid of the Ifs to risk more than petty games of chance, but here, luck is *everywhere*. Droger crews crowd around tables, betting on who can drink the most rotgut; a gang I don't know – red scraps of fabric tied at their throats and boots – play stabberscotch outside a weapon's dealer; in a dusty corner a grubwoman bawls out the odds on a mantis fight, where the painted insects scuffle in a miniature ring and a wild-eyed man screams, '*Box for Papa! Box for Papa!*'

And everywhere, silver is changing hands. The Xoon coins, with their impossible proposition, flooding this moon like a wave, a virus already beneath the skin… I stagger, my head reeling with it and I have to step out of the thoroughfare, against a rough, sparkling wall to try and calm my breathing.

After a few breaths, a dry clattering noise filters into my hearing. One that's uncomfortably familiar, like the voice of someone I once knew well but have forgotten. Looking into a narrow vein off the main cave artery, I see a prop lamp outside an alcove. It spins and cycles through colours, turning the mica in the ceiling marrow white and leaf green, sharp-toothed vermillion. Entranced, I take a step towards it and the sound of the thoroughfare drops away. Inside the tiny cave, a figure with lank curling hair sits hunched over a small table. As I watch, they scatter dice across a worn black cloth like stars.

'Care to play?'

Their voice seems to come from somewhere else.

I draw back. 'It's dangerous.'

They laugh and sweep up the dice with scarred hands. 'Not for you.'

Without meaning to, I step closer. Beneath the figure's coiling, grey-black hair, I see a glint of dull metal, like lead. Their coat is made of old snakeskins. In the rainbow light it seems to writhe.

'What do I do?'

'Ask,' a hoarse voice says. 'Roll.'

I shouldn't do it. Already I can feel the strange greasiness in the air, as if the world has turned and I'm on the wrong side, looking at its weft. *Ask*.

I hold out my hand.

Will what I saw come to pass?

Six objects fall into my palm, knobbed and uneven. Not dice. Bones. Human knucklebones.

I drop them in horror, scattering them across the table and it's too late, I have already played and *they* are here, waking, watchful.

The teller's fingers spider over the bones, deciphering the language of dead hands.

'Death in the desert,' they whisper, 'a trade, one life for nine. And him. Him or Hel.'

They raise their face to mine and their eyes are gone, the eyeless sockets in-filled with silver, their flesh grey as a corpse. I stumble back as they open their mouth, dark sand spilling from their tongue…

Hands grab me as I spin, panicked. 'What's wrong with you?' a familiar voice demands and I blink to see Rouf staring up at me. 'Are you completely cracked?'

I turn, but there is no cave, no lantern, and no figure. Just solid rock, sparkling with black mica, giving me back my own shadow.

'I…' I close my eyes. 'I don't know. There's something wrong with this place.'

'Yeah well, you're the one who wanted to come here.' Rouf sighs. 'Can you keep it together for another minute? We're almost there.'

Every part of me wants to turn tail and run for the light, back to the desert where it is safe. But I know it's an illusion. If what Esterházy showed me is true, there will be no safety there, for me or anyone else. I nod to Rouf and we walk on, into the cave.

I smell the Barebones before I see it, a spoiled dairy fug that competes with the tunnel's other ripe odours. Two huge silver churns stand on either side of a cowhide-curtained doorway.

'What is this place?' I ask, as we approach.

'Brovos joint.' Rouf makes a face. 'Hope you like cows.'

Inside, the smell is even worse. There's leather everywhere, on the bar, the stools, even the floor is covered with cowhides.

And it's crowded, so many faces that they curdle in my vision, until I see that many of them bear augmentations and body modifications, glowing blue at temples, throats, earlobes.

'Well?' Rouf demands. 'Where's this contact of yours?'

I turn, staring through the gloom. 'I don't know.'

Nothing for it. Swallowing down some sticky air, I inch into a space at the bar.

'Hey,' I call to the bartend, a woman with hair slicked to her skull and a bolt-gun at her hip. Her thickly glossed lips downturn as she takes in my appearance.

'No scabs.'

'I'm looking for someone.' Cursing myself for giving Rouf the last breath bead, I take an ampule of painkiller from the kit and slide it over. The woman raises an eyebrow, looking at me closer.

'Yeah?'

'She—' What would Gabi even go by, here? 'She works for Malady Falco.'

The bartend's lips squeeze together. Along the bar, I see a burly Peacekeeper turn my way, a new Xoon Futures gun sparkling in their holster.

'You want to be careful who you say that name to here.'

Nerves flood into my stomach as I realise just how many people in the bar are wearing silver. 'Forget it,' I murmur, turning to Rouf. 'Let's go.'

I manage two steps towards the door before someone grabs me. Instincts kicking in, I spin, snatching the scalpel from my belt only for a small, callused hand to seize my wrist and disarm me, as easily as someone taking a toy from a child. I look down into Gabi's dark eyes. Glaring at me, she pockets the scalpel and shoots a syrupy smile in the direction of the bar.

'Don't mind her,' she says sweetly, wrapping an arm around my shoulders. 'She's mad. Weaker than Prosper tea. Come on, auntie, let's get you sat down…'

Her fingers dig into my arm as she pushes me through the crowd towards a table in a private cubbyhole, concealed behind a cowhide curtain. She has obviously been here for some time, the surface littered with empty plates and bowls of gelatine cubes.

'Can't you go *anywhere* without attracting attention?' she hisses.

'Why do you think I've been living in the U Zone?' I lower myself stiffly into a chair, trying to calm my thumping heart.

She surveys me. For all her hard mouth and deep frown something flickers in my chest at the sight of her. Almost happiness. I must be smiling because her lips twitch a little in response as she takes a seat and pours a measure of cloudy liquid into a cup.

'You look like shit. Smell worse. Here.' She pushes the drink towards me.

I take a sip of it and wince at the odd, dairy tang of milk liquor. 'Kosmos?'

She shrugs apologetically. 'Only thing they serve.'

I nod, and drink again. 'We had hard travels.'

'We were almost eaten alive by Road Agents,' Rouf says, pushing through the curtain and grimacing as they sit.

Gabi stares at them hard before switching her gaze to me. 'Who is this silverfish and why are they talking to me?'

'Rouf Cinque,' they say at once, polishing their metal hand on their grimy chest and holding it out.

She ignores them. 'You brought them why?'

'Because they worked for Xoon. They were hired by the Alcaide here to join a group of Metaldogs in the U Zone.' I swallow back the memory of blood. 'They were part of a gang that attacked my town, Paranoia.'

She sighs, but has the grace not to say *I told you so*. 'The place with the clinic. Many dead?'

I nod.

'The Metaldogs?'

'Your auntie here went loco and killed most of them.' Rouf scrapes up some gelatine from an empty bowl before eyeing the Kosmos bottle. 'Some of them were alright, you know.'

'She's not my auntie. And it seems she didn't kill *you*.' Gabi shakes her head. 'One day, Low, you'll learn that youth doesn't mean shit. How come you didn't run away?' she asks Rouf.

They shrug painfully. 'Tried. But it seemed like too much effort in the end. Plus, I needed a ride.'

She just rolls her eyes. 'What were they paying you? Xoon Futures, the Alcaide?'

They flash her a gunmetal smile. 'Eighty a week.'

'Silver or scrip?'

'Scrip,' they admit.

'Alright. I'll pay a hundred a week, in silver, if you work for me instead.'

Rouf's eyebrows almost disappear into their ragged curls. Looking at me, they shrug. 'Done.'

'Good.' Gabi leans back. 'You can start by telling me what your orders were from Xoon.'

'Think I know the man?' Rouf mutters, rubbing at their wrist. 'Just heard that people were getting recruited as mercs here and there was good money in it. So I came.'

'And then?' Gabi's voice is steely, some of the commander she once was returning.

Rouf shifts uncomfortably. 'We were given a bunch of arms, told to run them into the U Zone and equip a gang, help them take a few settlements, report back when we'd cleared them out. Don't know why.'

'Because Xoon Futures can't get what they want in Accord-controlled land.' She meets my eyes. 'Xoon started setting up research outposts all across Factus about six months ago. He tried to do it in the towns first, but the Accord balked. They don't like the idea of him having access to something they don't. So he tried to drop some into the Barrens. None of them lasted long before they got hit by Seekers or...' Her smile stretches. 'Others.'

'Falco?' I ask, my neck prickling at the memory of the bartender's scowl when I mentioned her name.

Gabi smirks. 'Someone in Xoon Futures must bear a grudge, because we keep getting tip-offs about locations. Let's just say the G'hals have been moving a lot of Delos tech through the markets lately.'

'Shit,' Rouf says, looking at Gabi, impressed.

'So now it looks like Xoon's grabbing land in the U Zone because he knows he can operate unmonitored there. Beyond the Accord's reach. *If* he can keep his bases safe. Hence your Metaldogs.'

Research outposts. Thinking of the abandoned base and its record of countless deaths, my stomach sours. 'I don't think it's the first time Xoon Futures have tried something like this.' In my pocket, the two-faced coin weighs heavy, the memory of blood and war all too present. Would Gabi believe me, if I told her what I saw in the Suplicio? Or call me crazy like she always used to? 'What are they looking for?' I ask instead.

'That's what we're trying to find out.' She raises an eyebrow at Rouf.

'Search me.' They shrug. 'I'm just here for the cash. Are you eating that?'

Gabi sighs testily and shoves the remains of a Brovos steak towards them. 'Xoon's been collecting data. We know that much from what we snatched from the outposts. Some of it standard stuff, atmospheric pressures, meteorological stats. Some of it seems random. Endless lists of probabilities…'

Reaching into my pocket, I pull out the steel eye; Lazar's parting gift. Rouf swears, dropping the last bit of steak.

'That's Muck's eye.'

I ignore them and hand it over. 'This belonged to one of the mercs. Might have information on it.'

Gabi examines it, before giving me a strange look, half-puzzled, half-amused. 'Glad to see there's a bit of spy left in you.'

'You were a spy?' Rouf asks, gaze travelling between Gabi and me. 'Goddam.'

I feel heat creep up my scarred neck. 'I don't know how we'll access it, though.'

'I do.' Gabi pushes back her chair. 'Follow me.'

The Personal Notes of Pec "Eight" Esterházy
Lunar Body XB11A – now "Factus"
Lutho-Plex Outpost

Where was I? The bunkroom. Yes. We should have known there was something wrong the moment we saw it. Twenty-five beds to sleep fifty and only twenty-three of us. Not that the rest of the inmates seemed to care. Most rushed to claim their own, arguing pointlessly over the best spot. Others sagged against the flimsy walls in relief, sweating. Some had been on the hulks for so long they'd been robbed of their horizons, couldn't stand to be beneath the sky.

The bunkroom was just that, an empty room full of beds. Wasn't exactly clean either; there was a layer of dust over everything, drifts of sand in the corners.

'Pec, over here.'

Harri gently helped Mollusc onto a lower bunk and heaved herself to the upper of the next one along. It clanked as she did, but she looked satisfied once she was there, like a ship's cat on a favourite perch.

She jerked her chin at the bunk opposite. 'Upper's better than lower, I reckon. Out of the draught.'

I took the bed between Harri and the man with the living tattoos.

'Mind?' I asked.

'Whatever, grandma,' he grunted.

I let it go. He'd find out soon enough.

The bunks were unmade, of course, a pile of bedding dumped in the centre of the room — tough synthetic sheets and a wad of thermal blankets. Inmates fought over the best. By the time I got there, Bigmouth Lon was hurrying away with three in her arms. Not that it mattered. There were plenty to go around, so many that a few of the resourceful inmates were already forming capes or wrappers from the shiny fabric.

I started to fold my sheet corners properly, the way I learned working the cleaning shift on the long *Decader* voyage, only to see something gleam inside a tear in the mattress pad. I reached in and pulled out metal.

It was a coin, or something shaped like one. I sat on the bunk, turning it in my fingers. A snake eating its own tail. The number eight.

'What's that?' the tattooed man demanded.

'Don't know.'

'Let's see.'

I handed it over. My palm tingled where it had rested.

He sucked his teeth. 'It's for playing Snakes and Eights.'

Of course. Popular game in the Western Systems. Simple and cruelly compelling. Place your bet, toss the coin. Snake eats all. I'd seen people lose their whole lives to that viper. But this coin looked different; the snake was an ouroboros and the eight was on its side. Eternity and infinity. No choices at all.

'Keep it,' I told the man. Call me superstitious, dragging tattered fears and frailties all the way from Earth, but the idea of carrying those two symbols made my skin crawl.

He looked at me warily. Generosity didn't exist, on the hulks.

A second later, Harri let out a shout of laughter and disgust as a pair of pink fibreglass teeth clattered from the pillow pad.

'What the hell?'

Moll picked them up with a smile. 'Looks like someone forgot their teeth.' They chattered them at the room. 'Anyone interested?'

That set off a frenzy, as inmates began to turn the bunks upside down in search of hidden loot. They were rewarded. Items were hidden inside bedframes and behind loose wall panels, under the flooring and knotted into blankets. Treasures: a twist of salt, a battered story almanac, a bundle of wires and components, some long-preserved meat. Within minutes, the bunkroom became a market, fierce trading taking place between the beds. Moll – despite their delicate appearance – haggled with the ferocity of a Delos scrapper, until they had traded the fibreglass teeth for a lapful of contraband.

'Maybe this place won't be so bad.' They smiled, dabbing some kind of balm onto their chapped lips.

I looked down at those items, prised from their hiding places, and felt uneasy. 'Don't you think there's something wrong about all this?'

''Bout what?' Harri asked, gnawing on the preserved meat.

'These things all belonged to people.'

'Yeah, idiots.'

But the tattooed man stared at me thoughtfully, tossing the coin in his hand. 'She's right. If this was mine, I wouldn't have just left it. All this shit probably belonged to whoever was here before us. To Cohort One.'

'So what?'

'So, why did they leave it?'

'Commander said they were re-deployed.'

The tattooed man sneered. 'If you believe that, you're slack in the skull. Something went down here. Something bad.'

Moll glanced at me. 'What do you think, Pec?'

Facts were facts. Inmates from the hulks had so little; scraps like these were treasures, not likely to be left willingly.

'I'm not sure,' I murmured, but even then, my gut told me that the tattooed man was right. Something bad had happened here, and whatever it was, Lutho-Plex did not want us to know.

'ARE YOU SURE talking to a data broker is safe?' I ask as we walk.

'Of course it isn't.' Gabi snorts. 'Simon Pure's a snake. But he's the only one with a decent unregistered connection to the wire. And he knows to play nice if he wants to stay in Falco's graces.'

'Who's Falco?' Rouf asks her, hurrying to keep up. 'Your boss?'

'Malady Falco,' Gabi says, as if talking to a drunk. 'She runs half this moon, dryskull.'

'She's the leader of the G'hals,' I explain quickly.

'Alright.' Gabi stops just inside the cave's entrance. 'You two, stay in earshot but out of sight. Don't want Pure getting any ideas.'

I watch her stalk through the crowd, all elbows and impatience, towards a booth wedged into an alcove in the rock. Jerking my chin to Rouf, we follow at a distance.

Simon Pure the data broker sits in the armoured booth like a soft-bodied crab squashed into a discarded shell. The tiny space looks like a dozen wire stations smashed together, cables and screens and carbon printers everywhere, even an old radar system pulled from some downed fighter.

I draw back a little further into the gloom at the edge of the cave. Data brokers collect secrets like shrapnel to a magnet, pulled from deep beneath flesh. One of the reasons why I never asked Lazar for news from cities, or mentioned the names of people I once knew.

'Pure,' Gabi greets, rapping her knuckles on his window.

I see the broker smile. No tattoos of rank on his bald head, no prison scars either.

'Mx Orts,' he says in mock surprise. 'Been a while.'

Gabi takes an airtight from her pack and thumps it on the counter.

'Any more trouble from the Muldoons?'

Pure eyes the can greedily. 'No trouble, thanks to your G'hals. What cause for this visit? Are Falco's little snitching snakes not hissing the right tunes?'

Gabi's eyes narrow.

'Of course,' Pure says hurriedly, 'I'm more than happy to share anything they could have missed. It's a big system, after all.'

'Xoon Futures' interests on Factus. What do you know?'

I see Pure's shoulders heave as he shrugs elaborately. 'Only as much as you must have found in your, ah, recent dealings with them. Land purchases, strange choices of location.'

'Not for the first time.'

There's a pause. When Pure speaks, his voice is alive with interest. 'No indeed. They were majority shareholders in a mining concern, back when Factus was still an unnamed rock. Lutho-Plex. Bad investment, Xoon's mother lost the family fortune, people say.' I see him lean forwards. 'Not many people know that.'

'Bad how?'

'Accidents, misadventures. Story goes that Xoon's mother took her own life over it. Couldn't face the shame of bankruptcy. You know, on Delos, tin is everything.'

Gabi just grunts, giving nothing away. 'Need a read-out on this.'

I watch as she rolls the steel orb through the slot in Pure's window.

'Can't believe you took Muck's eye,' Rouf mutters beside me. 'He loved that thing. One time he once used it to cast some porno onto the side of a truck—'

'Shut up,' I hiss, straining to listen.

'…raw data,' Pure is saying. 'Of course, that will take a while.'

'Just the most recent, then,' Gabi snaps. 'And hurry it up.'

Pure's head twitches towards me and I press myself back, into the shadows. From the booth comes the sound of carbon bulletin sheets being spat out by a printer and torn away.

'Obliging as ever, Pure.'

'My pleasure, Mx Orts. May your thoughts be clear.'

Jerking my chin to Rouf, I slip into the crowd on the other side of the cavern entrance, keeping our distance until we are well away from Pure's booth.

'That toad,' Gabi grunts, peering down at the read-out. 'He knows far more than he's saying.' She lets out a noise of frustration. 'This doesn't make any sense.'

'What is it?' Rouf asks eagerly, leaning close beside her to look.

138

She moves away from them with a grimace. 'It looks like whoever was wearing it was recording something. Probabilities, again. You know anything about that?'

Rouf blinks at being addressed. 'I dunno. Muck used to make people flip for things, sometimes.'

Cold creeps through my belly. *Heads or tails.* 'Flip for things how?'

'Like, sometimes before he shot someone he'd let them flip for their life…' They lapse into silence at the look on Gabi's face. 'Don't know why.'

'Freaks,' Gabi mutters, folding the paper into her jacket. 'We'll deal with this later. Right now, there's something more important we have to do.'

'What?' I ask, nerves growing with every step.

She slides a glance at me. 'We need to see the Alcaide.'

'In person?' Rouf whistles. 'She's a tough woman.'

'She's a mercenary bitch,' Gabi snaps. 'Right now, she's playing the court. Taking Xoon's money, making profit from *our* enterprises. But if she joined us, we could cut off Xoon's access to the U Zone. That might be enough to dissuade him from trying to take more towns. We just need to get her on side.'

'How?'

She turns to face me, nodding at my chest. 'We have to offer her something no one else can.'

'No,' I say, taking a step back. 'I told you, I can't control the Seekers.'

'Then why are you here? Anyway, that's bullshit. I've seen you make deals with them.'

'Once.' *And you don't know what it cost.*

'Once is one more time than anyone else on this moon.' She takes my arm, her voice earnest. 'Low, we need her. This could end things. This could save lives.'

I turn away, knowing that she's playing me like she intends to play the Alcaide. The problem is, she could be right. Behind my eyes I see it again, the war Esterházy showed me, Gabi, dead… Perhaps there is still time to steer this reality onto another path. 'Alright,' I murmur. 'But no promises.'

'Did I ask for any?'

We follow her towards a vendor selling airtights from a wagon. Two familiar figures stand before it, the neon greens and yellows and pinks of their mockingly customised army surplus jackets marking them out as G'hals. One of them, small-statured with a bright scarf wrapped tight to her head squints.

'Doc. Is that you under all that muck?'

Warmth flickers in my chest. 'Bui. It's good to see you.'

The second G'hal turns, smiling sheepishly. 'Alright, Doc?'

Something like happiness swells in my chest. 'Peg?'

Pegeen – Malady Falco's partner and second-in-command – grabs me into a G'hal hug with a laugh. Their pale hair is still bushy and unkempt as ever, and there are new white lines fanning from the corners of their grey eyes, evidence of long hours sharpshooting in the saddle. When they step back, I see the bullet scar on their collarbone beneath their loose tank top: a souvenir from the last time we travelled together.

'I'm sorry about Rat and the others,' I say softly, remembering what Gabi told me about the G'hals lost at Landfall Five.

'Bastards are going to pay.'

'How's Falco?'

Peg smiles wryly. 'How do you think? Pissed off.'

'Gabi,' Bui interrupts. 'We can't find Silas.'

Silas. A crush of emotions fills my chest. Shame, hope, guilt, longing. 'He's here?'

Gabi flicks a look my way. 'What do you mean you can't find him?'

'Who's Silas?' Rouf asks, staring at the G'hals.

'Our flyboy,' Bui retorts. 'Who the hell are *you*?'

Peg frowns. 'He went to pick up a shipment from Vlad's place hours ago.'

Gabi snorts. 'The hophead's probably smoking away his cut in some century lounge. He'll turn up. Listen, we're going in to see Baba. If we're not back in half an hour…'

Peg adjusts the rifle on their shoulder. 'We got you.' They jerk their chin at Rouf. 'What about this one?'

'They're with us now.'

Bui grins, showing real teeth. 'Want us to babysit?'

'No, I'll take them. Proof of another victory over Xoon.' She frowns at Rouf, as if seeing them for the first time. 'What the hell is in that bag you're lugging?'

'Rowdy,' I tell her, feeling dazed.

'What happened to him?'

Rouf shrugs uncomfortably. 'Casualty of war.'

She gives them a look of disgust. 'Bui, put it on the mare. We might have to move in a hurry.'

With a strange pang I watch Bui shoulder the sack, before Gabi leads us away through the winding passageways of rock.

Silas. Memories rush through me like notes played out of order. Black hair resting against my cheek, the smell of a century pipe and green chilli and real coffee, hands rough with fixing engines touching my face, holding me without judgement for a few precious days, gone too soon… The letter I left behind as I walked away into the desert.

'Low!' Gabi's voice drags me back. We have stopped near the edge of the mine, where a brand-new construction of metal and glass dazzles. A lift, I realise. A couple of guards lounge beside the platform, one filing their nails, another drinking lavishly from a glass bottle of water that makes my throat cry out in envy. They are the cleanest people I have seen in a very long time. Even the weapons at their belts shine.

'Here to see the Alcaide,' Gabi barks at them, one hand on the charge pistol at her belt.

The guard looks me over in revulsion. 'Get lost.' Their voice is tinny through an expensive respirator.

Gabi leans into the guard's space until they're forced to look at her. 'Tell them it's Orts.'

The guard's nose wrinkles, but they reach up and touch their ear. Not an ear, I see dizzily, their ear has been replaced by a silver crescent, winking with a blue light. A recent augmentation, the skin around it still swollen and healing. A shiver runs through me when I see the infinity symbol stamped into the metal. Still sneering, the guard waves a hand and the metal doors slide open. 'Go down.'

With a smirk Gabi steps into the elevator. Swallowing dust, I follow her, Rouf at my heels.

The deeper we sink, the more my unease grows. Whoever the Alcaide is, she is obviously powerful and very likely dangerous.

'I hope you know what you're doing,' I murmur to Gabi.

'I won't bother to answer that,' she retorts. 'Just don't do anything crazy.'

As we slide to a stop, I catch my reflection in the glass and for a heartbeat it is not me, it is an old woman, her eyes wide in the darkness of a cave as a silver coin clatters…

The doors slide open and oxygen washes over me, purer than anything I have breathed in years. Of course the Alcaide would have her own supply. I take a deep breath and feel my brain sparkle and spin. It is scented too; a fresh smell of wet green branches, that makes my body cry out for mist and leaves and forests.

'Don't pass out,' Gabi mutters as Rouf sucks great breaths into their lungs.

'Got to get my money's worth,' they say.

There are more guards here, at least six. My shoulders tighten as I realise how hard it will be to fight our way out if…

Stop, I cut the thought off. *No doubts. No questions.*

We reach a glass door. A guard opens it with an augmentation at their wrist, motioning us through.

Moisture hits me first; the air is so thick with it, breathing feels like drinking. I step into the swirling steam, mica sparkling from the walls and ceiling and floor until it is like walking in a cloud-strewn night sky. Gabi seems unfazed, striding across the wet tiles, her boot heels clacking.

'Baba Guelo,' she calls.

Deep water sloshes. The sound of utter luxury. Through the clearing steam I see a bath, sunk into the rock. A woman reclines against one edge, her long black hair wet. Impossible to tell her age; her skin is full and flushed with good food and good air. Standing there, I feel like a filthy desert toad left out to shrivel in the sun.

'Orts.' Her voice is lazy. 'You're back again.' She takes a glass from the bath's edge and fills it from a gently running fountain in the wall. 'Will you join me?'

Rouf steps forward eagerly, but Gabi stops them with a hand to the chest.

'I said I would bring you proof of what we can offer. Here she is.'

The Alcaide glances through the steam. Dark jewels glitter on her forehead. Not jewels, I realise, implanted lenses. Half a dozen eyes to catch everything that happens around her. Such an augmentation must have cost a fortune.

'*This* is your secret weapon?' She laughs, showing mica-washed teeth.

A shiver runs through me at the word. 'I'm no weapon.'

She only smiles. 'Orts here says you are allied to the Seekers.' She lets water drip from her fingers. 'She says you can sense the Ifs.'

There are not many who will willingly speak *their* name, especially this close to the Edge. I glance at Gabi's face, but she gives away nothing.

'I feel *them*, yes.'

Baba Guelo, the Alcaide, smiles. 'Is that how you killed a dozen of my recruits?'

'It was defence. They attacked a settlement.'

'They were simply suppressing local hostility. I can see the confusion.' She glances at Rouf. 'Though I see you spared a runt. How kind.'

Languidly, she rises from the pool and strolls across to a couch strewn with fabric, water cascading from her body. Gabi clears her throat. I can see from the ropes of strain in her neck that she is controlling her temper.

'We can offer you protection from the Seekers, Baba.'

The woman laughs as she shrugs into a fine, pseudo-silk robe. 'Xoon can offer much more than that.'

'What do you mean?'

'Just that he is a man with great vision.' Baba Guelo looks over her shoulder at me. The crystals glitter. Recording us? 'He'll be very interested to hear that I've met *you*.'

Trouble, Rowdy would have barked if he were alive. I can feel threat bubbling beneath the surface, and with it the knowledge that this woman can change reality in the blink of an eye. I meet her gaze.

'Xoon Futures will be responsible for the deaths of thousands,' I say.

'And the Seekers aren't?'

I feel a pulse of nausea. 'It's different. Seekers try to keep the balance, to give life.'

'And Xoon Futures are simply trying to establish law and order. Are you really telling me this place will be *worse* for their presence?'

'Stow it, Baba,' Gabi barks. 'Lutho's drowning this moon in scrip. He'll turn it into another Delos, unless we act.'

The woman says nothing as she buckles lightweight body armour over the silk, pulling on boots and gloves to keep out the dust. 'Alright,' she says easily, stowing a pistol in a holster. 'How about a little test? To prove that your weapon here is what she says and not just another mad Zoner?'

'No,' I croak at the same time that Gabi says, 'What do you have in mind?'

Baba Guelo smiles. 'This way.'

∞

We follow Baba Guelo and her guards through a maze of sparkling clean tunnels and finally, into another glass-doored lift. All built with Xoon's money, I realise. No one else could afford to ship materials like this from Delos. As the doors close, Rouf takes one last long snuff of that good air.

'Where are we going, Baba?' Gabi demands. Despite her youth she looks battered beside the Alcaide.

Baba Guelo smiles as she clips a delicate respirator to her nose. 'You'll see.'

When the lift doors open on the surface of Sagacity, my lungs heave and complain at the clogged, budget air. We have emerged onto a platform that runs above the streets – a private thoroughfare. Night has fallen and the mine's passages and tunnels are alive with solar lamps and the red glow of planchas, cook smoke spiralling towards us, frying protein steaks, spitting grubs on skewers, the fug of buzz sticks and century smoke mingling in the cold desert air.

We turn a corner and light blinds me; I squint in the sudden glare of hot white sodium floodlights, illuminating a roughly circular space cut into the high rock walls.

'The hell?' Rouf swears over the sound of voices, hundreds of people shouting and laughing, haggling, fighting.

I step to the edge of the platform and look down.

Below, a stage has been erected, a handful of the Alcaide's guards lounging at the edges of a barrier to keep back the crowd.

'What's going on?' I hear myself ask.

'An experiment I've been conducting on behalf of Mx Xoon,' Baba Guelo says. 'We're calling it a Luck Tribunal. I think you'll be interested.'

Gabi's face is hard, a jaw in her muscle twitching. I grab her arm. 'What is this?'

She just shakes her head at me.

My words of protest are lost as someone in the crowd starts to bellow out odds. A bet-taker. I have never seen one on Factus before, did not think anyone would dare for fear of summoning the Ifs. But this one stumbles through the throng, a clear glass canister protruding above their head, filled with tokens from across the system: Accord triangles and Prosper blues, pink freight-exchange dockets and even white marrowpence from Brovos. They're exchanging them for silver, I see in horror, passing out Xoon coins faster than I can blink.

Luck Tribunal. I grab hold of the rail as those two-faced coins wink and shine everywhere, clutched in every fist. The air is turning thick, my skin shimmering as it always does in the moments before *they* appear.

'We have to get out,' I call, but the crowd are too loud, the bet-takers whipping them into frenzy. I try to take a step away, but one of Baba Guelo's guards pushes me back, the woman herself watching me eagerly, and the pressure in my head is growing until I feel as if it will burst.

Then, through the clamour, a bell rings and the crowd surges forwards. The doors to the mine swing open and a figure appears, clad in a silver snakeskin coat that sweeps the ground, make-up shining in swirls and patterns across their cool brown skin. They stride forwards, holding up their arms and the crowd hollers and bawls, wanting entertainment, emboldened by liquor and lights.

'Drogers and mongers,' the MC cries. 'Farmers and Factans, Prodorians and pit-dwellers, Rooks and raggers, welcome to Luck Tribunal number two!'

My heart starts to beat hard. Beside me, Gabi's face is pale beneath the windburn and the grime. Rouf just stares, open-mouthed at the spectacle.

'By the authority vested in me by our Alcaide—' A great cheer goes up as Baba Guelo acknowledges the crowd. 'And by our generous benefactors Xoon Futures, I hereby present the following, who stand accused under the laws of the First and Last Accord.'

They point a finger at the mine's doors. They swing open, and this time people emerge – five of them, six – all squinting hard in that bone-white light, some of them bloodied, some of them barely walking, shoved along by armed guards. Each one has a number hanging about their neck, stamped out in metal.

'Number one, Pentita "Babyface" Blaize,' the MC yells, 'for murdering an officer of the Accord.'

The crowd boo and applaud in equal measure.

'The accused Five Wiseall, for grievous bodily harm against a Xoon employee.' The crowd yell, Xoon coins spilling between fingers as people place wild bets.

Sick to the stomach, I realise what's about to happen. 'What is this?' I turn on Baba.

She smiles. 'Justice.'

No. Everything in me rebels, and I reach for the scalpel at my waist, ready to fight my way out of here if I have to, when the third prisoner stumbles through the doors. The hot white light falls on a tall individual with untidy black hair falling into their face, a scrubby black beard and deep shadows beneath the eyes.

All the breath goes out of my lungs.

'Silas?' I whisper.

'The accused Silas Gulivinda,' the MC bellows, 'for flying an unregistered ship, receiving stolen goods and participating in the armed robbery and destruction of a Xoon Futures outpost.'

'Baba, you bitch,' Gabi hisses, turning on her.

'Easy, little G'hal,' the Alcaide warns, and I see the steel that lurks beneath her soft flesh. 'Don't forget where you are.'

'You know he's with us.'

'Is he a G'hal?' the Alcaide challenges. 'No? Well then, I'm breaking no word to Falco. And we caught him smuggling stolen Xoon Futures goods. What was I supposed to do?'

'Call it off.' My heart is crushing itself against my ribs.

'I told you there would be a test.' She smiles her chilling, mica-flecked smile. 'What are you so worried about? Just ask the Ifs to save him.'

It doesn't work like that, I want to cry. *There's a price, there's always a price*.

I lean hard against the railing, staring down at the man I left behind five years ago. Apart from a few threads of silver in his black hair, he looks the same, thinner, maybe. One of his eyes is swollen shut, one ear crusted with blood. He sways, as if drunk, staring murderously at the MC.

Silas. I strain forwards, but the lights are in his face, the crowd too loud, and I feel myself start to tremble with rage, with fear, because something is coming.

Baba Guelo's blood flows red. Screams fill the night. Dust and fire.

'Stop,' I gasp.

But Baba Guelo's eyes are shining. 'It's different because you're here. Already, I can feel it. I can feel *them*. Ready, doctor?' she calls down to someone.

I follow her gaze to the back of the stage, where a lean figure with grey hair stands over some kind of monitoring device. They look up, light reflecting from their spectacles and for a second I see an infinity-blazoned flag flapping in the wind, I taste arak. Then the vision is gone.

'One of Lutho's scientists,' Baba Guelo says. 'An expert in Factan phenomena.' She holds up three fingers to the MC.

I turn desperately and meet Gabi's furious gaze. She gives me one, tiny nod. *Be ready.*

'Then, in my capacity as legal representative of the Xoon Futures Sagacity Mining Camp,' the MC is bellowing, 'I call for this tribunal to commence!' The roar of the crowd is deafening. 'Prisoner number three,' the MC cries, holding up a Xoon coin. 'Snake or eight?'

Silas raises his head and spits blindly up at the railing. 'Fuck you, Baba.'

The crowd are shouting advice while a guard readies a rifle, all of them standing on a blood-stained platform. A shudder runs through me and I realise that *they* are here, vast and numberless, clawing at the cracks between realities as a man's life hangs on the flip of a coin.

'Silas!' I scream.

He jerks as if stung, face dropping into confusion. 'Ten?'

'Eight it is,' the MC cries and throws the coin into the air.

A cry dies in my throat. Something – countless somethings – turn towards me, and just for an instant I see Silas as *they* must, his existence unspooled into a million glittering threads of chance that stretch across the system; a knot about to be cut.

No, I tell them savagely and pull the scalpel from my belt. In the split-second before the coin hits the MC's upturned palm, I turn to meet Gabi's eyes. I see them flare in warning but I don't wait. Instead I spin and slash the blade across one of the guards' wrists. They scream, dropping their charge pistol and I am ready: I snatch it up, aim and pull the trigger, shooting the MC in the arm before they can open their fingers.

Their scream merges with the roar of the crowd as panic bursts like a flood across the space, as *they* descend, ravenous, feeding on the fear and doubt. I see a woman collapse, clutching her head, another person vomit in terror.

'Factus!' someone bellows from the crowd. 'Factus!'

My head snaps backwards as a guard seizes the scarf around my neck, but my body remembers long-ago training as I twist and barrel into their torso, sending them crashing to the platform, my scarf still clutched in their grip.

'Get down!' Gabi bellows.

I throw myself flat as one of the guards from the stage opens fire, blasting open the rock above my head.

'Don't hurt her,' I hear Baba yell. 'We need her alive!'

I look up, vision blurring. Gabi is a whirlwind of fists and charge pistol as she breaks a guard's arm and hurls them from the railing, as she shatters their jaw and kicks them backwards, every decision she could make all happening at once.

Rouf too, I see them run away, see them vault over the railing, see them grab up a fallen gun and turn towards me.

'Hundred a week!' Gabi yells and all those possible worlds coalesce into one as Rouf turns with a wild grin and slams their metal fist into the throat of a guard aiming at my head.

A charge bullet explodes inches from me and I roll, trying desperately to see a way through the chaos. Down below Bui vaults the barrier to slug a Xoon guard in the face and take their gun while Peg is already on the stage, freeing the prisoners who leap to join the fray, battering the Xoon mercenaries with the shackles about their wrists. The monitoring machines are going haywire, one of the technicians down, blood running from their ears, another cowering beneath the casing. I look wildly for Silas and see him directly below me, staring up.

'Ten!'

I roll a second before the green light of a stun charge fills my vision. Baba Guelo fires again and *I slump unconscious, I am dragged to a ship, I slash her throat, I stab her in the guts.* I get my feet under me and hurl myself towards her, slamming us both into the platform, before she can fire, slashing at her arm with the blade as I try to get the gun. With a scream she drives her head into mine and I tumble backwards, pain exploding through my forehead, doubling my vision until I cannot tell which world is real, which reality is the one I have to take…

A pistol whines. Through the chaos I see Baba aiming at me, blood running down her face, the crystals in her forehead sparking and flickering out.

'Enough,' she pants. 'Xoon won't want you damaged.'

The scalpel is still in my hand, but there's something in my other hand too, which I don't remember picking up. I open my fingers. The blank loops of an infinity symbol look back at me.

Choose.

I meet her eyes, and toss the coin.

Everything slows. Eternity coils, infinity twists forever and I step into that maelstrom of possibilities – a needle threading worlds – and carve the path *I* choose.

In the endless moment before Baba fires, I step forwards and turn the gun towards her own chest.

She pulls the trigger.

The Personal Notes of Pec "Eight" Esterházy
Lunar Body XB11A – now "Factus"
Lutho-Plex Outpost

On our first morning in the camp, an alarm woke us before sun-up. Santagata slammed on the bunkroom lights, blinding us all as we opened our eyes.

'Boot room in five minutes,' she barked.

'Cold bitch,' someone spat as the door clanged shut.

I stifled a groan. I felt like death, a headache pounding at my skull, eyes and mouth dry as dust. A hangover with none of the fun.

In the boot room, a jumble of heavy outdoor shoes awaited us, along with a crate of protein pouches.

'Fish flavour.' Moll grimaced, sucking down a little of the stuff. 'Why is it always fish flavour?'

I tried to swallow down a few mouthfuls. After two years of prison protein, my daydreams about food were lurid, vivid. Breakfast aboard the *Heavenly Rest* was always a lavish affair, with dishes of eggs and rice and canned meats and syrupy cakes and juice that tasted almost fresh, and coffee – good, contraband coffee – lifted from the high-class freight consignments.

The memory just made the paste taste worse. I gave the rest to Harri.

'Water rations.' Santagata banged a tap. 'Half a canteen each per day. Let's go.'

One by one we lined up, shivering in the pre-dawn air. Santagata turned the tap sharply between each ration, not allowing a single stray drop to hit the ground. The canteen on her belt, of course, was twice the size of ours. Already, I could hear people muttering, wondering why we had left the hulk for this shit, but for all the discomfort I was glad.

Because when I took a breath, the air was sharp as ice and once we were out beyond the gates there were no walls, no soul-deadening metal corridors, just space and a luminous dawn as beautiful as any I could remember, streaked gold and rose and lilac, like the cellulose-silks my workers once saved their tips to buy.

On the horizon Brovos hung like a huge gleaming eye, ringed with red. The sight brought a strange ache to my chest. The famous navigators of the ISSB might have been the first ones to set foot on this moon, but ours would be the hands that built it.

We were set to work assembling some kind of huge monitoring device, lugging it out into the wastes beyond the camp, hauling cable to attach it to a generator, digging its spindle legs into the hard-packed dirt. Its silver body bounced the light savagely until we were all half-blind with sun-flare. My muscles trembled as I hauled and heaved alongside the others, old wounds and injuries waking up to groan.

Beside me, Harri took Moll's share of the work, carrying enough for two. She worked hard and reflexively, pounding rivets with ease, never minding the sweat that ran from her thick, red hair. As the day grew hotter, some of the inmates started up an old work-song about an engineer with only ten breaths left, until Santagata put a stop to it, telling them they were wasting Lutho-Plex's oxygen.

After what felt like hours, our team of five was allowed a rest. We trudged towards the tiny tarpaulin shelter set up to protect the tools rather than us. The tattooed man – Scratch – collapsed beside the tool crate. Harri chafed at Moll's hands, sharing her canteen. A man I didn't know watched her ministrations with a look I knew to be envy.

'Think this is hard?' he muttered. 'Try being inside a rigging suit for nineteen hours straight, only water whatever comes down the pipe from the last man, hands so scorched they stick to the gloves.'

'Cry me a gallon,' Scratch mocked. 'You were the one stupid enough to sign up.'

The rigger made to stand, ready to smack his face. Smirking, Scratch lifted a mallet from the tool crate. The handle caught the light.

'Give me that,' I said.

'But, Ma, we were playing.'

I snatched it from his grasp. He grunted in surprise at how easily I took it, but I ignored him, turning the handle, looking for what I had just seen, letters scratched lightly into the metal: a name.

'Six Nguyen,' I murmured.

'What?'

'Must have been another prisoner,' Moll said, lifting their head from Harri's shoulder to see. 'From the last cohort.'

'Where did you get this?' I asked Scratch.

He frowned. 'Tool crate. Why—'

'Harri.' I shifted myself over towards the crate. 'Keep an eye for Santagata.'

Reaching inside, I rifled through the tools, pulling out any that seemed worn. On a spanner I found another name, *Pest Cox*, on another a series of numbers: #239703.

'Why the hell do you care who used them before?' the rigger grunted.

'Because it might tell us what happened here, you glomb,' Scratch said, squinting at a worn chisel. 'What's this?'

I took it and peered at the words.

Μην τρέχεις. Αυτοί είναι παντού

'Looks like Greek.'

'Is it a name?' Moll asked.

'Don't think so. Does anyone here speak Greek?'

'Five!' Scratch said at once. 'Five Farai. Didn't he used to run with a Hellenic transit crew?'

Before I could speak, Harri let out a pointed cough. I shoved the chisel into my pocket, knowing that if they found it on me, I'd be adding years to my sentence. Santagata's shadow loomed outside the shelter. 'Alright, crabs, back to work.'

It took another exhausting, sweltering hour before I was able to get close to the inmate called Five Farai. He looked older than some of the others, a patch of grey in his thinning black hair.

'Esterházy.' He nodded, sweat dripping from the prison collar. I nodded in return. Didn't recognise him, but that wasn't unusual in my lines of work.

'You know her?' Scratch was surprised.

Farai grunted. 'So would you, if you were any good. Best fence in the Western Systems.' He met my eyes. 'What you got?'

I slipped the chisel into his hand. He glanced down at the faint letters and his face went still.

'What?' Scratch demanded. 'What does it say?'

He dropped the chisel to the dust, wiping his hand. 'Drivel. Always a mad one in the batch.'

'Farai,' I said quietly. 'Tell me.'

He looked at me, and swallowed. 'It says, "Do not run. They are everywhere".'

STAND AMONG THE stink of smoke and hot metal and rock dust, staring down at Baba Guelo's unmoving body. Everywhere people are fighting, screaming, dying, hurt. The price. The cost of *their* presence.

'There!' someone shrieks, and I look up, eyes stinging with blood, to realise I am isolated on the platform, my scarf gone, the Seeker scar stark on my chest and a bloody blade in my hand.

'It's her,' a voice cuts through the crowd. 'It's Hel!'

The screams increase, panic sweeping through the fighting as people try to flee down the narrow passageways of rock. The platform shudders under me as silver-clad Xoon mercenaries race from the other end towards Baba Guelo, the one she called the "doctor" at their backs. 'Don't kill her,' he yells, as their weapons whine red. 'Take her alive.'

'Down!' a voice yells and I drop as Gabi flings herself around the corner, firing with deadly accuracy, taking down two, three guards... shoving the scalpel into my belt, I gasp a breath and scramble over the railing, dropping ten feet into the crowd below.

I hit bodies, not ground, falling in a tangle of limbs and boots and dust. The ragged-looking man I have fallen on flails at me only to stop, reddened eyes fixed on the symbol carved into my chest. With a choke of terror, he covers his head.

A hand grabs my shoulder and I spin, ready to strike until I meet dark eyes, one of them swollen. Among the melee, Silas and I stare at each other and I feel the weight of everything in that gaze; that I left with nothing but a letter to say goodbye, that I stayed away all this time, that I am still alive… A shot shatters the wall above our heads and reality crashes back.

'This way,' he yells, pulling me to my feet.

The fight has swelled into a full-blown riot, Factans attacking Xoon mercenaries, tearing down anything with an infinity symbol. One merc jumps for the stage, only to be dragged down by the crowd, silver armour no match for fists and envy and a rage bred from long neglect. Silas elbows and pummels a path down the passageway, but as soon as people see the mark on my chest they scatter, backing up as if I'll carve their hearts from their bodies then and there.

'Gabi,' I choke. 'We need to find her.'

'The stables.'

We stumble on through a sea of violence. I see a group of gang members smashing their way into a container emblazoned with the Xoon Futures logo; see a woman with the scars of a recently arrived convict seize up an armful of protein packs from a barrow only to be blasted in the chest by a hawker. The air is filled with smoke and the stench of scorched metal and mica dust and blood. As we barrel down a rock passageway in the direction of the stables, a G'hal war cry splits the air and the crowd scatters as two neon-painted mares roar through the chaos, Bui and Peg on one, Gabi on the other, Rouf clinging to her waist.

Peg's pale hair is bloodied, but they're grinning wildly, holding a brand-new Xoon Futures rifle, another slung over their shoulder. Gabi too looks dishevelled, black hair thick with rock dust, her eyes shining with adrenalin.

'Get on, gutspills,' she yells.

Gunfire streaks through darkness after us as I scramble awkwardly onto the back of the mare, clinging to the packs. The moment I am on, Gabi revs the engine, sending us hurtling forwards through the crowds. Every second I think we are going to hit something as she zigzags recklessly through Sagacity's winding passageways in the direction of the docks. Rouf lets out a whoop of excitement as we skid around a corner, sending up an arc of dust. At last, through stinging eyes I see the docking platforms rising ahead, ten stories high, a rattling, clanking network of gantries and elevators, the ground below a mess of spattered propellant.

We race through the gates, into the heat blasts of engines. Through the haze, I see a familiar ship docked at the end of the lowest platform. The *Charis*. Charges strafe the air behind us and I look over my shoulder to see a silver-plated truck come skidding through the gates.

'Go!' I yell.

Gabi revs the mare even harder, sending us leaping up the gantry steps and onto the walkway. I cling on to keep from falling as metal flashes past, rattling underneath as we race towards the ship. Gabi slams on the brakes so fast that Rouf tumbles to the ground.

'Move it, flyboy.'

Silas staggers towards the *Charis*.

'Can he even fly?' Rouf demands.

'I can fly.' Silas jabs at the keypad beside the ship's doors with a shaking hand. The other is held awkwardly to his chest, the fingers ballooned and swollen. The lock flashes and releases, the door creaking open with a protest.

'Then get us the hell out of here,' Gabi barks, running the mare into the *Charis*'s hold.

'Gladly.'

I race after Silas as he staggers onto the flight deck. Inside, it is just as I remember, except more worn, messier, as if Silas spends long weeks aboard. His flight jacket hangs over the back of the chair, and for a moment, the smell of the place – old century smoke and oil and sweat and distant spices from the kitchen – threatens to rip the heart from my chest.

He collapses into the chair with something between a sob and a laugh, and starts the ignition sequence.

'Hold on.'

Before I can take a breath he slams his palm to the booster. Metal squeals horribly as the *Charis* snaps the cables holding her in place, straining away from the edge of the dock. I lose my footing as we lurch, slamming into the navigation panel. For one, horrible second I think we're going to plunge nose-first into the dirt, but then Silas wrenches the yoke, dragging us up into the air. Charges pepper the *Charis*'s belly, red in the darkness, but they are too late. Bui and Peg let out whoops and hollers, yelling G'hal war cries down at the truck below as we wallow into the sky, leaving a trail of debris behind us.

∞

Washed up on the ebb tide of adrenalin, I slump in the co-pilot's chair. I know that I am hurt, that there is dried blood crackling on my forehead, pain blooming through my muscles, but it doesn't seem important. I close my eyes. *Deathbringer*. How many dead on the streets of Sagacity? How many injured or dying because of me? My fingers find the marks of the tally upon the backs of my hands. One more, for Silas. Even a single life can spawn a hundred worlds; a single person might save another, might save hundreds in a way I will never know. Every subtraction a tragedy. Every addition is worth it. It has to be.

'Any sign of pursuit?'

I look up to see Gabi leaning over the flight panel, looking – in her crumpled black duster – like the commander of a fleet, rather than a member of a bandit gang.

'Nothing so far,' Silas says shakily. 'I've got the scramblers running.'

'That was *amazing*.' Rouf bursts onto the flight deck, their eyes shining. The wound on their chest has opened again, bleeding through the stained dressing but they don't seem to care. 'You were amazing,' they tell Gabi. 'Where'd you learn to fight like that?'

Gabi ignores them, turning her burning eyes on me. 'What the hell did you do? You were meant to *convince* Baba Guelo, not shoot her.'

THE BOOK OF THE TRAITOR

'I had to,' I say dully, remembering the feel of her hand beneath mine, the jolt as the stun charge went through her body.

'She'll be pretty convinced when she wakes up,' Peg says, throwing themselves onto one of the jump seats.

'Yeah,' Bui adds. 'Convinced she shouldn't have tried to play us.'

'And you.' Gabi turns on Silas. 'If you hadn't got yourself caught—'

'I wasn't exactly expecting Baba to throw me in some crazy tribunal,' he snaps back. 'And I'm alright, thanks for asking.'

'Bet you regret being with her now.' Bui smirks.

'You were with Baba?' Rouf looks Silas over doubtfully. 'I thought she had standards.'

'Oh, she does,' Peg says. 'He might not look it but flyboy here is Jericho royalty. Slumming it with us Border Mooners.'

'I wasn't *with* her,' Silas mutters, flicking a glance at me. A sort of pang goes through my chest that he might still be thinking of my feelings, after everything.

'He likes strong women,' Bui tells Rouf in a mock-whisper. 'They remind him of his mothers.'

'Ha ha,' Silas says, fumbling through his jacket until he finds his century pipe.

'What kind of people do *you* like?' Rouf asks Gabi, pushing at their tangled gold hair.

'Ones who don't kill dogs.' She doesn't even wait to see their face fall. 'Flyboy, set a course for Angel Share. Peg, see if you can raise a signal on the wire, get a message to Falco.' I feel Gabi's dark eyes on me. 'Say that we've got her.'

As the *Charis* bears us away from danger, I let the medic in me take control, opening the kit to treat wounds with numb efficiency. A new dressing on Rouf's chest, a cocktail of anti-inflammatory and painkiller for Silas, disinfectant spray for Peg's grazed knuckles. Finally, I look to myself. I am filthy from the days riding the U Zone, sand from the Edge and dust from Sagacity and dried blood caking my skin. I wipe it free as best I can. In the *Charis*'s scratched metal mirror, a ghost looks back at me. A dead woman, summoned back to the world of the living. Carefully, I patch up that body too, dabbing sealant onto the swelling cut across the forehead, shooting drugs into its veins, pulling my awareness back onto those bones a slow minute at a time. Finally, exhausted, I collapse into the co-pilot's chair and close my eyes.

I must sleep, because when I open them again the flight deck is dark around me, the *Charis* on autopilot.

The sound of laughter and the hiss of frying food and the smack of bitter coffee spirals out of the tiny galley kitchen. I imagine Bui and Peg in there, burning off the last of their adrenalin and wish I could be like them. An easier life, one where I didn't care about the lives taken, or could nod them away as necessary, as Gabi seems able to. My fingers go to the marks of the tally, always present in my mind.

A shadow shifts, and I realise Silas is standing in the doorway, watching me.

'Still chasing redemption, Ten?'

'Still paying my debt.'

With a dry laugh, he limps forwards and gropes around under the console. It is as messy as I remember, the floor littered with bits of trash, protein wrappers, ash from his pipe, an old sock. After a moment, glass clinks and he straightens holding a bottle of bright green liquid. Unscrewing the top, he pours a few drops onto the floor before taking a swig, and another and passing it over.

The liquor is fiercely sweet and bitter like herbs all at once, with a chemical aftertaste that tells me it's adulterated with something.

'What is this?' I ask, as the heat spreads through my throat.

'No idea. The hawker called it "Super Green". Don't tell the others I have it, or it'll be gone in about a minute.' He takes another drink, the slosh of liquid filling the space where words could be.

'So I heard you're some kind of witch doctor now,' he says at last.

I manage a scrap of a smile. 'Hardly. It's just what folk thought, in the Zone.'

He shakes his head, at the idea or the fact I have been living in the Zone, I can't tell. 'Because of *them*?'

'Yes,' I admit. I have never been sure of how much Silas believes, when it comes to the Ifs. 'I thought if I stayed away, stayed alone, *they* might leave me be. But *their* presence just keeps getting stronger.'

'Is that why you didn't come back?'

I can feel it, the hurt that he is trying to keep down for my sake. I nod. 'It was safer there.'

He snorts. 'You're the only person I've ever met who's called the U Zone safe—'

'Not for me. For everyone else.'

He has no answer, just turns the bottle in his hands.

'Back there in Sagacity,' he says at last. 'Someone called you Hel.'

My chest aches. 'Yes.'

His brown eyes are searching. 'And are you?'

I asked Esterházy the same thing, the night she died. *We are all Hel*, she had told me.

'I don't know,' I whisper my fears. 'I don't think so. Not yet.'

Slowly, he reaches across the distance between us. When his hand touches mine, warm and dry and roughened by repair-work on the ship, I feel something inside me begin to crumble. A wall built from cleaned wounds and mended bones, held together with stitches and newly healed scars.

'Most people are more than the worst things they've done.' His fingers tighten around mine. 'One day, I hope you'll see that.'

The Personal Notes of Pec "Eight" Esterházy
Lunar Body XB11A – now "Factus"
Lutho-Plex Outpost

News of what we had discovered among the tools spread fast. Words became theories, theories wild stories. "They" meant Lutho-Plex, some insisted. Others whispered about strange creatures, about gangs of riggers gone mad and living in the desert, surviving on the flesh of escapees. When the gates finally clanged shut behind us, I felt an absurd sense of relief, like a child hiding beneath a blanket.

Story or not, real or not, the words lingered in my mind. *Do not run*. Meaning others before us had tried to and failed?

'Paranoia,' Moll declared as we scrubbed our faces in an inch of water, shared between the four of us. 'Remember what Crazy Fran used to have written all over her cell walls?'

I smiled back, and tried to believe they were right.

Dinner that night was unruly, people trying to elbow aside their fears and doubts about this strange, empty moon with loud talk and filthy jokes. Bigmouth Lon horsed around, starting some competition to see who could eat their chilli-flavoured protein slop the fastest. Warden Santagata stood by the door, eyes hidden behind her ever-present shades and her hand always on her weapon. Now and then she would bark orders at an inmate who fiddled with something that looked like a projector at the back of the room. I turned away with a sour smile as people began to speculate on what they were going to show us. Whatever it was, I doubted it would be for our entertainment.

Instead, I spent time scanning the room for signs of whoever was here before us. I found traces in the faint grooves of boots on the floor, in a line scratched into the table top, a silicone spoon dented with tooth marks. Down the table, talk eventually turned to people's home moons and planets. I turned away and forced myself to eat until Harri nudged me.

'What about you, Pec?' Her sunburned face seemed carefree, happy in this moment of eating and chatting. 'Where you from?'

'Earth.' It was from my mouth before I remembered that it was easier to lie. Because there it was – the usual silence – followed by the questions. When did you leave, which country, which city, what was it like, then? Did you see the storms?

'Tell,' Moll demanded.

I sighed. 'Won a lottery place on the *Decader* when I was eighteen. Spent the voyage on the janitorial staff. I didn't understand inflation insurance so by the time we arrived on Jericho...' I didn't need to go on. It was the usual story.

'What was it like, Earth?' Harri asked, leaning forwards.

I stirred the synthetic protein, the slop that sustains so much of this system.

'I remember how it smelled sometimes, the rain on hot pavements, or the dying leaves – like sweet tea at night and old paper by morning.

It was sad. And beautiful, like looking at the face of someone you love and seeing they've grown old. So much beauty and so much loss.'

Scratch let out a belch. 'Well I'm Jerichan. Born and bred.'

'As if a pathetic gas-stop satellite like Sugartown is the same thing as being from Jericho,' Moll said with a snort.

'It's an official sub-domicile, you void-born piece of shit.'

Harri started to leap up, but Moll put a hand on her arm. 'Better born in transit than with a face like the back end of a waste unit.'

I laughed with the others, for a moment forgetting where I was and what might wait, outside the doors.

'Quiet!' Santagata roared. 'Eyes up. You will now watch a recording from the head of Lutho-Plex, Ms Frida Xoon herself.'

She waved impatiently at the inmate who stood by the projector. Laboriously, they started to crank the handle until the thing's motor kicked in and a pale square of light fluttered into being on the far wall. Santagata slapped off some of the lights.

The Lutho-Plex logo spun eyelessly, before being replaced by a woman's smiling face. She was younger than I expected, perhaps in her mid-thirties, with silver-blonde stubble and weird silvered eyebrows that must have been fashionable on Delos. She smiled, glossy lips stretching like elastic pulled taut.

'Cohort Two.' Her voice fuzzed out of the cheap speaker. 'Welcome to Outpost Eleven, Lutho-Plex's newest installation on Lunar Body XB11A, or Factus. I hope you are adjusting well to the moon's atmosphere. I would like to take this opportunity to thank you for joining our programme, and to remind you that your efforts are at the cutting edge of scientific development: I am confident that what we discover here on Factus will change the course of human history – and human development – forever...'

'Hey,' Scratch hissed over the woman's voice, jerking his chin to Moll's tray. 'Gimme that.'

Moll narrowed their eyes. They had barely made a dent in the protein, and already looked nauseous, but still, they toyed with the spoon. 'What's it worth to you?' they murmured.

'Moll, you gotta eat,' Harri whispered, but Scratch had already taken something from his cuff. The coin.

'Play you for it,' he whispered, glancing at Santagata, who stared rapt at the recording. 'Snake eats all. Eight I give you a share of whatever else I find in this shithole.'

There was nothing strange to it, the type of wager made a hundred times a day on the hulks, but for some reason, my stomach churned at the thought of those symbols – eternity, infinity – spiralling through the air.

They are everywhere.

'Wait—' I started.

Too late. Scratch flipped the coin. The serpent coiled, the infinite loop turned.

Snakes hissed and writhed in lamp-lit darkness, their grey bodies scarred. A light blinded me, sharp-toothed vermillion stars cut into my flesh. A figure with cold, black eyes and blood-soaked hands leaned towards me, her chest carved with a strange mark, to rip the organs from my body...

The coin hit the table, and everything went black.

People yelled, shrieking in panic, and in that instant I knew — with some gut-deep, animal knowing — that we were not alone. Something was in the room with us. No, not one thing. Many, everywhere in the darkness, all ravenous, all with jaws opened wide to swallow us down. I couldn't see, but I could feel them, coursing through the hysteria.

Light dazzled as the projector went toppling, Frida Xoon's face warping as it was thrown onto the ceiling, her voice booming through the chaos. I flinched away as the red sight of a gun cut through the darkness and, inexplicably, I saw what was about to happen. I saw Santagata's face go slack with terror as she fired wildly. I saw the charge sear through the air towards me, saw it split my skull open and my life — everything that I was — spill onto that grimy floor.

No, someone said. My own voice, or another's, I couldn't tell. But my hand shot out and grabbed the heavy food tray, using it to shield my face. The charge blew it from my hands, ricocheting away at an angle into the room...

A shriek, a gasp, followed by a noise that chilled me to the soul. A death-gurgle, air bubbling from a ruined throat.

It could only have been a few seconds before the back-up generator kicked in, but it felt like an eternity. The lights flickered on to chaos, revealing inmates huddling terrified under tables and in corners, some soiled by piss and vomit. The recording had frozen, Frida Xoon's face lost in a mass of static. But most of all the light showed me the dying inmate, lying in a pool of her own blood, her throat blown open by the charge that was meant for me.

I stared until I knew that she was dead and *they* – whatever *they* were – had gone.

GABI WAKES ME by kicking in the door to the storeroom. 'Rise and shine, traitor,' she says cheerfully. 'We'll be landing within the hour.'

Squinting, I lever myself from the bunk. My head throbs; every muscle feels as stiff as year-old snake jerky. There were dreams, I'm sure of it, but right now all I can think about is the smell of coffee coming from the galley kitchen. Slowly, I make my way outside.

The *Charis* feels alive, voices and footsteps echoing through her bones.

'Haven't you got anything to eat on this shitheap?' I hear Rouf yell from the galley.

'I wasn't exactly expecting company,' Silas shouts back, pipe in his mouth. Seeing me, he nods to a tin mug on the console. 'Saved you some.'

'Thanks.' I lower myself into the pilot's chair. 'We're going to Angel Share?'

He nods. 'One of the only guaranteed non-Xoon places left. Falco's been using it as a base since Landfall fell.'

'It's that bad out there?'

'Worse than we know, probably. Every day there's another story of a settlement burned up or bought out. Half the places I used to trade in don't exist anymore.'

Rouf appears on the flight deck, a bag of sev in their hands. 'This is stale,' they say through a mouthful.

'Hey, I was saving that.' Silas snatches it from them. 'You can't get it anywhere out here.'

'I'm not surprised—'

Leaving them to bicker it out, I take the coffee into the corridor and stand at the porthole window, watching the desert rush by below, shimmering pink-gold with dawn.

Angel Share. The name brings back memories of a blue house, the taste of pálinka, Esterházy's inscrutable smile, good food, and comfort. But those memories soon burn up, replaced by others. Fire and panic, a face twisted in hatred. Blood on the sand. A bullet in my shoulder. Esterházy's body in the rubble.

I blink stinging eyes.

Should have stayed hidden, Deathbringer, a voice whispers. *Should have stayed alone.*

Too late now.

Draining the coffee, I go to find the others.

The sun is fully up by the time I see Angel Share in the distance. A rusted docking platform in a maze of shipping containers, it stands on its own in the northern wastes of the U Zone; an illegal port, an oasis for smugglers and less-than-honest freighters to offload their more suspicious cargoes and get their landfall stamps, away from the eyes of the Accord.

But as we come in to land, I immediately see that something is wrong; the docking platforms and landing pens are full, crowded with ships from across Factus. Not just of drogers and water-haulers but gang birds of all kinds; ex-Accord fighters and huge, wallowing Albs and even – I see with a sick jolt – the grease-black forms of the Rooks. Hastily made habitats and hovels crowd what was once a patch of empty dust, cook smoke from dozens of campfires and stoves rising into the air.

'What's going on?' I ask Gabi, as Silas brings the *Charis* down into the dust.

'Refugees from Xoon Futures.' She glances over at Rouf. 'Better cover up that hand.'

They look like they're going to retort, but think better of it, looking around for something to use.

'Here,' Silas says, tossing a welding glove over his shoulder, before giving me a wink.

The second the hold doors clang open, the smell of the place hits me: a cocktail of propellant and metal, human waste and wet dirt and the scent of melting plastic. As Gabi and Bui roll the mares out into the dirt, I falter, not wanting to bring trouble into this place. Before the next second there are G'hal cries and hollers from the compound up ahead, and the dust gives up figures, running towards us. G'hals – with their wild haircuts and brightly dyed military surplus and rivets sparking in the sun. I can't but smile as they surround Peg and Bui and Gabi, leaping onto each other's backs, punching arms, kissing loudly. With them stands a woman dressed in a tie-dyed ex-army jacket and orange snakeskin trousers. Her scalp is shaved smooth, ochre-brown skin glowing in the light of a new day.

'Saw you come in,' she calls, one arm around Peg's shoulders. 'One day that old bird is going to get you killed, hophead.'

Silas laughs around his pipe. 'She hasn't yet, Mala.'

Falco smirks and then turns her gaze on me. Guilt and uncertainty fills my chest as I step forwards. 'Mala,' I start. 'I—'

She does not let me finish, just strides forwards and grabs me around the neck with one arm in a hard G'hal hug. I return it, my head against hers, feeling the heat of her, the strength like coiled wire. She smells of sun-baked clothes and gun oil and the violet-scented balm she uses on her hands and I hold on, not realising until now how long I have ached for someone to touch me in friendship.

'Doc,' she says, pulling away. 'You look like you fell off a leichenwagon.' Despite the greeting, her gaze is sharp as she looks from me to Rouf. 'What trouble have you brought in this time?'

Before I can say anything Rouf sticks out their hand. 'Rouf Cinque. You're Malady Falco? What happened to your eye?'

I see Bui stiffen, but Falco only smiles, the skin crinkling around the toughened pink-brown scar tissue that fills one eye socket.

'Doc here took it out. Along with the bullet that was in there.' She reaches forwards and rips the welding glove free, seizing Rouf's wrist where metal meets flesh.

'You brought us a Xoon bird,' she says coldly. 'I wonder, will it sing?'

Rouf twists. 'Let me go, you crazy bitch!'

'They're with us now,' I say quickly.

Falco raises an eyebrow.

'It's true,' Gabi calls over her shoulder. 'I recruited them in Sagacity. They fought with us there.' Her lips twist. 'They're alright, I guess.'

Rouf stares at her, seemingly forgetting to struggle. With a grunt, Falco lets them go.

'If you double-cross us, I'll cut off the other hand,' she says smoothly, before beckoning us on.

Together, we walk from the dock, through the new shanty outside of Angel Share, filled with the sounds of arguing and crying and coughing, onto the settlement's dirt street. The heat thuds down, reflecting back from the metal-walled houses. 'There are folk here from all over,' Falco says as she walks. 'Snake ranchers, rat breeders, half of Drax, people from settlements as far as the Worrad Pits…'

For the first time I notice how tired she looks, beneath the bright make-up, lines of tension I don't remember about her nose and mouth.

Angel Share's few stores are crowded with people, some bandaged and gaunt, others dust-worn, bargaining, haggling for whatever they can get from almost-empty shelves. As we walk some turn to stare at us. I feel their eyes on the Seeker mark that scars my chest and hear the whispers as I pass. Some make a protective sign over their eyes, more hurry away. 'Temporary hospital over there.' Falco points to what were once the stables. 'I'll show you later. For now, let's get you clean.'

The moment I see the blue breeze-block house at the heart of Angel Share, grief almost stops me in my tracks. It has been re-built just as I remember, except the hand-painted sign above the door now reads *PEC'S*. When the door swings open I half expect an old woman to step out, leaning on a rifle, her grey hair blowing on the wind. But Esterházy is long dead, her body turned to dust. Instead, a young man emerges, skinny as a rail, with black hair dyed an iridescent blue.

'Gabi, Peg,' he calls, rushing forwards, a bit of bulletin paper in his hands, 'you're back.' There's relief in his voice, and panic. He thrusts the paper at Gabi. It's wet with his sweat. 'This just came through on the wire.'

As Gabi frowns down at it, I stare at the young man, a memory stirring of a shy little boy, playing with Gabi as if she were a child just like him, and not someone who'd had their youth stolen from them.

'Franzi?' I murmur.

He stares at me as if I am a revenant, face pale beneath the wind-tan.

'What is it?' Falco demands. 'What's happened?'

Gabi turns and holds up the bulletin, a strange smile on her face. '*She* happened.'

A grainy picture tops the bulletin sheet. I squint at it in the hard light and feel a sick jolt. The picture is of me. My face stares straight from the paper, my eyes dark as hollows, the Seeker scar livid on my chest. Captured by Baba Guelo's lenses.

WANTED

BY XOON FUTURES

THE INDIVIDUAL KNOWN AS

HEL THE CONVERTER

500,000 CREDITS

FOR INFORMATION LEADING TO HER CAPTURE

∞

I stand beneath the vapour shower, blasting grime from my flesh. It comes away in layers, dried blood and mica, sweat and dust from the long days on the road, leaving me raw and bare. I am almost afraid to see it go. I need that coating of Factus, that facade of sand and desert. I am not sure what remains underneath. This body has borne so many names.

Medic. Spy. Traitor. Murderer. Convict. Killer. Seeker.

Life.

Ten.

Hel.

Slowly, I rub some soap between my palms – good, floral-scented stuff, Falco's doing – and lather my freshly shorn scalp. Water beads my body, lean as a desert snake's, patterned light and dark by sun and fabric. Is it even mine anymore? Or does it belong to the Seekers, to *them*? I close my eyes and try to remember what it is to be human.

I step out of the bathroom dressed in clean, sun-stiff G'hal clothes, fresh sealant on my wounds; no longer a ragged witch doctor from the wastes. My head feels light without the hair, but better for it, as if I've shed some of the woman who caused chaos in Sagacity. I walk quietly along the corridor. In the past, Esterházy ran a casual brothel from these rooms, renting them to freelance workers who arrived on the freighters, but now, they are full of people who have lost their homes, seeking shelter of a different kind.

As I walk down the stairs I hear familiar voices from the bar. The thought of cool drinks, frying spices and roasting grubflesh makes my mouth water, but I hesitate, not yet ready to be seen, to become what they want me to be.

Are you Hel?

Heart kicking at my ribs, I walk into the bar.

The scene is so like my dreams, during those long exiled years in the U Zone, that it stops me in my tracks. A table laden with food. Airtights – the majority of Falco's smuggling empire – stand open, gleaming cherries in syrup, oranges bobbing in juice, fish in brine all the way from the hydrofarms of Prosper. Fresh flatbreads dripping with real butter, huge fried slabs of Brovos steak, protein grits, grubs with chillies, fried crickets and thick coils of snake meat covered in pseudosalt and spices. Gabi slouches at the table, one leg over the arm of her chair, black hair wet and freshly braided while Silas pours her a shot of Falco's famous benzene. Bui and Peg set places and clatter plates while Rouf hovers apprehensively behind Gabi's chair, mouth half-open as if trying to think of something to say. They're wearing one of Silas's faded floral shirts, I see with a smile, and have polished their hand to mirror brightness.

As I step among them, a woman with dyed black hair and a threadbare floral dress looks my way, the holster over her shoulder creaking. Bebe, Franzi's mother and the current head of Angel Share, who was here the night Esterházy died, who knew the truth about what – *who* – she was. For a heartbeat, I think that she will ask me something I won't know how to answer. But then her eyes go to the scalpel at my belt and her face melts into a smile. 'Doc. You are welcome.'

'Thank you,' I tell her.

'Ten,' Silas says in a rush, 'come and eat.'

For a few minutes, all is lost to the scrape of spoon on tin, protein and bread and grubs gluing teeth together. Bui launches into a lurid description of our flight from Sagacity, lingering with great relish on details of Xoon mercenaries getting beaten up. Rouf tries to interject here and there, watching Gabi for some kind of reaction. I let more benzene slide down my throat and soon whatever cocktail of chemicals it contains gets to work, loosening my muscles, unknotting the tension in my belly.

'…knew Baba Guelo was malicious,' Bui is saying, 'but flipping for someone's life—'

'She didn't do it out of malice.' I raise my head. 'She said it was an experiment. For Xoon.'

The table goes quiet.

'There was an old guy there,' Gabi says, 'the one she called "doctor".'

'Glasses, long grey hair?' Silas asks. 'He came into the cells. Took blood samples from all of us.'

'And they had one of those machines, Mala,' Peg says. 'Like the one we nabbed a few weeks back.'

The benzene sticks in my throat as I swallow. 'Do you know what it does?'

Peg shrugs. 'Some kind of data collecting. Nothing that made sense, just strings of numbers.'

'Same as from that merc's eye,' Gabi says, pouring herself more benzene. 'Calculations. They look like probabilities.'

My entire skin goes cold. *Probability. Odds. Chance.* The abandoned base, the records of deaths, the two-faced Xoon coins filling Sagacity, life and death hanging on the flip of a coin.

'He's trying to summon the Ifs.' My head spins. 'That's what this is all about. The experiments, the research —'

Rouf snorts. 'That's crazy.'

But Gabi doesn't laugh. 'Could he summon *them*?'

I return her gaze. In the past, she has dismissed *them*, laughed and called me insane, but now I know her military brain is dissecting the chilling prospect – however outlandish – of a person like Xoon being able to somehow use *their* presence for his own ends.

'I don't know.'

'He who controls the present, controls the future,' Falco murmurs. 'No wonder he wants Hel alive.'

Fear sweeps through me. 'I'm not her.'

'Tell that to every hunter from here to Prodor's ass who's going to come looking for that bounty.'

'They wouldn't dare,' Silas mutters.

'For five hundred thou credits they might,' Rouf says, mouth full of crickets.

I meet Falco's eye. 'Rouf's right. My presence puts you all in danger.'

She smiles, orange-painted lips lifting. 'Maybe not. Maybe this is just what we've been waiting for.'

'Don't see how,' Bui mutters, dropping a cherry into her cup.

Falco takes the bulletin sheet from her jacket and flattens it on the table. 'We needed proof that the Seekers would stand against Xoon, didn't we?' She jabs a finger at my image. 'What better proof than this – Hel the Converter herself inciting a riot against Xoon in Sagacity.'

Gabi nods, and I can tell her mind is racing, her tactician's brain calculating how best to use this to advantage, how to fight a second war of spin and propaganda while the bullets fly and the bombs fall, just as the Accord taught her.

'I didn't mean to incite anything,' I tell them all.

'Who cares?' Falco retorts. 'You did. And more than that, you made Hel real.'

'Hel's always been real,' Bebe says softly from the bar. The hairs on my neck stand up, as if Esterházy waits just over my shoulder.

'No, she's been a story, a legend that scratchtooth ranchers tell to frighten each other. Why do you think the Accord keep claiming to have caught her?' Falco leans forwards. 'Because they're scared. They're scared of what she represents.'

'What does she represent?' Rouf frowns.

'The truth. The fact that this moon is barely under their control.' Her eye shines. 'Until now, there's never been a reason for the gangs to unite, fighting over our little scraps of turf. Too many ideologies, too much greed. But what's the one thing every gang on Factus has in common?'

Gabi leans back in her chair. 'A fear of the Seekers. A fear of Hel.'

She looks at me and I feel it again; that her presence is a touch-paper, ready to blaze a path across the future.

'With you on our side—'

'I told you, I can't control the Seekers. I can't control *them*.' But I know that everything they are saying is true, and it scares me.

'Don't know much about Xoon,' Rouf says, picking their teeth. 'But he's a businessman, right? What if you, you know, negotiated?'

'Oh, he's negotiated before.' Falco's voice is soft and deadly. 'He negotiated for the Accord to look away when his private army burned Landfall Five and butchered three hundred people, including five of my own. All those people out there in the dirt are the ones who made it out alive from his negotiations. So I'm not inclined to give him anything. In fact, I'm more inclined to take anything of his that hits dust on this moon.' She looks across at me and her gaze is hard as diamond. 'The question is, *Doc*, why did you come here, if not to help us?'

I stare back, the lines of the tally and the visions of war and the promise I made to the Seekers colliding in my mind until I can't stand it anymore. I push back my chair and walk out without a word.

In the scrappy courtyard behind Esterházy's house, I breathe, trying to still my racing pulse. It feels almost safe here, peaceful, just the distant sounds of Angel Share, the evening heat as soft as spiced honey, ship lights winking through the terraform. Leaning my head against a wall that radiates the day's warmth, I look up at the stars. Hard to fathom that millions of lives are being lived out there, in their own tight orbits around a million brains, billions of realities fracturing every second. Warehouse cities seething on Jericho, long grass rippling in Brovos's endless fields, and somewhere in time and space, a child with my face is looking up at the stars and wondering at tales of the far-flung Border Moons.

The door squeaks open, there's a flicker, a hiss and the smell of strawberry buzz stick fills the air. Gabi watches me, her eyes lit by the pink flare.

'Don't let Falco see you smoking that,' I say.

'I'm not a child,' she grunts. 'Or an idiot.' Stepping forwards, she jerks her chin skyward. 'What are you looking at?'

'I don't know.' *Everything*.

'You know your lights?'

I can't help but smile, a little. 'Some.'

'Alright.' She jabs the stick at a patch of sky. 'What's that group of stars, past Delos?'

'Qureshi's Throne, isn't it?'

'Very good. And there?'

'The Great Gat. And that square group is the Troyerik Spires. And beyond them, the Far Stars…'

I trail off, looking towards the Void, the great chasm of darkness that yawns in the sky.

'You know,' Gabi says, her voice dragging me back. 'I still remember my first solo interplanetary flight. I can't describe the feeling, Low. To be in charge at the helm for as far as a ship could take me… It felt like freedom.'

My chest aches. 'How old were you?'

'Nine.' The lines around her eyes deepen as she squints through the smoke. 'Realised I was wrong about the freedom part, soon enough.'

Clamping the buzz stick between her lips, she reaches into her duster to take out a tin. Inside is a small injector gun, a few phials. I watch as she slots one in, bares her wrist and shoots a dose into the skin.

'My own special compound,' she says, putting it away. 'Counteracts my reliance on the Accord's medications. Keeps everything' – she waves the stick at her head – 'steady.'

I smile at this young woman who cheated death. 'I'm glad for you, Gabi.'

She doesn't answer right away, just takes a drag. 'You know what I was doing while you were wallowing in the Zone?' she asks eventually. 'I was looking for others from the Minority Force. Not just from C Class, from the whole Force. Can you guess what I found, after two years of searching?' She flicks ash. 'Nothing. Not one other surviving member. Just stories of "accidents" and ship crashes and illnesses. They got all of us, Low. Except me. I'm the only one left.'

I want to reach out to her, but I know she'd push me aside. 'I'm sorry.'

'I'm not. I'm alive.' Her eyes burn into mine. 'You were there, in the Suplicio when we died. You said *they* wanted us to live. Why, if not to fight for this place?'

'You're talking about a war.' The tally is rough beneath my fingers. 'I can't let that happen.'

She tosses the buzz stick into the darkness and turns towards the house.

'Not even if it's a war that should be fought?'

She walks away and leaves me alone, those ten words raging through my brain like fire over tinder.

I don't go straight back to the bar. Instead, I slip inside and walk on quiet feet to an alcove at the end of the corridor. It's lit by a string of solar lights and a fat yellow candle made from real tallow. It illuminates a grainy photo, a wanted picture, I realise with a smile. In it, Esterházy smiles into the lens, an old woman with wild grey hair, a faded crescent moon tattooed around her eye and an expression that challenges and pities all at once. *Ma Esterházy* the caption beneath it reads. People have left offerings from across the system: chunks of semi-precious stones from mining asteroids, freight tokens all the way from Jericho, a full bottle of pálinka, even – I see with an odd pang – a string of carved plastic prayer beads from the Congregations. I brush them, wondering if someone I once knew made these while listening to my fathers preach their sermons, whether they are even still alive.

Reaching into my pocket I find a coin, Xoon silver, like the one she showed me.

Choose.

Closing my fingers around it, I turn and walk back into the bar. 'Alright,' I tell them all. 'I'll do it.'

The Personal Notes of Pec "Eight" Esterházy
Lunar Body XB11A – now "Factus"
Lutho-Plex Outpost

After the riot in the canteen, I spent the night in the brig.

A pointless exercise. The warden knew there was nowhere for me to run. But the dead inmate – Leech, I learned her name was – had friends, and the mood in the canteen was violent enough that Santagata and Song were only able to keep control by using the collar throttles.

I closed my eyes, trying not to remember the dead woman's face. I have killed before, no use me denying it now, but always in self-preservation. This was the same, but it felt different. Leech shouldn't have died in that moment. I should have.

Accident. Fluke. Bad luck. Freak chance. That was all it was. There were no *things*, just an empty moon and not enough oxygen to stop my own frayed mind from running wild. That's what I told myself. But in three decades of fleeing across the stars, of sucking in life and squeezing through the cracks in the known system, I had still never felt anything like this.

Do not run. *They* are everywhere.

The next morning I was summoned to MacOboy's office. He sat at his desk as if he had been dragged there. His fingers twitched constantly, his face covered in a sickly sheen of perspiration. If I didn't know better, I'd have said he was a junkie in need of a fix. Santagata stood against the wall, her face as blank as plastic.

At the sight of me, MacOboy flicked on a bulletin recorder.

'Interview with inmate Peccable Esterházy,' he mumbled, as if talking to someone, 'further to the incident previously described. We have investigated the death. Warden Santagata, fearing for her safety, fired a warning shot not knowing it would be deflected.'

I stared at Santagata and said nothing though I knew it was no warning shot. She showed no sign of discomfort. Did she feel any remorse about the dead woman?

She didn't kill Leech, an insidious voice said. *You did. You saw what would happen, and you chose.*

'Further year added to Esterházy's sentence for violent resistance,' Commander MacOboy mumbled. 'Punishment detail, Song has the orders.'

He could have sent me out into the desert to be executed and no one would have done anything more than stuff my record into an archive. He was letting me off lightly. I watched him, waiting for what I knew must come. Nothing for nothing: the first rule of the Outer Systems.

When he swallowed, it sounded as if someone had a grip around his oesophagus.

'For the record, state events as they occurred from your perspective, Inmate Esterházy.'

Was this a trick? Wardens never let inmates speak. Which meant

MacOboy wasn't doing this because he wanted to, but because he had been ordered to. Someone up there was listening. Someone like Frida Xoon.

Knowing that, I made the gamble.

'I saw something last night in the mess hall. It happened when Inmate Scratch flipped the coin he found.'

MacOboy's lips tremored. 'State what you saw.'

'Felt is a better word. I felt a presence. Presences. Others felt it too.'

'You have been made aware of the symptoms of hypoxia. Audio-visual disturbances, hysteria—'

'I know what I felt. It wasn't hysteria.'

'Then what?' MacOboy snapped.

Something else. Something not human. I looked at the recorder.

'I don't know, sir. But we're not alone on this moon.'

Thanks to my actions, the entire cohort was given punishment duty: fetching a spare generator and supplies from Lutho-Plex's mining site, some hundred kliks to the south. Which meant a whole day on the back of a heavy transport ox, with no food and no water, beneath the blazing sun. Santagata was sent as our driver and guard, which made me suspect she was being punished too.

Safe to say it didn't make me popular. I felt the stares of the other inmates as I crossed the parade ground, heard the mutters about me. I didn't exactly blame them. Leech's death clung to me like tar.

I could still see her wide eyes, her neck blown open, orange hair wet with her own blood. A hand touched my elbow and I twisted around, ready to strike, but it was just Harri.

Eyeing her bulk, some of the inmates moved away.

'About Leech,' I told her. 'I didn't know what would happen.'

'It's okay, Pec. Song told us. A tragic accident, is all.'

'Bullshit.' Scratch interrupted from across the ox. 'No one can move that fast. No one sees a charge before it hits.'

I stared him down. Finally, he worked some saliva in his mouth and spat over the edge of the truck.

'No one blames you, Pec,' Moll assured me.

'Some of them blame her,' Harri put in. 'We just heard Lon say she was a freak—'

Moll gave her a hard glance. 'We're all wound up right now. Things will settle down.' But they didn't look convinced.

Anyway, there was no talking after that. Santagata revved the engine and the ox bellowed into life, taking us through the metal gates – our illusion of safety – and out onto the moon's desolate wastes.

We drove south, towards a series of rugged foothills. It had been years since I travelled on solid ground, and despite the dust and the burn of the prison collar about my neck, I felt the brush of freedom. That horizon sang to me. Through the heat-haze I thought I saw a blue house, and tall, metal structures, ships landing like insects. When I swallowed, I tasted pálinka.

The ox stopped with a jolt, almost throwing me from the seat. I blinked hard, surfacing from the drowse. My face and scalp were already sunburned, my eyes dry in their sockets. From the sullen shifting and swearing among the group, the rest of the cohort felt the same. Moll looked dreadful, beet-red, despite Harri's attempts to shade them with her arms. Scratch had removed his jumpsuit entirely and was using it as a parasol, revealing his lean body, inked armpit-to-heel.

Santagata appeared, a portable respirator on her back, the oxygen tube clipped to her nose. Her dark glasses reflected the sorry sight of us.

'Alright,' she barked, clutching her gun. 'Site's up there. You got an hour to get the stuff on this manifest.'

She slung a cracked tab at the nearest inmate – the big man named Filch – who fumbled for it. Ahead of us a dusty slope glittered in the hard light like snow.

'Why don't you drive up there?' one of the inmates complained. 'This truck could make it.'

Santagata sneered in response and touched the transmitter at her waist, connected to the collars. 'Get on with it. Any funny business and you get the choke.'

'Trigger happy bitch,' hissed Scratch as we scrambled down. 'She just wants to watch us suffer.'

'Isn't it kinda stupid, sending us out with just one guard?' Lon asked, rubbing at her scalp.

'Would be if there was anywhere to run to,' another inmate answered as we started up the slope. 'Unless you like the taste of dust?'

Within ten steps I was sweating, losing what precious liquid I had left. The inmates ahead kicked grit back into my face, but I ploughed on, boots sliding in the ruts and soon I started to overtake them. Three decades spent clinging to the margins of space did a lot to toughen a body.

Still, the glittering dust was terrible — coating my tongue like chalk until I could taste it deep in my lungs. Within minutes, all of us were wheezing like air-sick birds.

'What is this stuff?' someone choked.

'Mica,' Lon answered, a hand over her mouth and nose. 'Don't breathe.'

'Goddam it!'

I squinted back to see Moll collapse face first onto the slope. Harri rushed to take one arm. 'Help me,' she croaked to Scratch, who just spat in disgust. Coughing, I skidded back down to take Moll's other arm and drag them to the top.

Finally, the mining site came into view.

'What the fuck?' someone swore.

The place looked abandoned. I'd expected a functioning operation, ready for us to work ourselves to death, but it was nothing of the sort. Three huge digging machines hunched in the dust, paint already pitted by the sun and the wind. Rubble scattered the path, among pipes, girders, fixtures, all of it left out to decay.

Scratch kicked at a crate, stamped with the logo of Lutho-Plex. Dust cascaded from the sides. 'This ain't right,' he muttered.

'No one's been here in months,' another inmate agreed, unearthing a length of chain from beneath the sand. 'What the hell were Cohort One doing, if not mining?'

'Whatever,' Filch said. 'Let's grab what we need and get outta here.'

He sounded uneasy, and he wasn't the only one. Harri and I propped Moll in the shade of a boulder and went to join the others at the mouth of the mine.

No one was moving.

'What is it?' I asked.

Scratch nodded at the doors. They were pitted silver, emblazoned with the Lutho-Plex infinity symbol. 'Not locked,' he said.

'So?'

'So, there could be anything in there.'

'Like what?' another inmate demanded. 'Sand?'

He scowled. 'Just don't get why it isn't locked.'

'Why would they need to lock it?' Harri asked. 'Ain't we the only ones on this moon?'

'I heard there was a Prosperian Army outpost, somewhere to the east,' Lon mumbled. 'And the remains of the ground base for the rig, with a caretaker. But apart from that...'

The silence that followed her words was dangerous. The idea that we were alone here – a few people on a vast moon and no one to come looking for us – it was enough to make desperate people do stupid things.

I glanced around at the faces and saw that many were staring back down the slope at the ox.

Do not run.

As if he sensed it too, Filch leaned down, grasped the handles, and swung the doors open.

Scratch flinched as they banged softly against the rock, but nothing happened. The air that billowed out smelled dry, slightly stale. Boxes of supplies stretched into the gloom: components and engine parts, coolant, fuel, spare parts, tools. Even water drums, protein bars, oxygen canisters. A few of the inmates immediately started jostling for the water drum, trying to work out how to release its seal.

'Enough here to last years,' someone said.

Enough that they can abandon us here. I pushed the thought away.

Scratch flicked a customs tag, still intact. 'I don't get it. Why's none of it been touched? It all looks new.' When no one answered him, he turned to me. 'Something ain't right about all of this, Pec. You know it. Why the hell are we even here? Delacey hated my guts. He'd never put me forward for transfer.' He licked dry lips. 'Look at this place. We ain't here to mine. We're here for something else, and whatever they did to the poor bastards before us, they'll do to us too.'

'We don't know that,' I muttered.

'We know something.' He faced me down. 'What really happened, in the mess hall?'

'I saw something,' I admitted.

'Something?'

'Things. Presences. Not human.'

I expected him to scoff but he only stared, breathing harder and I felt it: fear, crawling into all of us like a parasite.

They are everywhere.

'Hey,' Harri called, a few paces down the tunnel. 'There's something here.'

Everyone stopped. More than one inmate immediately backed out of the mine, into the light. But I had to see. I strode forwards, unhooking a torch from the wall as I went.

Harri stood where the light failed. Beyond her, a vague shape was just visible on the floor.

I wound up the torch, shone it into the darkness, and saw the body.

WE TALK LONG into the night, as Gabi and Falco and Peg plan a council of war: a meeting of all of Factus's most notorious gangs and cult and bandit leaders, the likes of which has never been seen.

Over the next few days the word goes out across the U Zone, via bird and mare and mule as Silas and the G'hals fly sorties into gang territories, even via coded messages on the tangle.

I pass the days treating the wounded who continue to pour into Angel Share, while Gabi prowls the place, amassing ammunition and weaponry into a cache, poring over maps of Sagacity and its surrounding terrain. Falco works with Bui, "auditioning" new recruits to the G'hals, while Peg trains them in sharpshooting. In the exhausted evenings, we gather around the table in Esterházy's house drinking pálinka and benzene and eating meals of airtights and jerky, taking comfort in idle talk, and placing bets of bottle caps and sweets on Franzi's battle beetles including his oldest – a scarred creature called Voivira – named by the General when she was just a child.

I look around at that room full of strange, vivid life; Falco reclining in her chair while Peg massages her leg, Gabi flush-cheeked and bright-eyed with liquor, reconstructing military campaigns with the salt canister and the syrup bottle and bits of bread for a raptly listening Rouf, Bui and Silas, and the other

G'hals tinkering with their souped-up mares outside the doors, and I can't help but smile, even while a pang of sorrow goes through my chest. If the council goes to plan, I will have one job – to summon the Seekers – and it terrifies me. Because there will be a price to their help, as there is a price to seeing the world through *their* presence. The last time it was five years alone in the wilderness.

This time, I fear it might be forever.

I fear, but I don't say. I keep the words locked behind my teeth. And when Silas offers me his pipe I take it and draw deep until billows of green century smoke carry me away, into his arms, and into sleep.

Hours later, I wake to pale light, warm and drowsy. For a while I lay still, listening to the mouthing of the night wind against the sides of the *Charis*, to Silas's steady breathing as he lies in the bunk beside me. I am about to roll over, to rest my chin on his shoulder when I realise that we are not alone.

In the darkness beyond the bunk's curtain, someone sits on the flight deck, watching me. Her clothes move in a breeze I cannot feel.

'Pec?' I whisper.

A flash, like eye shine, something outstretched in the darkness. Silver. I reach out and touch metal, a snake, infinity, the symbols worn almost flat. It slips through my fingers, cycling through those endless states, those choices that are none at all, and in that second I feel *them*, waiting.

I sit up. The fight deck is empty, the night quiet, but still my heart pounds.

Silas murmurs something as I ease from beneath the tangled blanket, but doesn't wake. My head a fug of exhaustion and century smoke, I creep through the ship on bare feet and step out, onto the night-cold sand.

The sky is black as ravens' feathers, dawn a forgotten promise. Beyond the landing pens Angel Share finally sleeps, even the most die-hard drinkers rolled up in their emergency blankets. The night wind slides over my scalp, twines through my fingers, coils around my bare arms, calling me back to the desert…

I'm about to step inside when movement catches my eye: a light on in the old mechanic's shed. Remembering an old man who once sat there, I walk across the sands, picking around spots of spilled fuel. I realise that it has been years since I dared walk barefoot on this moon, where boots are life or death.

I peer inside the shed, expecting to see Horse, the old mechanic. Instead I'm surprised to see a slight, lean figure, tangled gold hair falling over their face as they bend over something on the floor.

Rouf grins when they see me. 'Couldn't sleep?'

I lean in the doorway. 'Just wanted some air.'

'You and everyone else on this rock.'

I smile, my eyes still heavy. 'What are you doing?'

'Wanted to work on this when it was quiet.' A red flush creeps down their neck. 'Wasn't gonna say anything 'til he was finished.'

They shuffle back to show what they've been making. A familiar shape rocks on uneven legs. I stare. 'Rowdy?'

Rouf flicks a switch and Rowdy whirrs, the sound so familiar it hurts. One of his eyes flickers faintly and he comes clanking towards me. I bend to rest a hand on his warm, metal back, feeling the scars of remaking on him.

'He still looks like a bit of a glomb,' Rouf says gruffly. 'Had to use a few different parts. But he's a solid model, guess he'd have to be to last out down here.'

I look up in amazement, at this person who I might have killed in an instant. They smile crookedly. 'Only thing I didn't fix was his gun. Figured you wouldn't want that.'

My eyes blur, stinging in the workshop fumes. 'Thank you.'

They shrug as if embarrassed and step away. 'Wait there, I got his collar.'

Kneeling lower, I put my face close to Rowdy's working eye so that he can see me, my only companion for so long. His eyes flicker at me.

Trou-ble, his old voice croaks. *Trou-ble*.

'I think he's still a bit confused,' I tell Rouf. 'Have you —'

I break off as the walls of the shack start to shudder with something that roars beneath the wind.

Engines.

Rouf meets my eyes and we stumble outside as a handful of birds tear from the sky, circling Angel Share like vicious raptors before making for the top of the docking platform.

'Who are they?' Rouf asks.

I peer into the docking platform's floodlights. The ships are small and sleek and fast, painted with grey and brown stripes, hung all over with hooks and nets.

'The Butcherbirds.' Turning, I hear another sound on the wind: the grating rattle of dirt mules. I push Rouf towards Esterházy's house and set off for the *Charis* at a run. 'Go get Falco, tell her the gangs are coming!'

There is barely time to wake Silas and shove my feet into boots before the crews start to roar into Angel Share. I rush through the swirling dirt, keeping to the edge of the buildings as the Sand Eels tear along the strip on their low-slung dirt buggies and the itinerant Dhūḷanā śētānō lope through the gates, hoods pulled down low over their heads. I recognise a few of the saner crews from the U Zone: the Barranca Boys with their wreck-salvaged vehicles and welding-scarred hands, a couple of Shadow Riders in night-vision goggles.

As the hours pass, other more powerful gangs arrive too: the Rooks in their grease-black birds and the infamous water baron Yarrigan Quan who rolls into town in the cab of a huge armoured tanker. The stores that had closed for the night are hastily re-opened, the owners handing out bottles of liquor and plates of grubs and wads of century faster than they can keep an eye on their stock. Nerves start to writhe through my stomach.

'We're sure this was a good idea?' Silas asks from the upper windows of the house, watching one of the Butcherbirds bite the head from a live cricket and spit at her crewmate.

Falco stares, her eye narrow. 'Want to tell them to go home, flyboy?'

Gabi walks in, thick kohl around her eyes and the black duster stirring at her boot heels. 'We're ready?' Falco asks Peg.

They smile and nod at Bui. 'We're ready.'

By the window, Gabi swears violently and reaches for her gun.

'What is it?' Rouf asks eagerly. Squeezing in next to them, I peer down.

A charabanc has stopped in the middle of the street, painted all over with pictures of snakes. As I watch, figures dressed in black and grey snakeskin leap down, followed by a taller person, oiled curls hanging to their broad shoulders, silver twisted jewellery catching the lights.

The writhing in my stomach turns into a swell of nausea.

'Valdosta.'

Boss of the Pit, Factus's most notorious outlaw hole. The Augur, to some, the Viper to others, feared even by the gangs for their mad obsession with the Ifs, for the way they'd throw a person into a cage as live tribute for the Seekers on the roll of a dice, the flip of a coin...

The last time I saw them, they were lying unconscious on the floor of their own office, among the mess of augury and superstition they used to try and summon *them*. Now, they smile, looking up at the house. A shiver goes through me.

'What are they doing here?'

Rouf shrugs. 'Must have heard about it on the tangle.'

'We need to get rid of them,' Gabi snaps. 'Bui, Peg—'

'No.' Falco's face is hard as stone. 'We said every gang willing to join against Xoon. If that includes the Vipers, so be it.' She slides a knife into a hidden sheath at her boot. 'But watch them. And, flyboy, go get your heap ready, just in case.'

With shaking steps, I follow the others down towards the bar. Even from the stairs I can smell the stink of too many people, barely masked by sickly-sweet buzz sticks and century pipes that Falco would never normally allow people to smoke in her presence. A gesture of cooperation.

'Where do you think you're going, silverfish?' Gabi says, blocking Rouf's path as they try to step inside.

'With you.'

She smiles sarcastically. 'I don't think so. Wait outside.'

Muttering to themselves, Rouf stomps away through the back door. I let the others step into the bar without me, hanging back behind the leaf-fibre curtain that covers the doorway. The heads of the gangs are seated: a woman with the black eye-stripe of the Butcherbirds; a dirty-nailed man I recognise as Six Lagarto, leader of the Barranca Boys; Yarrigan Quan in his pseudo-silk suit; Valdosta, smiling dangerously, the sack tied to their belt writhing as whatever snake they carry tries to escape.

Weapons are piled in one corner, watched over by G'hals, but still, this place balances on the knife edge of violence…

Bullets shatter glass, Valdosta smiles through bloody teeth.

I wrench my mind back to the room, breathing hard. No doubts. Not now.

At last, Falco strides from the doorway to the head of the table. She looks resplendent in her G'hal best, neon pink snakeskin trousers and an orange-dyed Accord jacket, matching paint on her lips. The room goes quiet. She sloshes some benzene into a plastic cup and raises it high.

'Egészségedre.'

The heads do the same, mumbling their own toasts, knocking shots back or sipping them down.

Falco remains standing, her hands on the table. 'I won't waste time. You know why you're here. To discuss Lutho Xoon.'

Some of the gang members shift, but Falco ploughs on. 'We have all lost territory. We have all lost people. Good people. It has gone too far. Xoon wants control of this moon. And thanks to turncoats and cowards, he's already halfway there.'

'He can have it,' one of the Sand Eels spits. 'He wants to ship me to Delos, fine, I'll kiss his metal ass.'

'You think it's better there? You want to live on scrip?' Six Lagarto demands, his voice rough as rust. 'Took me ten years to get out of the scrapyards. I'll eat lead before I go back.'

Falco's voice snaps over the dissent. 'Any of you want to bargain with Xoon Futures you are free to. But know that it makes you fair game for me and my G'hals.' Her dark eye roams the faces. 'We might have ended up on this moon for different reasons, but I'll bet we've stayed for the same. Because here, we can be more than what the Accord label us. And I'll be damned if I let some chrome doglord take what we've built.'

The Barranca Boys let out yells and hisses, some of the bandits thumping the walls, showing fibreglass teeth.

'No one can doubt your zeal, Lady Sickness,' Quan says, moving the gold-plated buzz stick holder in his mouth. 'But skirmishing with someone of Lutho's capital is cracked.'

'It's true,' the Butcherbird says. 'We've got a larder full of silver vipers, and all Xoon Futures do is send more.'

'Which is why we hit them at their heart.' Gabi stands, her hair slicked back tight to her head, young face hard with authority. 'We hit Sagacity. Baba Guelo is Xoon's factotum here on the ground, and our snitches say she's allowing Sagacity to be used as a port for shipments of personnel and materiel from Delos. It's a strategic position. If we take it, we control the northern sector—'

'What about the fact there's six hundred Xoon mercs there, plus the Metalbitches, plus whatever other loco marshals and Peacekeepers they've deputised?' The speaker is a tall man, his bald head smeared with engine oil. I know him. Amir, current chief of the Rooks.

'Much as I hate to say it, the greasewing's right,' the Butcherbird says. 'Even if we did join forces, they'd still have double our numbers.'

'Suicide,' Quan agrees. 'There aren't enough of us.'

Falco's gaze flicks to me, and I step into the light. For once, my neck is bare, the Seeker scar stark for all to see. A ripple goes through the room. Some make signs of luck against their chests;

others stiffen or reach for weapons that aren't there. Valdosta only smiles, eyes glittering.

'There will be,' I say.

Swearing, Amir shoves back his chair. 'I'm not staying here with *her*. She's cursed. She killed Moloney.'

'Sit down, Rook,' Gabi barks. 'Moloney killed himself through sheer stupidity. We were just there to watch.'

Lip twitching, Amir lowers himself to the seat.

'She's Hel the Converter?' one of the Sand Eels says sceptically. 'I heard Hel was dead.'

'I heard Hel was worth half a million credits,' Quan says slowly.

'I heard Hel was mad,' one of the Butcherbirds observes, toying with a buzz stick as if it were a blade.

'Wouldn't you be mad,' Valdosta asks in their showman's voice, 'if you rode blood for the Seekers? If you walked with *them*?' They meet my eyes. 'That is her. The Blood Doctor herself. Hel.'

Silence falls across the room. I avoid Valdosta's gaze. 'Xoon believes he can claim Factus for his own ends and use the Ifs to shape the future, but I have walked the Edge and seen the war he will bring, the lives he will take in pursuit of it. Lives that should feed *them*.' I swallow. 'If you fight, the Seekers will fight with you. Now and always.'

'Yeah, right before they cut out our livers,' Amir snarls. 'They're deranged.'

'We pay tribute.' Bebe stands from behind the bar. 'We offer the Seekers what blood we can. And they leave us be.'

'The Seekers are closer than any of us to the truth of this place.' Valdosta's hands move ceaselessly, sending a Xoon coin dancing back and forth over their scarred knuckles, the silver clinking against their rings. 'Isn't Mx Xoon only trying to do as they do by attempting to understand *them*?'

'Stop that, you freak,' Amir spits, reaching for the coin in Valdosta's hand. With a flourish of fingers, Valdosta spirits it into the other palm.

'He wants to use *them*,' I say.

'And you don't?' Their eyes gleam. 'Mx Xoon has the vision we have long needed. With someone of his resources behind us we could finally lift the skin of this reality and peer at what's beneath. We could communicate with *them*.'

A shudder runs through me. There is too much danger here.

'*They* can't be communicated with.'

'Ah, but *they* can. Or how else are you here, Hel?' They smile at Gabi, showing a new chrome tooth. 'How else does the Dead General still walk among the living?'

Gabi starts forwards, reaching for her gun.

The coin turns in Valdosta's fingers, balanced upon their black thumbnail. They meet my eyes.

'No—!' The shout bursts from me, too late. They send the coin spinning into the air.

I don't see how it starts; I only see endings as the room erupts into chaos, bandits and gang members drawing concealed pistols, knives, overturning chairs, glass shattering as assailants lunge for the G'hals who guard the weapons.

And *their* presence rips through me as worlds end and split and spawn until I cannot see, and stagger blind, realities tangling about me.

'Get her!' Quan yells and *Falco shoots him in the gut, he spins and fires first, hitting Peg in the throat, he runs towards me, a snub-nosed pistol raised, a Butcherbird shanks him in the spine and turns to me blades drawn…*

With a cry, Gabi tears through possibilities and headbutts the woman before me, sending her crashing backwards.

'Move!' she says, already aiming her pistol.

There are G'hals at every door, all of them wearing body armour beneath their jackets, all of them ready and it will be slaughter, the floor will run with blood. Unless I act…

For a split-second, a path opens between the crush of bodies, a clear way to the front door. I take it, ducking my head and throwing myself across fallen furniture and limbs to burst out into the night.

'Low!' Gabi's yell follows me, but it isn't all. *They* are with me as I run for the shadows of the buildings.

I make it to the stable, I am shot in the back, I sprawl to the dust, a bullet bursts open my leg… Throwing a glance back over my shoulder, I see bandits tumbling from the door of the house, racing to follow me. If I can lead them away, if I can get to the *Charis,* if I can even the odds until my friends are out of danger…

I hurl myself around a corner and skid to a stop. Valdosta blocks my path, their chest heaving, forehead slick with sweat.

'Hel,' they say, their eyes flicking over my shoulder.

I spin and get one glimpse of Rouf's face, teeth bared behind a charge pistol, before a flash fills my vision and everything goes black.

The Personal Notes of Pec "Eight" Esterházy
Lunar Body XB11A – now "Factus"
Lutho-Plex Outpost

The body lay on its front, head and hands so covered in mica they were barely visible.

Behind me, inmates cursed and shoved to see, staggering away when they realised what we had found.

'What the fuck?' Scratch swore over and again. 'What the fuck?'

'Get another torch,' I told Harri, and knelt down in the cold, glimmering dirt.

There was no smell. That meant the body was either fresh or... Taking a shallow breath, I reached down and rolled it onto its back.

The corpse was desiccated, skin like fabric stretched to creaking. Impossible to tell much about them, now. The eyes were gone, the sockets filled with dust, the jaws yawning open, as if they had died screaming.

The prison collar had cut into their flesh. Throttled. I peered down at the nameplate.

Cad Jimpson. #8572. Inter-System Penal Vessel Tyrintha.

Something gleamed silver between the corpse's shrivelled fingers. Harri retched as I forced the digits apart with a crack to pluck it out.

A coin. Eternity and infinity.

When I looked up, Scratch's face was livid with fear, tattoos dulled by the mica.

'Knew it. Didn't I say this wasn't right?' He let out a wild laugh. 'We're all going to die here.'

I could feel it, the terror and panic rising, infecting us all.

'We don't know what happened.' My voice sounded older than ever. 'Whoever this was, they might have tried to escape a work detail, set off the choke—'

'Bullshit.'

Filch's head jerked upwards. 'What was that?'

No one moved. Then, after an endless moment, I heard it: a distant clatter of metal on metal. It was coming from the mine.

I shifted forwards a step, gently scuffing at the dust with my boot to unearth a cable, running into the darkness.

'There's something in there,' I said, voice rebounding from the walls.

'Fuck this,' Lon muttered, backing away, her face almost blue beneath the sunburn.

'Pec,' Harri hissed. 'Let's get out of here. Back to the ox. It's nothing to do with us.'

Us...

Them.

I stared into the tunnel, lit only by the shivering torch's beam and I remembered MacOboy's face, the whirr of the recorder as it took down every word I said, to be transmitted somewhere. To someone. Scratch was right. We sure as hell weren't here to mine.

Anger gave me the heat I needed. 'Who's coming with me?'

'I will.' Scratch grabbed a crowbar from the wall, held it in white knuckles. 'I'll kill the bastards.'

'I don't like this,' Harri whined, but she didn't move away like the others. Three against whatever was in there. It would have to do. Taking a breath of the bone-dry air, I crept forwards.

Every step took us further from the scorching light, until the mine entrance disappeared, leaving us in darkness. The walls glimmered strangely, like ice. Dust streamed from the ceiling, disturbed by our passing.

'This ain't right,' Harri whispered. 'I worked a mine, once. It weren't like this.'

'Shut up,' Scratch hissed.

His breathing was coming hard, like mine. There was even less oxygen here, and my head started to spin, vision turning cloudy. Everything cried for me to give up, to return to the light and the air when I heard it again: a metallic clatter, closer now. It sounded like coins falling, tossed in a wager...

'Up ahead.' Scratch's voice was rough. 'The tunnel's wider.'

Ten paces on the rock walls yawned into a cave. As soon as we stepped inside, I heard the hum, low and steady. The cable we had been following ran into the back of a squat, grey box. A generator of some kind, battery powered.

'The hell?' Scratch swore softly, his torch beam raking the darkness. 'There's nothing here.'

Metal crashed and clattered, sending my skin leaping, my eyes flooding with terror. I braced for – something, some danger – but nothing came. Just the generator, humming endlessly. I edged my way to its front.

A small cage sat on the dust, a metal plate beneath it. My torch's beam caught on a single object within, so familiar that I could only stare, wondering if hypoxia had finally caught me after all.

A single coin lay quietly on the metal plate. As I knelt down beside it the generator whirred, a light flashed and the plate jerked a few inches into the air, sending the coin flipping, eternity over infinity to land on *snake*.

A tiny light flashed – a camera maybe? – before the machine settled back into its low murmur.

'Pec,' Harri whispered. 'What is that?'

Before I could answer, a choked noise echoed through the cavern. Scratch stood near one of the walls, his shoulders heaving.

Five bodies lay on stained mattress pads, all of them covered in dust. Detritus strewed the ground around them: water canisters, airtights, hygiene powder cans, buckets... All of them had been throttled, the prison collars locked about their throats, hands splayed into claws of agony.

For a long moment, none of us moved or spoke, confronted by everything we had feared. I had to be sure. Knees cracking, I bent down beside the closest corpse.

'What are you doing?' Scratch demanded as I reached between the curled fingers to get at what I knew lay within.

The same coin, stamped with infinity. Stamped with eight.

'Snake ate all,' I croaked.

'Why didn't they run?' Harri's voice was thick with horror. 'The doors were unlocked. Why didn't they run?'

'Their collars,' Scratch said. 'That's what happened to the one in the tunnel. There must be a proximity sensor here, set off his choke.'

I looked at that grey machine, humming to itself at the centre of the cave. 'Someone was playing with them. Gambling with their lives.'

It came back to me as easy as breathing, that old anger at everything – everyone – who saw us as nothing but useful meat, cheaper than robotics, easily disposed of, small numbers in a ledger. *Ballast.*

Striding towards the machine, I slammed the torch into its casing, again and again until the bulb smashed and the light went out. Something heavy crashed into the side – Harri's boot – and then Scratch's as the three of us attacked the thing, sundering the metal. Finally, I grabbed a broken edge and together we heaved it free.

The machine's cold brain whirred and clunked, whirred and clunked, recording every moment, every coin toss, the proximity sensor that linked it to the dead convicts' collars glowing a steady blue. Harri swung back her boot, but I stopped her, took her torch and shone it down into the machine's workings.

There, stamped in silver, were five words.

PROPERTY OF F. XOON, DELOS.

A PATTERING WAKES ME, like drops of rain on the roof of a tent. Rain means Prosper and the Accord training camp, means sleeping out on the levees between the hydroponic fields like the rest of the trainee medics, but not like them, so unlike them that I sleep with a retainer in my mouth, for fear I should talk in my sleep and give myself away to my bunkmates.

But pain follows. Pain that arcs through my skull in raking red fingers until I want to retch. I heave in a breath through my nose and open my eyes. Everything is blurred and hazy but I am moving and that's wrong, and it's light and that's wrong too. It was before dawn and I was running and Valdosta…

With a lurch I try to sit up only to find my body won't move. My wrists are tied with something rough and every bone feels filled with lead. My lungs heave with panic as I hear the deafening roar of an engine. When I fight my eyes open again, I see a grey tarpaulin roof, swaying above me. Rolling onto my side, I find myself eye to eye with a pit viper.

The oily fabric stuffed into my mouth muffles my scream. I try to spit it free as I squirm away from the hissing snake but I can't, and there is not enough air, just dust and I'll suffocate.

Some distant part of me takes over, the part that could carry out my missions with steady hands and a cool head while I shook with terror inside. That part tells me that the snake is inside a plastic cage, just like dozens of others around me. I force myself calm, taking control of the panic a second at a time, making do with each rapid breath until my lungs stop straining and my pulse begins to slow.

Valdosta. Rouf. The green light of a stun charge. I am in Valdosta's wagon.

A throbbing takes up in my head, like a fist on skin. *Are you there?* I call silently, trying to stretch my awareness out to *them*, but my mind is like static.

At last, the wagon slows to a halt. All around the snakes bump and coil in their cages. I lie still with my eyes closed, listening to the crunch of boots on sand, waiting until light slides across my face and hands seize my ankles to drag me out.

Snapping my legs back I kick out and feel my boots connect with flesh, as one of Valdosta's vipers goes tumbling into the dust, clutching at her face. Nausea flooding through me, I worm forwards and crash down to the dirt before I hear the unmistakable whine of a gun.

I roll onto my back, breathing hard.

Rouf stands above me, a pistol pointed dead at my chest. Set to kill now, not to stun.

'Stop fighting, Doc,' they say miserably. 'This doesn't have to be hard.'

I stare up at them, trying to reconcile this tight-lipped figure with the person who brought Rowdy back. Keeping the gun on me, they give a sharp whistle.

More boots approach through the dust. I watch Valdosta through burning eyes. In the harsh early morning light, they look older, kohl seeping into the fine wrinkles of their face.

'Hel.' They smile. 'It won't be long. They're watching for the signal.'

They. Xoon Futures. I look back to Rouf.

Their silver hand gleams. 'Sorry, Doc. Two hundred and fifty thou is enough to clear my debts, my family's debts. And anyway,' they glance at Valdosta, 'they say Xoon wants you unharmed.'

'Of course he does,' Valdosta says, fixing their hair in a small mirror. 'Mx Xoon is a most enlightened person. I have never met anyone – save yourself, Hel – who shares my interest in *them* the way he does.' They beam. 'He has been so anxious to meet you.'

You don't understand, I try to say, but all that comes out is a muffled plea.

Rouf's face creases. 'Can't we take that off?'

'No way.' Valdosta's viper wipes fresh blood from her nose. 'She'll call to those *things* and do that loco shit again.'

Frantically, I look around but there's nothing. We are far out in the badlots beyond Angel Share. Even if I did run, without a hat and water, I wouldn't make it far.

A steady roar joins the pounding in my head and for a while I think I am about to pass out before I realise it isn't the blood squeezing through my brain; it is coming from above, on the hot, hissing air. The sound of engines.

'Thank Lux,' Rouf mutters. Sweat has broken out on their chest, matting their gold hair. Ships appear in the blind white sky, descending towards us at speed. Three silver Xoon birds, painful as needles in the sun.

Valdosta's eyes follow them hungrily.

I try again, forcing my mind outside of my skull. *Where are you?* But there's nothing. When Valdosta's viper hauls me upright I strain to reach for my pocket and the coin that must be there, but my hands are too tightly bound.

The ships' engines make the air shake, rattling my brain inside my skull as they start to descend. The dust they kick up is so thick that I turn back towards the wagon, pressing my face into the greasy tarpaulin side to keep from choking. Huddled there, rage finds its way through the fear; how much of my life have I already given over to *them*? How often have *they* hounded me across the wastes? How many years did I spend alone, for fear of hurting the people who might shelter me, smile at me and call me friend? And now, when I need *them*?

A noise of anger and frustration tears from me and I force my eyes open. The ships have touched down and a dozen mercs are running through the stinging dust, silver as molten metal. At their centre walks a familiar figure, lean and stooped, eyes hidden behind smoked lenses. The doctor from Sagacity. A chill raises the sweat-slick hairs of my neck.

'Doctor.' Valdosta's eyes gleam, as they toy with a Xoon coin from their pocket. 'An honour.'

The doctor gestures with a gloved hand. 'Take her.'

'You got our money?' Rouf's voice is sharp-edged with fear as they glance at Valdosta.

One of the mercs tosses a silver case onto the sand. Rouf edges towards it and fumbles it open. Inside, rolls of silver Delos credit tokens gleam, reflecting onto Rouf's face like water.

Blood on sand.

I blink and find the doctor standing before me, an injector gun in his hand. Before I can stumble away strong hands seize my shoulders, the viper holding me still as the man shoots a dose of something into my arm.

'Alright.' The doctor's voice is softer than I expected. 'She's safe.'

Whatever he injected into me is spreading through my body faster than I can think. My body feels limp as two mercenaries come forwards to seize me under the arms and drag me towards the ships, the heels of my boots carving tracks through the dirt.

'We done?' I hear Rouf call.

'We're done.' The doctor nods to Valdosta. 'Mx Xoon is grateful for your assistance.'

Through the rushing black tide of the drug, I raise my eyes as Valdosta glances at Rouf and flips the coin. It hits dust.

'Snake,' they say, and reach into their jacket.

'What?' Rouf frowns, looking up.

My gagged scream is lost as Valdosta draws a pistol and shoots them twice in the chest.

Rouf spins to the ground, blood spattering the silver tokens.

I scream again, straining towards them but my vision is clouding black, guards dragging me away.

'You bitch,' Rouf chokes, teeth stained red. 'You bitch—' They reach for the charge gun but Valdosta fires again, and they lie still beside that bloodied bounty.

'A price, Hel,' they mutter as I am dragged away. 'There is always a price.'

THREE

THE
BOOK
OF
THE
KING

THE SMELL OF metal hits me, then clean, stale air. I peel open one eye and see nothing but swimming shapes. There are voices, now close, now distant. A steady hum. I try to drag myself awake, fingers slipping on the edge of consciousness and – finally – force my eyes open. Stained metal walls and a metal floor. I try to rub at my aching head, only to find my hands cuffed with some high-tech-looking device. It drags on my wrists as I scrabble at my neck, but there's no collar there, just flesh.

Awkwardly, I worm my way onto an elbow. I'm in a cramped, dark space, empty save for the metal bunk and a toilet in one corner.

Something trails in my vision, a tube, tethered to me like a ship's fuel line. A saline drip. I stare at it, utterly lost, until images creep back to me; Rouf. Valdosta. The price.

This isn't a cabin. It's a cell.

Terror floods through me, curdling with whatever knocked me out. A cell means the hulks, means that I'll die inside a clanking metal tube twisting through space, my sins unanswered, the debt unpaid. It means tracing the lines of the tally on my cell walls until madness takes me.

I make it upright and immediately a sick tug in my stomach tells me this is artificial gravity. In disbelief I stagger to the eye-wide strip of window and stare out, into darkness.

We are off-moon, in space. For a moment it is so incomprehensible I think I must be dreaming, but then – past the few lights of orbiting vessels and broken satellites – I see a distant moon. Factus. I cannot be here, not when I should be *there*.

The saline drip tugs, stretched to its extreme as I take two steps towards the riveted steel door and drive my boot into it, kicking until my throat closes and I slump against the wall in exhaustion.

The door slides open with a hiss. Silver-uniformed legs and gun barrels crowd, hands haul me by the cuffs and dump me back on the bunk. Before I can think to fight, there's another sharp punch of pain and I look down to see a wrinkled hand remove an injector gun.

'A precaution,' the doctor says softly, without meeting my eyes. 'We want no accidents.'

Accidents. He means *them*.

'Rest.' He re-settles the catheter in my arm. 'We'll be there soon.'

He turns away and his hands are those of a corpse, his neat grey jacket spattered with blood.

'Don't do this.' My voice is thick and slurred. 'If you do, you're going to die.'

He glances over his shoulder. 'We're all going to die.'

Sick, I fall into nothingness.

∞

A long darkness, filled with endless, sharp-toothed stars and white points of light. And among that darkness, images of other worlds where a woman with my face lives out her life on the satellites

228

of the Congregations, raising children in the communal homes, crafting beads, writing religious pamphlets to send out across the stars. Another, where a young recruit never does what her handlers ask of her. Another, where she accepts her sentence and lives, forgotten on the hulks. Another where she sits inside a rattling tin shack with her dog, haunted by visions of a war she cannot bring herself to fight or prevent.

I feel all of them at once, those versions of me knotted across the stars. I feel *them*, vaster than it all and for a strange moment, in *their* endless presence, I feel peace.

I open my eyes to daylight.

Light means we are no longer in space. Light means we are planetside. Experimentally, I move my body. There isn't much pain, which seems odd, just a dull ache behind my eyes. No cuffs. No collar. No saline drip, either. I am in a bed, a real one, with smooth cellulose sheets and a blanket. Pushing back the sheets I realise that my clothes are gone. I'm wearing what looks like a plain hospital tunic. There should be panic and fear but all I feel is curiosity. A chemical taste on my tongue tells me why that might be. Drugged, with something.

Tiny silver electrodes scatter the wind-burned skin of my arms, among fresh bruises from a cannula... I touch my face and find electrodes there too, stuck to the scarred skin of my temples. My fingers trail across to the split in my forehead from Sagacity. There's barely any swelling, just a hard scab. A prickle of unease finds its way through that drug-induced calm. How long have I been here?

Where? I have no idea. The room gives no clues, empty save for the bed and a metal chair and a wide window.

There's a traitorous freedom in the blankness. As if I have been cut loose from all of those other possible lives, and can begin anew, unburdened by the past and unfulfilled promises. Standing gingerly, I walk across cool mica-flecked tiles to look outside.

A city spreads below me. Wherever I am, it is high up, so high I cannot see the ground. Silver fills my eyes; towers and scaffolds, chimneys and smoke, a metropolis of metal winking with a million lights. Stilted Air Line tracks snake like arteries, shunting along great iron slugs of freight. In the distance, refineries send up gouts of flame one after another, the oil fields stretching off into red dirt.

This is Ithmid, Tin City, the capital of Delos. Which can only mean one thing: I am in the hands of Lutho Xoon.

Almost as soon as I think it my skin starts to tingle, my feral, Factus-sharpened senses telling me that I am being watched. Turning, I catch movement: my own reflection in a large mirror. I walk towards it. In the grey hospital tunic, with my shorn head and the silvery electrodes, I look like a patient from the War Homes, too haunted to return to reality. My pupils look too large against the reddened whites, and within the darkness I see her – the woman with hands of blood, who wants to wear this skin, who has saved me more times than I can count. I reach towards her and she reaches back, until my fingertips touch the glass.

The surface changes and I am not looking at the woman, but at a stranger who stares back at me with silvered eyes.

Eternity spinning, blood on sand, mirrored eyes reflecting death.
Lutho Xoon smiles through the two-way glass.
'Hel,' he says. 'At last.'

The Personal Notes of Pec "Eight" Esterházy
Lunar Body XB11A – now "Factus"
Lutho-Plex Outpost

We gathered at the mouth of the mine.

'Some sick experiment,' Scratch spat. 'That's us. We're rats. We're rats in a goddam maze.'

I looked back into the darkness, knowing I should say something to stop us spinning into hysteria. But this wasn't a rowdy night aboard the *Heavenly Rest*. It was something else and Scratch was right to be mad with rage – perhaps that was the only sane response when you learned that your life depended on a coin toss.

'He's telling the truth,' I told the other inmates. 'There's some other life form on this moon. I think they're using us to try and study it.'

'What the fuck do you mean?' one of the inmates snarled. 'Aliens? Fucking demons?'

'Study it how?' Lon demanded.

'With these.' I tossed one of the coins at her. She caught it, dropped it almost as quick. 'Whatever they are, they appeared in the mess hall when Scratch flipped.'

'You're out of your mind,' Filch said, backing off. 'You're fucking crazy. Didn't Song say we'd imagine things—'

Scratch seized a fistful of Filch's jumpsuit. 'We didn't imagine six dead cons, you gutspill.'

'"Do not run",' one of the other inmates murmured. '"They are everywhere".'

Feverishly, Scratch shoved Filch away and strode to the tools that hung in the entrance of the mine, ripping down a wrench.

'What are you doing?' Harri demanded.

Scratch pointed the wrench at her. 'I'm not staying here to die like those bastards.' He raised his voice, turning to the rest of the inmates. 'Think about it, we might never get another chance like this. Twenty-five to one. We ice that bitch down there, take the ox and drive for the rig base.'

'What the hell are you talking about?' Lon said, tears in her eyes. 'We'd never make it.'

But others were listening. Too many of them. Don't run, that's what the message said. Don't run. Things were slipping out of control.

'Santagata's got a gun,' a woman with no teeth said. 'And the choke.'

'Yeah, and how many shots you reckon she could get off if we took her by surprise? Once we have the transmitter, there's nothing she can do. We get to the rig, force whatever poor sack got left behind as caretaker to boost us off this rock in a freight pod and—'

'No.' My voice rang through the hissing dust. 'We can't run. We have no idea what's out there.'

'And what do you know about it?' the woman with no teeth retorted. 'How do we know you ain't their snitch? Why the hell else would they send a dried-up old hag to a mining detail?'

I rounded on her. 'I told you, we have to stay calm.'

'We'll vote on it,' Scratch declared, knowing he had me. 'All in favour of staying here to die?'

No one raised a hand, though many looked nervous. Even I couldn't argue with that.

'Thought so,' he said.

I felt sick. All around me, the inmates were grabbing weapons, picks, wrenches, metal bars. Someone shoved a screwdriver into my hand. I saw the woman with no teeth grab a canister of acid.

'We load up the generator, get that weed Moll to distract her, then—' Scratch slammed the wrench into his palm.

Harri gave me a despairing glance, even as she hefted a mallet. 'I don't like this, Pec. Moll might get hurt.'

I shook my head at her. We were outnumbered. All I could do was watch as they heaved the generator onto a trolley, grabbed Moll by the arms and took off, down towards the ox.

With a last look back into the mine, I followed.

Santagata stood waiting at the bottom of the slope, the gun slack in her hands, face red despite the shade of the vehicle and the extra oxygen. Scratch was right, she looked hot and slow and sluggish.

'Pick up your feet,' she ordered lazily.

No one spoke. Hands clutched hidden weapons, ready to strike, to rip our freedom from her grip however we could. I looked over at

Scratch as he panted, the tattoos on his face shining like they were newly inked. He opened his mouth to speak and dark sand poured from his lips. He was dead, his head clotted with blood and sand, eyes clouded and vacant.

'Ready?' his corpse mouth clacked silently.

The reeling sensation in my head became worse. Hypoxia?

'Ma'am,' he called whiningly. 'There's something wrong with Mollusc.'

With a huff, Santagata bent to roll Mollusc over. For a moment, her head was lowered, only one hand on the gun. Scratch raised the wrench.

Footprints lead into hell. Lives lost that could have been lived – realities wasted that could have split and branched and bloomed. A woman with eyes like the Void and a hand full of bloody organs...

I lunged, shoving Santagata aside. The wrench missed her skull, smashing into her collarbone and as she screamed in pain I ripped the gun from her grasp and pointed it at Scratch.

'Knew it!' the woman with no teeth cried. 'I knew it, she's one of them.'

Against my skin, the collar buzzed and began to tighten. Harri snatched the transmitter from Santagata's sweating hand and threw it to Moll, who scrambled to turn it off. As Santagata squirmed in agony and rage, Harri put one heavy boot on her neck.

Adrenalin thudded through me, my head a mess of visions and bad air. 'I'm not *with* anyone,' I told them. 'You're making a mistake. If you go out there, you'll die. I saw you dead.'

Scratch's face twitched. 'She's mad. Going senile.'

'Wh—what do you mean, you saw it?' Lon called.

'Can't you feel *them*?'

'Bullshit,' Filch muttered, but his face looked drained and I knew he must feel something.

'Ask her,' I said, jerking my chin at Santagata. 'Ask her what happened to Cohort One.'

That got their attention. In the struggle, Santagata's smoked lenses had come off, and I looked into her eyes for the first time. They were as blue as cobalt.

'Talk,' I told her.

She spat. 'You're dead, old woman.'

'Right now, I'm all you've got. So talk. Where are Cohort One? Were they transferred?'

Her lips twisted. 'No.'

'The inmates in the mine,' I insisted. 'What happened to them?'

'Don't know what the hell you're talking about.'

'Liar,' hissed Scratch.

But when I looked into her eyes, I saw something beneath the rage – fear.

'What did Lutho-Plex tell you, before you came?'

Her gaze flicked to the other inmates, to their makeshift weapons. 'Last cohort disappeared.'

'Disappeared how?'

When she stayed silent, Harri pressed down harder on her neck. 'Don't know!' she choked at last. 'Gone when we got here. Only one we found was the former Commander. Still sitting at her desk. She cut her own throat.'

Harri let go, leaving Santagata to wheeze and spit on the ground.

'We're getting out of here,' Scratch told me, backing up. 'And you can't stop us.'

Some of the inmates joined him at once. Others hesitated. I kept the pistol trained, ready to fire at anyone who took half a step towards me. After a lot of hesitation, Bigmouth Lon raised her hand.

'Pec,' she said uncertainly. 'If I stay here...?'

'We'll send a distress signal to the base. You'll be dehydrated, but alive.'

'And the rest of them?'

'I told you.'

Looking ill, Lon ducked her chin and joined me. As, to my surprise, did Filch.

Sneering, Scratch climbed into the ox, Santagata's glasses on his face. I saw myself reflected in their glare, a dark shape against the sand, a crow, a bird of prey. For a second, my shadow seemed to move without me.

Scratch spat from the window and revved the engine into life. I watched them take off in a cloud of dust, knowing – with a certainty I couldn't explain – that the next time I saw them they would all be dead.

XOON'S SMILE GROWS as he leans towards the mirror.

He is and is not what I expected, unassuming at first glance, with his round shaved head and pale skin so smooth and polished it could be marble. He wears a loose grey suit – one that might see him mistaken for a mendicant preacher on some way-off satellites and Border Moons. It is only when he moves that he reveals himself. When the light catches Xoon's face, he shimmers. His irises have been silvered into mirrors and his skin has a blue undertone as if – for all the softness of flesh – he is made of steel beneath.

Impossible to tell his age. No pores or wrinkles or lines. He has had his humanity removed.

Deep inside, something is screaming, telling me to run, to attack the glass with my fists, even though there are armed guards on either side of the door and the doctor stands behind Xoon, medical kit prepared. Thanks to the drug, I simply stand and meet the man's eyes.

There, I see myself as he must: a ragged woman with Factus ingrained beneath my skin and the mark of a cult upon my chest.

He nods to the room behind me. 'I hope you don't feel too many ill-effects from your stay?'

'How long have I been here?'

Xoon smiles, as if pleased that I have spoken. 'What is it now, Ess? A little more than a week?'

The doctor nods. Where Xoon's eyes reflect everything, his are hidden by smoked glass. 'Eight days.'

A mote of rage finds its way through the numbness when I think of Factus – Silas waking to find me vanished, Falco and Peg and Gabi and the G'hals at the mercy of their own theories about me. Rouf, their corpse drying in the brutal heat.

'What did you do to me?' I ask.

'A full array of tests. Brain activity, bloods, nervous response to various exposures and stimuli. Ess has the details.'

'I should kill you.'

'I know your comrades would like that. But you won't. Ess tells me his special cocktail will prevent it.' I find myself staring at his fingers. They are the only part of him that look as if they belong, out here. Peppered with old burns and scars, one nail replaced by a scale of shining silver. 'We've found that heightened states of emotion can act as a conductor, to make an individual more susceptible to *their* presence. What's in your system now should keep you entirely stable, Hel.'

'I'm not Hel.'

Xoon breathes a laugh and focuses on the two-way mirror. Parts of it becomes a screen. He must have tech in his eyes, a subtle and unimaginably expensive augmentation. Footage flashes up – a grainy moving image that shows a woman with filthy strings of hair and a bloodied face. A recording from Baba Guelo's lenses, I realise. As I watch, the woman blinks out of existence for a fraction of a second before appearing again inches from the screen. A faint chill creeps across my skin. It could be a glitch, a skipped frame in the recording. But at the same time I remember the feeling of stepping into chaos, of walking worlds. Close up, the woman's eyes are featureless as the Void and as I stare into them, I see something move, deep within. A hand, reaching…

There's a flash and the recording disappears, replaced by an image of my face captured only seconds before. I watch with distant horror as some programme starts to run, and who knows what data Xoon has access to, prison or military logs that might return a match on my face and with it a name, a sentence: *Life W.P. Lowry. Life, Without Parole.*

Instead when the screen flashes up a confirmation, it is an image of an old woman, with a crescent moon tattoo and grey, ragged hair.

Peccable "Eight" Esterházy, the system declares me. *Deceased.*

As I smile Xoon's face falls into something that's almost fear.

'Who are you?' he demands.

I stay silent.

'Tell me! Why do they call you Hel? How can you communicate with the entities known as the Ifs?'

'I can't.'

'Don't waste my time,' he barks. 'We have the data from Sagacity to prove it.' He leans forwards. 'I have been collecting reports. People say you can reach *them*, use *them* to see the future —'

'*They* can't be used.'

His eyes snap to my face at the interruption. 'Anything can be used. You think I am the only one trying to find a way? The Accord might deny *their* existence officially, but behind closed doors there are others who see *their* vast potential. Would you rather they develop *them* into a weapon?' He leans forwards again. 'What do you want? I can offer anything. Name it.'

I look into his eyes, this man who can kill thousands with a flick of a hand, who is drowning Factus in his money, who will cover its surface in silver and build another moon like Delos, over the bones of the dead.

'There is nothing you could give.'

He only bares his whitened teeth in a smile that doesn't reach his eyes. 'We'll see.'

∞

The hours pass as I lie with my back to the room, wrapped in a blanket so the cameras cannot see me. Every time there is a clank in the building, the rattle of a door, I expect them to come, to transport me to a lab, a medical room, some other form of torture. But they don't. As the smog-filled daylight wanes I force myself to walk circuits, checking every screw and window panel for a possible means of escape. But there is only one door, and even if I did smash the window, it would only mean a sickening drop of hundreds of feet. Outside, night falls, turning Tin City into a blurred carpet of lights and flame, a tapestry of life and commerce of Xoon's making. I concentrate on walking. With each step I take, the numbness slips from me.

As I pass the two-way mirror, I see the reflection of a woman standing in the empty room behind me.

Is this the way? I ask her. Is this what *they* wanted?

She doesn't reply. That is the way of *them*, the curse. *They* show the what but not the how. The result but never the cost.

What if they *don't exist?* a small voice hisses. *What if you went mad, all those years ago on the hulks?*

A shiver goes through me, and I retreat to the bed, dragging the blanket aside. Something tumbles to the floor with a soft clatter. A coin, older than any other I've seen, roughly carved and worn by decades. Esterházy's coin.

When footsteps clang outside the room a few minutes later, I am waiting.

Doctor Ess steps in flanked by four armed guards. 'Mx Xoon would like to see you.'

I nod, standing. One of the guards tosses some folded clothes onto the bed. Real silk. Loose grey trousers and a short robe. I have never felt anything so soft before. No shoes, of course. I have just finished pulling them on when Ess approaches, an injector gun in his hand.

'More of the same. Mx Xoon wants to be sure.'

I extend my arm willingly, the coin clutched in my other hand. Ess frowns for a moment, before sending the needle shooting into the flesh.

It won't help, I feel like telling him.

'Follow me,' he says.

Once, when I lived a double life, I would have taken note of the route we walk through the building, every exit and escape point through the twisting corridors. Perhaps it's the drug in my system but the way passes in a blur, until I am shunted into a private elevator, its doors etched with an infinity symbol.

A penthouse, I realise, as we come to a stop on the top floor. Of course.

The room is made of glass. Floor-to-ceiling windows that look over the entire city, high enough above the smog that stars and ships shimmer through the ceiling. A telescope stands in one corner, trained upon a distant ball of ochre dust, barely visible through the darkness.

Factus. The sight tugs at my chest.

Xoon sits at a glass table. When I see what litters the surface, my steps falter. It is covered in games of chance – packs of tarot cards, straws, dice, tokens, knucklebones, even a grey dove that coos nervously in a cage. Drug or no drug, the hairs on my neck rise with the threat of what's to come.

'Ah,' he greets. 'Hel.'

'What are you doing?'

He waves a hand. 'I have tried so many ways to connect with *them*.' He sifts through the objects on the desk. 'Spent a fortune on scientists, collected endless data, only for them to lose their minds or come up with nothing. We have tried it all – Galton boards, random generation, even all of this superstitious nonsense, but we found nothing conclusive.' He nods. 'Until you.' He beckons Ess forwards. 'You change the rules.'

I watch as Ess opens a silver box beneath the desk. Dry ice

billows out, and he straightens holding a bag full of blood. My heart starts to beat harder, the drugs no match for the horror rising in my chest as I realise that the blood must be my own.

'What are you doing?'

Xoon barely winces as Ess slides a needle into the crook of his elbow and raises the bag. 'I have heard the stories about Hel the Converter; that she cannot be killed.' Nausea rolls through me as my blood slides down the tube, into Xoon's body. 'I want to test that.'

As Ess hooks the bag to a stand, Xoon reaches into the desk drawer with his other hand and pulls out a silver-plated pistol.

He levels it at me.

I take a step back, knowing that the elevator is the only way out, knowing that armed guards stand in the way.

'Mx Xoon—' Ess starts, but Xoon ignores him, flicking the pistol open one-handed. Inside are eight gleaming slugs and one empty chamber.

'This pistol was my mother's. She gave it as a gift to a man she thought would help her. Of course, he didn't. And so, before it was too late, she used it to join *them* in the only way she could.'

He flicks the chamber shut, spins it and arms the pistol. Even mirrored, his eyes are too bright. Beads of sweat slick his pristine forehead, and as he aims the gun at my face, I realise he is intoxicated. 'Eight deaths and one life. Can you choose, Hel? Can you call on *them* to save you?'

A shudder runs through me, my body trying to turn itself inside out. I feel control slipping away from me as *they* descend, until I realise I have a weapon of my own. Something of Xoon's to use against him.

I reach into my pocket, pull out the coin and throw it high just as Xoon pulls the trigger.

The Personal Notes of Pec "Eight" Esterházy
Lunar Body XB11A – now "Factus"
Lutho-Plex Outpost

Song found us at the mining camp when the light had faded and the blessed relief of sunset had turned to the torture of a freezing desert night.

Santagata cursed at me when I helped her to her feet.

'Remember who saved your life,' I croaked.

'Fuck you,' she wheezed back.

Song looked sick when we told him what happened, but he didn't waste time on talk. Water, a sachet of protein each, and we piled on to the mule as best we could, Santagata howling as we jostled her broken collarbone.

Each mile back to the base was a fight against the wind. The night was vast, threatening to snap the tiny needle of the mule's headlight, our only hope of making it through the darkness.

But at last, we saw flimsy metal walls and rolled through the gate, exhausted, burned and frozen, but alive. As *they* promised.

Five of twenty-five.

In the bunkroom, Lon sat on her bed looking lost, before realising she could help herself to the others' possessions. Moll passed out as soon as Harri lowered them to the bunk, their mouth hanging open like a bird dying of thirst. Filch lay with his back to the room and didn't speak, though I could see he was shivering hard. One cohort, mirroring another. We'd fled our fears and run into them head first.

I found Song alone in the infirmary, where he'd finished treating Santagata. The place was in darkness, except for a small work lamp. He didn't look surprised when I entered.

'You've felt *them* too,' I accused.

I thought he would throw me out, but instead he went to a cabinet and pulled out an unmarked bottle. I smelled alcohol when he opened it, sickly and cheap.

'I hoped I was going crazy,' he said.

'What are *they*?'

He wiped his lips. '"They" are lack of oxygen, bad food, paranoia and the chemicals used to treat the water—'

'But *they're* not.'

'I don't know.'

'Lutho-Plex know. We're not here to work. We're here as bait.'

He frowned at me. 'What do you mean?'

'Cohort One. We found six of them in the mine. All dead. All with one of these.' I flung the two-faced coin down on the metal table. 'They couldn't leave. Some sick machine gambled for their lives.'

The coin seesawed to a stop. A snake, staring up at us as it ate itself.

'I didn't know about that,' he said.

'Who's F Xoon?'

He stared as if seeing me for the first time. 'F for Frida. Owner of Lutho-Plex. The one bankrolling all of this.' He drank. 'Didn't you see the recording? All that talk about collateral, sacrifice in the name of a new frontier of humanity.' He laughed into his bottle.

Realisation came then, cold as a blade. Lutho-Plex didn't want workers because workers had families, had unions. Convicts were different.

I grabbed the bottle away from him. 'You have to contact them. You have to ask them to send a rescue shuttle.'

'Why the hell would they do that?'

'You and MacOboy and Santagata — you're civilians.'

'You don't understand, do you?' Slowly, he reached up and unbuttoned the high collar of his jacket. On his neck were two new scars; the sort left behind by a prison collar. 'Removal was a perk of the transfer. Not that I had a choice. It was this, or a decade on the hulks.' He let go of his collar and reached for the bottle again. 'If I'd known, I would have taken the years.'

I stared at him. 'The Commander—'

'Him, Santagata. White collar jailbirds, just like me. Just like you, Peccable. All of us are expendable.'

One day at the base turned into two, with no sign of the other inmates. We tried to distract ourselves: sweeping endless sand from the corridors, carrying crates from one side of the camp to the other for no good reason. Even in the heat, none of us complained. We were just glad to be within the walls. As if it made a difference.

No one talked much. When they did it was careful, as if every word were flammable and our tongues were rough with sulphur. No one wondered aloud, or questioned or asked "what if?". All of us were scared of doubt, of accidentally summoning *them* by chance. Now, no one even wanted to ask which was better, tomato-flavoured protein, or fish.

Filch broke the stalemate.

Sometime in the night, I felt the air in the bunkroom change, smelled old body odour and fresh fear-sweat and knew someone was standing over me in the dark.

When I opened my eyes, Filch sucked a breath, but did not cry out. His eyes bulged like blisters. There was no one nearby; Harri snored at the far end of the room, Moll breathed softly ten bunks away.

'Where is it?' Filch demanded, breath stale on my face. He held a shank made from a shard of metal.

'What?'

'The coin, Pec. Give it to me.'

My blood ran over the synthetic sheets, I was buried in the desert, a woman stared back at me, her eyes like empty sky...

I blinked away that rush of images. 'Under the pillow.'

He scrabbled beneath my head. I felt his fingers find it and draw back as if it burned before snatching it up.

'It won't work,' I told him. 'Whatever you are planning—'

He didn't listen, just turned and ran from the bunkroom without another word. A few minutes later, I heard the squeak of the gate, the roll of silent tyres, the far-off cough of an engine.

I closed my eyes.

We found him the next day, half a klik from the base, the mule he had stolen letting out a plaintive bleeping to signal that its lights were about to die. Throttled by the collar's proximity sensor, his face as purple as Brovos's shadow. The coin was clutched in his hand so hard it had cut into his flesh and left an imprint of infinity there. Lutho-Plex to the end.

We buried him as best we could, Moll singing some old, sad song as the shovelfuls of sand blew away as fast as we could lift them.

That night at dinner, no one ate. When an alarm pealed, it was almost a relief. Song – who had taken to eating with us – met my eyes. 'The emergency siren.'

Together, we turned out onto the parade ground, lit only by the fizzing sodium base lamps, the wind smashing against the metal fences like waves.

MacOboy stood there, jacket unbuttoned, silver pistol in his hand and a wild look on his face.

'Picked up a distress beacon,' he yelled when he saw us. 'You are now Search and Rescue. Suit up, boots and goggles. Prepare to move out.'

'He's out of his mind,' Lon murmured.

'Sir,' Song protested. 'If we wait until first light—'

'There'll be no first light!' He waved the gun. 'The sun never rises here. Santagata. Where is she? Santagata! I want them back. Dead or alive, but back. No loose ends.' His face was mottled from whatever emotion was trying to escape. His hands were bleeding from dozens of tiny cuts.

'Sir.' Song reached out. 'Let me give you something to help.'

'Get away from me, junkie.' He turned frantically. 'Santagata!'

'Here, sir.' She stood in the doorway to the staff quarters, tightening a shoulder holster with her teeth.

'Move them out. Anyone resists, it's insurrection. Permission to use force.' He looked at us again, gaze sliding as he backed towards his office. 'Go!'

'He's lost it,' Song told Santagata as she stalked across the dust. 'He's completely lost it.'

She shoved past him. 'Give me a shot of something good, or get out of my way, Yussef. You heard the Commander,' she barked at us. 'We're going out to find those traitors. Suit up!'

Moll grabbed for Song. 'Deputy, this is suicide. You can't send us back out there—'

'I don't want to,' he answered desperately. 'But if they've activated the ox's beacon, it must mean they're alive. And in trouble.'

'So what?' Lon looked pale. 'They knew what they were risking. They left us.'

'They did. Alive.'

He looked at me and I followed the meaning in his gaze. If we got them back, then maybe Lutho-Plex would want to hear what they saw out there, think twice about leaving us here to die.

'There are three mules in the stable,' Song called over the wind. 'I'll give you the exact coordinates of the beacon, and one of the tabs to navigate with. If you're not back by daybreak, I'll come and look for you myself. Deal?'

I nodded, although one thought played over and over in my mind.

If we were bait, this was a lure.

T HE GUNSHOT DOES not come. The coin does not land. Instead it turns and turns in the un-light of the Edge. Xoon stares around. His desk is gone, the penthouse vanished; instead, there is nothing but dark sand, stretching endlessly.

'What…' he chokes. 'What is this?'

'You wanted a world where you live.' My voice sounds hollow as the wind through dry bones. 'Here, you cannot die.'

With a cry, he puts his hands to his chest. Blood blooms through his elegant suit, first a spot, then a stain, spreading across his torso, dripping to the ground. He looks up at me in terror.

Mirrored eyes reflect death.

Hel the Converter looks back, her eyes deep and black as coals.

'Eight,' she says, and takes up the scalpel to cut out his heart.

∞

A coin hits the marble floor. A pistol clicks on its one empty chamber.

For a heartbeat, no one moves. Then Xoon lets out a cry, dropping the gun to clutch at his chest. I don't wait: before he manages to recover I dash forwards and seize the gun, pressing it to the side of his head.

Behind me charge pistols whine; red gun-sights dance in my vision but I keep my eyes fixed on Xoon's as the coin seesaws to a stop on infinity.

'Don't shoot her,' Xoon calls. This close I can smell him: new linen and talc, and something sour beneath – cold fear-sweat. His breath comes fast, one hand still holding his chest. 'You killed me.'

'Tell them to drop their weapons.'

'Sir—' one of the guards barks.

'Do it!'

One by one, I see the guards lower their charge weapons to the floor. My head pounds with the knowledge that the second I let go of the gun, they will attack.

'Back away,' I tell them.

At a nod from Xoon they do, stepping away from the elevator doors.

'You,' I bark at the doctor. 'Get that out of his arm.'

Face pallid, the doctor edges forwards and detaches the cannula with trembling hands.

'Yussef,' Xoon hisses.

I tense, expecting the doctor to make some move, but he does nothing, just steps away as the tube swings free, my own blood spattering the marble floor.

I press the pistol harder into his skull. 'Move.'

'Please,' he pants, stumbling forwards. 'You won't get out alive. They'll have to kill you. I don't want that…'

I shove him towards the elevator knowing he is right – that I'll be facing a building full of armed guards with only an antique pistol.

Not me. A shiver goes through my body. Hel. All I need to do is let her in…

With a chime the elevator doors slide open to reveal two armour-clad Xoon guards in full respirators. My stomach drops.

'Stop her!' Xoon screams as I drag him away.

The smallest of the guards hefts their charge gun. 'No.'

Before I can take a breath, they spin and fire straight into the group of guards. Chaos breaks out as the other armoured figure leans from the elevator and opens fire on their own, sending charges searing through the air, hitting legs, shoulders, face visors...

'Low!'

I spin to see one of Xoon's guards raising a stun pistol towards me. As they open fire I hurl myself to the ground, losing my grip on Xoon. A green charge smashes into the wall and there's nothing I can do to stop him from scrambling away behind the metal desk.

Glass shatters, marble splinters and I lurch to my feet, searching for cover. Someone grabs me and pulls me down behind a side table.

Before I can raise the pistol, they drag the respirator from their head, revealing sweat-matted black curls and a face that's old and young at once.

'Gabi?'

She bares her teeth. 'Xoon might be rich, but the discipline here is atrocious.' Charges fly over our heads, ricocheting from the glass. 'Where is he?'

I point to the desk and she surges up, shooting one guard in the leg as she goes, kicking another backwards through a glass sculpture.

An alarm is screaming, the pistol is slick in my grip as I try desperately to sight through the gun smoke and the shattered glass.

As Xoon emerges from behind the desk I fire – too slow. The shot bursts the bag of my blood, spattering his chest. I sight again as he slips and staggers towards the elevator and I have one chance…

From the corner of my eye, silver sparks: one of the fallen guards raising themselves on an elbow to take aim at Gabi's head.

Choose.

With a cry, I swing the pistol away from Xoon and shoot the fallen guard in the arm before he can fire.

The doors chime. The last thing I see are Xoon's mirrored eyes staring into mine, his hand pressed to his bloody chest as the doors snap shut.

∞

And all around is death, guards wounded, dying; the vast, complex knots of their lives cut through. I watch as one of my rescuers pulls off their helmet. Falco – sweat gleaming on her smooth scalp – kicks a gun away from a groaning guard and stuns them with a shot.

'Goddamit!' Gabi strides towards the lifts and slams a hand to the silver surface. 'You missed!'

I am shaking hard, adrenalin mingling with whatever is left of the drug in my system like oil on water. The pistol falls from my hand.

No, I chose.

But before I can there's a gunshot from across the room and a cry of pain; Falco drags the doctor out from under the desk and

256

slams him against the wall. Smoke and blood soaks one of his trouser legs.

'He was at Sagacity,' Gabi snarls.

'Wait,' he chokes, 'please—'

His spectacles have come off in the struggle. He looks desperately into my eyes and pulls up his right sleeve.

There, in the wrinkled flesh of his forearm I see an old, pale scar: the Seekers' mark.

'Stop!' I step forwards, head reeling.

'He works for Xoon,' Falco spits.

'No.' Ess gasps in pain. 'No, it was me, I'm the one who sent you the tip-off, the location of this place. I've been feeding you information for months.'

'*You're* the snitch?'

He nods frantically but she doesn't let him go.

'Bullshit.'

He turns his grey-brown eyes to me. 'I protected you, didn't sedate you like I was supposed to.'

I stare at him. He is telling the truth; if I had been drugged, I would not have been able to act.

Across the room, Gabi swears as the alarm peals louder, slinging guns over her shoulders. 'We need to go!'

On the floor, the dove flaps madly in its cage.

'Falco.' I grab her arm. 'He has the Seekers' mark.'

Her eye narrows as she presses the gun into his neck. 'You better be telling the truth, old man.'

Somewhere close there's a clamour of voices and Gabi curses, kicking at the elevator doors.

'They've disabled it. You,' she barks at the doctor. 'Get us out.'

Shaking, he slings the medical bag over his neck. 'Not that way.' Teeth gritted in pain he bends to release the door of the dove's cage. It bursts free in a flurry of feathers. 'Follow me.'

Limping badly, he crosses the room towards one of the glass walls, pressing a shaking wrist to the dark glass. With a hiss, it slides open, revealing a spindly metal staircase that clings to the edge of the building. Noise and cold air rushes in, thick with fumes and smoke and the smell of metal. Outside of Xoon's clean, controlled shell, Tin City roars – a carpet of industry hundreds of feet below.

'Hurry,' he gasps.

Gabi plunges through the doors, her weapon primed and ready. For a heartbeat, I stare at the old man with the Seekers' symbol, remembering Esterházy's words the night she told me who – *what* – she was.

We never truly let anyone go, once we recognise them as one of us.

'Move it, grandpa,' Falco yells and he staggers onto the stairs.

'Where are we going?' I yell as we run, our boots percussive through the metal skeleton.

'Landing pad,' Gabi snaps. 'Ten floors down.'

Ess lets out a choke of pain as he misses a step, crashing into the railings. I grab for him, my knees turning to water as I realise that one wrong step could send us falling to our deaths.

'A door bangs open somewhere above and I look up, into glowing gun-sights.

'Go!' Falco yells, spinning to aim and open fire.

Shoving the pistol into my pocket I sling my arm beneath the doctor's shoulder and haul him upright, staggering down the next two flights.

Charges ricochet, questing for our lives, but finally I see it below: a stretch of flat rooftop, ringed by lights. We almost crash into Gabi.

'What are you waiting for?' Falco hollers, firing over her shoulder as she runs. There's a scream and a guard plummets past us.

'It won't open!'

A metal gate stands in our way. Wheezing, the doctor waves his wrist but the metal doesn't budge. 'Revoked access—' he gasps.

'Get down,' Gabi barks and swings a blaster from her shoulder. I barely have time to cover my head before she plants her feet and fires, the whole staircase rattling and shaking. I look up through acrid smoke to see the gate blown to twisted metal.

'Well?' Gabi demands, swiping away blood from the shrapnel cuts that pepper her face.

We plunge from the staircase and onto a flat rooftop.

Pulling a torch from her stolen uniform, Gabi flashes it into the sky three times. 'Where the fuck are they—?'

There's a crash as a door bursts open, silhouettes spilling out. 'Down!' I scream and Ess hits the roof beside me as charges split the night, red as death. Rolling onto her back, Gabi lets out a blast of return fire with deadly accuracy and the shooting stops for the space of a few breaths before floodlights burst into life. There's a horrible whine as automatic gun turrets rise, swivel towards us.

'Move!' Falco yells.

Between us we haul Ess to his feet but there is no time; the turrets' tracking beams are at our heels, the guns spitting death. We are moments – split-seconds – ahead when Gabi stops and pulls something out of her jacket, lobbing it over her shoulder. It explodes with a flash, smoke billowing into the air behind us, sending the turrets' beams haywire.

'There.' She points to a refuelling platform, rising above the end of the pad.

'Suicide,' Ess chokes, 'there's no way down.'

Her eyes flash in the gun-light. 'We don't need a way down.'

She dashes towards it, dancing and dodging and leading the tracking beams astray, buying us time to stagger onto the rickety steps. Charges smash against the sheet metal as we crawl upwards on hands and knees, towards the tiny top platform, where Ess collapses, sweat and tears of agony soaking his face.

Across the rooftop, guards are streaming from doors, running to take cover behind the turrets. Ess was right, there's no way down, and for the first time in a long time I wonder whether Gabi is truly here, or whether the Accord programming has overtaken her mind and she is back on some lost battlefield.

I am about to call her name when a deafening roar fills the

darkness, drowning out the sound of the gunfire and a silver ship rises out of the smog. We are finished, utterly surrounded.

Falco grins. 'About time.'

My choke of terror turns into a laugh as I realise the ship above is the *Charis*. The hold doors hang open, the ship rolling wildly from side to side as every turret switches aim and starts to batter her hull with charges. Through the chaos something unfurls down through the air: the cargo net. Slinging the gun over her shoulder, Falco seizes hold of Ess and hurls him into it. Gabi leaps on like a cat and reaches down to pull us up beside her, into the net of greasy cellulose rope.

'Go!' Falco yells.

As the platform drops away I manage one look over my shoulder at a rooftop swarming with turrets and guards before the *Charis* banks, bearing us away into the clouds.

∞

I lie on the cold metal of the *Charis*'s hold, gasping for breath, my vision streaked with gunfire.

I look up as Gabi appears above me, her eyes bright as jewels, the stolen Xoon uniform spattered with other people's blood.

'You,' she says, holding out a hand, 'are more trouble than you're worth.'

She pulls me up with a reckless laugh, slapping me on the arm. My eyes sting and I can't help but laugh in return.

'Doc,' Falco says and pulls me into a brisk hug. As I pull away, I see her face is strained, bare of its usual bright make-up.

'You're here.' My voice shakes with the unspoken question.

She smiles viciously. 'No one steals from Malady Falco. Least of all that snake-headed freak.'

Behind us, Ess lets out a groan, still lying in the cargo net. Falco lets go of me to untangle him, the red hold lights painting her skin. 'Your intel was good,' she tells him. 'But if I even suspect you of double-crossing us, I'll kill you.'

He only nods weakly and fumbles for the medkit slung over his body. Rather than take out a painkiller, he produces a scalpel. I wince as he slides it into the skin of his wrist and levers the implant free, wires snapping.

'Take it,' he says, weakly. 'It's a tracker.'

Briskly, Gabi snatches it from him and strides away to eject it from the ship.

'Your name?' Falco demands.

He hesitates before telling her. 'Ess.'

'Hey.' Silas's voice yells through the comms. 'What's going on?'

I stumble through the hold and onto the flight deck, feeling the metal floor beneath my bare feet just as I did the night Rouf betrayed me, what seems like months ago. 'Silas,' I croak.

'Ten.' His face melts into relief as he turns in the pilot's chair. 'Thank god.'

Falco appears behind me, depositing Ess onto one of the jump seats.

'Where's Peg?' I ask. 'The gangs... what happened in Angel Share?'

'Later. First we have to get out of sight.'

'Working on it,' Silas says. 'Everyone hold on.'

The *Charis* dives, plummeting down through the thick layer of smog that covers Tin City, outside of any registered flight path. Falco lets out a curse as the ship almost clips the chimney of a refinery, flame searing the windshield, but then Silas is dropping us again, lower and lower until we're flying through struts and past the walls of the mile-high warehouses that form a labyrinth on the edge of the metropolis.

'Where are we going?' Ess wheezes as we narrowly avoid a low-altitude freighter, loaded to the brim with crushed rock that spits and scatters over us.

Silas's eyes are fixed. 'Skrammelstad.'

'The junkers' district?' Ess tries to push himself up. 'They'll shoot us out the sky. No one gets in without a contact.'

'Good job we have one, then.'

Falco jerks her chin to Gabi who disappears towards the *Charis*'s storeroom.

My body is coming back to me, breath by breath shedding whatever remained of the drugs, relief mingling with ebbing adrenalin. I'm about to speak again when Gabi appears in the doorway, behind a second figure.

Filthy blonde hair, shackles at wrist and ankle and neck, silver fingers shining in the light. I stare in disbelief. It's Rouf.

The hairs stand up on my neck. They are dead, dry skin and bones in the desert, but as they stagger forwards I see the thick bandages that wrap their chest, the weakness in their muscles.

'Rouf?'

They don't look at me and so I turn to Gabi instead. 'What...?'

'Found them in the wastes,' she says, her voice thick with derision. 'Looking like a vulture's breakfast. But then that's what you get for being stupid enough to trust Valdosta.' She gives Rouf a shove, and they stumble, blanching with pain.

'I don't understand.' I stare at their chest. 'You should be dead.'

They look at me through their gold hair then, shame and defiance and fear all mixed together on their young face.

'You,' barks Falco. 'We're coming up on Skrammel. Time to sing for your life.'

Rouf sways on their feet. 'Go to the west gate.'

Silas mutters and takes the *Charis* down, towards a sea of rust. When I was last on Delos, years ago, Skrammelstad was just a subdistrict; the lowliest of the city's barter yards. Now it's almost a city in itself, walls of scrap higher than buildings, the gristle and cartilage of an entire system's industry, sold and bought and ripped in half and sold again. Behemoth trash drogers slide by, their lights casting through the alleyways of junk like the eyes of vast, deep sea fish.

'Alright,' Rouf says. 'Start descending. Slow.'

Grimy walls rise towards us, SKRAMMEL WEST stencilled on the metal in huge white letters. Silas's jaw is clenched tight.

'You better be right about this, Cinque,' he murmurs. 'Never heard of anyone going this deep into Skrammel and coming out in one piece.'

A few seconds later, a low-altitude craft buzzes past the *Charis*'s nose, then another, skeletal buzzards that zip around us in the darkness.

'Shit,' Silas swears, trying to pull the ship up. 'Junk Harpies. They'll tether us, drag us down for scrap.'

The *Charis* lurches as something strikes the side with a deep boom.

Gabi's face twists as she turns on Rouf. 'You little shit—'

They look sick. 'Give me the comms.'

Jaw tight, Falco thrusts it at them. 'This is Cinque for Auntie E,' they quaver into it. 'Cinque for Auntie E, do you copy?'

A crackle emerges through the speaker, then a woman's voice, rough with disbelief. 'Roufy? That you?'

Rouf ducks their head. 'It's me, auntie.'

There's no reply, just a hiss of static before the tether releases. 'Vítejte,' the voice says. 'Be welcome.'

∞

A dozen figures stand, arrayed across the metal-flecked dirt of a scrap yard. Junk Harpies, Silas called them. Most of them are women, I think. In the light of a single sodium lamp, every one of their faces sparks with augmentations. Some are small: a riveted metal heart inset into a cheek, a finger, an ear, others larger, chins and skull pieces, fingers or whole hands and arms like Rouf. Limbs lost to Xoon Futures.

Behind the Harpies, a host of red lights wink in the darkness: mechanical hounds, if they can still be called that, strange creations cobbled together from models of all ages and sizes, some lacking legs, some just metal sausages lying in the dirt with flashing eyes and clacking jaws. A twist of sorrow goes through me when I realise this is where Rouf must have learned how to fix Rowdy.

'Are you sure this is a good idea?' Silas asks, shifting so that his ankle holster is within reach.

'Do we have any other options?' Falco mutters before striding out into the dust, one hand on the gun at her wrist. 'Malady Falco,' she announces.

One of the Harpies moves forwards. An older woman, her hair dyed jet black, skin stained silver-blue from mine work. She keeps one hand on her own gun, jaw working at something.

'Lady Sickness. Heard of you. Never thought we'd see a Factan Queen down here, though.' She spits into the dust. 'Where's my neiph?'

'Here, auntie,' Rouf calls from the hold, weighed down by shackles.

Immediately the woman's face changes, cold hatred seeping across her features.

'Alright,' she barks. 'What do you want for them, dust bitch?'

Gabi bristles, but Falco only holds up a hand, her eye glittering. 'Sanctuary. From Xoon Futures.'

Something shifts in the air then, the Harpies muttering to one another, a few edging forwards to peer at us more closely. My neck prickles under the scrutiny and I wish I were wearing my sun-bleached G'hal clothes, rather than blood-stained silk. I grip the robe tighter about my throat, covering the scars as the lead woman's eyes flick over us one by one, lingering with interest on Ess who sits, grey-faced on the floor of the hold.

Decisively, she spits in the dirt. 'You have it.'

Back straight, Falco draws her gun with her non-dominant hand and holds it out, grip first. The woman does the same. They walk towards each other until they are boot to boot, before exchanging guns, and kissing on both cheeks. The ceremony complete, everyone seems to relax a little.

'Eliska Nebosja,' the lead woman introduces herself, showing a mouthful of stainless steel teeth. 'This is my crew.'

The Harpies break up, several wandering over to inspect the *Charis*.

'Eyes off,' Silas grumbles to one woman who starts to tap at the hull with a set of metal fingertips. 'She's not for breaking.'

The Harpy smirks. 'Silver's not her colour.'

Falco nods. 'That's Silas, our flyboy. Ortiz, my second-in-command. Doctor Ess, recent turncoat. And...' She hesitates. 'This is Doc Low.' There is something in the way she says it that makes the hairs rise on my neck. As if it is no longer true. Eliska looks at me appraisingly before she turns her attention to Rouf.

'Well, grub,' she calls. 'What did you do this time?'

'Joined a Metaldog crew, shot up some settlements, killed a dog and then tried to sell us out to Xoon Futures,' Gabi says, lounging in the doorway. 'As you can see, it didn't exactly go to plan.'

Eliska just tuts. 'Roufy.'

Rouf's face is red with defiance and shame. 'It was a lot of money, auntie.'

'I'd hope so.' Her eyes linger on my face. 'Well, come in, we obviously got a lot to talk about.'

I cross the yard with the rest of them. My body aches all over, my head swimming from all that has happened. A house sprawls ahead, made from old containers, welded together. In the dirt, someone is trying to grow flowers – leggy ghost lavender and a few stunted marigolds. The sight makes me hesitate. This is a home; another place where my presence will bring danger.

'You're a real doc?' Eliska interrupts my thoughts.

I swallow. 'A medic.'

She jerks her chin. 'Down here.'

We follow her – Silas carrying a groaning Ess – down a corridor and into a tiny room lit by the blue glow of an antibacterial lamp. The shelves are crowded with black-market medicines – some stolen from the Accord, some stamped with that ever-present infinity sign, like empty eyes watching. In one corner, a cryo-cooler thrums, drawing my eyes.

'You run a clinic?' I ask.

Eliska snorts. 'No. We're not quacks. Just flesh mechanics.' Ess lets out a curse as Silas helps him onto the bed. 'What is it?'

Ess grimaces. 'Burns to the skin, severe damage to the peroneus longus—'

'Cooked leg.' Eliska nods knowingly. 'Well, use what you need.'

Silas steps aside to let her pass. 'Want me to stay?' he asks softly.

I shake my head. 'Thanks.'

He touches my shoulder and disappears, to join the others.

Slowly, I start to clean my hands with hygiene powder, sloughing away the blood. Whose blood? Gabi's? Xoon's? My own? The idea that Xoon holds some of my blood in his veins still makes me queasy.

'You don't have to do this,' Ess says weakly.

I don't answer. Instead, I cut away his sodden trouser leg to reveal a severe charge burn, down to muscle. The wound oozes sluggishly.

'I am sorry about your young friend. I didn't know they were in danger from that snake merchant. If I hadn't been so heavily guarded, I would never have brought you to Delos.'

'You have *their* mark,' I say. Easier to focus on facts, on my scarred hands, moving. 'Are you a Seeker?'

He sighs, an old noise. 'Not quite. I have tried to help, across the years. Doing what I can to save life.'

'But you worked for Xoon.'

'While working against him.' He nods to my throat, the collar scar. 'I thought you of all people might understand that.'

I say nothing, spraying the wound with antiseptic and filling it with sealant before finally wrapping it in some silver-soaked gauze. It will not heal neatly, but by the time I am finished Ess seems to be breathing easier, some of the pallid shock gone from his face.

With a grunt, he pulls his medicine bag towards him and reaches inside to bring out a silver flask.

'Egészségedre,' he croaks, and drinks.

I blink at him. 'What?'

'Something a friend of mine always said.'

The scar on his arm is old. 'Did you know Esterházy?'

'I did. Many years ago.' He hands me the flask. 'A remarkable woman.'

At a loss to know what else to do, I drink. Maybe it's the taste of arak, or the fading drug, or the strange feeling of kinship but I tell the truth. 'I was there the night she died.'

He nods, eyes heavy. 'I wondered.'

I have to clear my throat. 'I see her, sometimes. When I'm dreaming or…' I have to clear my throat. 'You probably think that's crazy.'

He shakes his head with an expression almost of longing. 'No. She walked the Edge, ran the road between realities, travelled further than any of us could ever dream. Who knows what we become, outside of time.'

Part of me yearns for what he speaks of, the freedom to leave behind what haunts me, to see further, to walk between worlds… But in the bare, blue light my scarred hands remain.

'Why did *they* choose me?' The words emerge from somewhere hidden.

'Who's to say *they* did?' Ess's voice is soft. 'Who's to say it wasn't you who called to *them*?'

I don't answer. There is too much inside my chest, too many fault lines that might cause everything to come spilling out.

'Here.' Ess hands over his medical bag.

'What's this?' I ask, looking down into it.

'Relics. From my earliest days on Factus.'

Inside, as well as the medical kit, I find some sort of portable beacon, old and battered and folded tight, the words SEARCH AND RESCUE stamped on the side.

'I don't know when "search" became "seek",' Ess says, with a twisted smile. 'But it still works.'

Beneath the beacon, there's an ancient, bulky bulletin tab. On the front a faded inscription has been scratched into the plastic.

To Song, E.

'Who's Song?'

He smiles, eyes drifting closed. 'I am. Ess for Song. You're not the only one to wear different names.'

I tap the screen until it bleeds into life, living ink words crawling across the screen a centimetre at a time.

The Personal Notes of Pec "Eight" Esterházy

'She gave it to me before she left,' he says. 'Said it might help me understand. Now, it might help you.'

The Personal Notes of Pec "Eight" Esterházy
Lunar Body XB11A – now "Factus"
Lutho-Plex Outpost

The mules' headlamps sputtered in the darkness, flickering as the wheels ground over dust and rock. Lon clung to me, her body warming my back, head tucked in close to mine. On either side I could hear the other two vehicles: Harri and Moll on one, Santagata roaring ahead on the third, steering one-handed, pumped full of analgesics and adrenalin. The wind howled, hooking its fingers into the fenders and dragging us into the night.

Into *their* night.

We followed our orders like good grunts, sticking to the coordinates and never driving more than a few metres from each other. Finally, through the darkness I saw a sickly orange beam. It grew larger, until I realised it was the ox. Santagata skidded to a halt beside it, drawing her pistol.

We rumbled up after her. I already knew what we would find.

Seven inmates lay dead, some slumped in the rear of the truck, others near the driver's door, which hung from one hinge. One – the rigger – sprawled on the sand, his head split open. Another had dragged themselves away, leaving a trail of dark blood on the sand.

'Fuck!' Santagata swore and kicked at one of the bodies. It was the toothless woman, mouth gaping dark from a slash to the throat.

'What happened?' Harri asked as Lon pulled the balaclava from her face to retch.

'They tried to mutiny against Scratch, that's my guess,' Moll said thoughtfully, poking at a corpse.

'Still thirteen of them out there,' Santagata raged. 'Get moving! Look for tracks!'

The torch shivered in my hand as I wound it. 'Whatever happens,' I murmured to Harri. 'Stick together.'

'Here!' Santagata howled. 'I've found the trail! Fan out, two on each side.'

The wind stirred up the dust, but beyond her I saw the indentations of deep tracks, made by running feet.

We followed them, our torch beams picking out splashes of blood, churned up sand, the beacon's light growing fainter behind us. The moment we lost its glow, something changed. The wind rose, raking us with claws of grit until I could barely see, drowning out Santagata's orders. I shone my torch into the darkness only to stop, fear rushing through me. A wall of sand was rushing towards us like a vast wave, hundreds of feet high, a maelstrom of lightning and dust...

'Go back,' I yelled to the others. 'Get back to the ox!'

I turned, managed ten desperate paces before the storm smashed into me. It slammed me to the ground, ripped the breath from my chest. I couldn't see, couldn't hear, could do nothing but curl in on myself as grit like broken glass lashed my exposed flesh, filled my ears, my nose, until I knew I was going to suffocate, sucked beneath the skin of this moon. Choking, I wormed my fingers into the jumpsuit and clutched the coin.

Then, everything stopped.

I T IS ALMOST dawn by the time I find myself sitting alone on the back step of the Harpies' house, Esterházy's words in my hands. With each page, I hear her husky voice, the accent unplaceable because it was from a country on old Earth that I have never, will ever, be able to visit. I hear her gallows humour, the quick crackle of her laugh, like silver paper around something sweet. And the more I read the more my heart tugs for her, this woman I barely met and spoke with only once, yet who wrote these words four decades ago to teach, to explain.

I see Factus anew through her eyes, not as a prison but a place that holds wonder. I see the dawn as she saw it. I read about their base, long abandoned, and know that I have walked the dirt of its yard. I read about a doctor, Ess for Song, and see him as he was, a young, jaded man, atoning in his own way. I see *them*, in all their rawness and terror.

Eyes blurring, I have to stop, leaning back against the doorjamb. The metal ledge once belonged to an airlock and the walls above still bear the Accord's symbols in warning yellow. Only now, there's no life-sustaining oxygen to escape, no vacancy beyond. There is only a rusted door propped open with an old boot and the smell of the meal we have eaten – bread fried in beef dripping, strong, bitter tea, lye hominy thickened with canned cow, augmented with a few of Falco's precious airtights.

Along the porch, Silas snores in a hammock made from old parachute, pipe dangling from his fingers. Inside, I can hear Falco and Eliska talking softly beneath a jab of metal as Gabi plays stabberscotch with a few of the Harpies. There's a thump beside me, and I look around to see one of the mechanical guard dogs collide with the wall, before wandering away.

When the door creaks open, I know who it will be.

Rouf steps down into the dust. Their shackles have been removed – as agreed by Falco – and they hold both hands pressed to their torso, as if afraid it will come apart.

'You should be dead,' I say.

'I know.'

Remembering their body, slumped in the sand, I shake my head. 'You're lucky Gabi found you before you bled out.'

Inch by painful inch, they lower themselves onto a crate. 'She didn't.'

'What?'

Wincing, they start to unwind the bandages from around their torso. I try to stop them but they ignore me, lifting the thick dressings with a hiss. Their chest is a patchwork of brutal stitches, puckered and swollen and dark, some of the skin a different colour to their own. Dark bruises line their arms – cannula marks, from where someone fed them blood.

'The Seekers?' I ask.

They look at me, scared. 'Heard them talking, Falco and that lot. They found me outside Angel Share, under the tribute post.

Reckon that's the only reason they didn't kill me over again.' Their face creases. 'Am I cursed now, like you? Will *they* follow me forever?'

'I don't know about cursed. Seems like you're lucky.'

'That's as good as cursed on Factus,' they grumble. Awkwardly, they start to re-wrap the bandage. I reach to help, securing the knot tightly.

'Sorry,' they mutter. 'It was so much money—'

I stop them with a dry smile. 'I know.'

'Won't be trying it again.' They look down. 'Think she'll ever forgive me?'

'Who?'

'Gabi.'

I push myself to my feet. 'Considering she sold me out herself once, I would say there's a chance.'

'She *did*?' Rouf gapes.

'She had her reasons.'

'I still don't get why *you* didn't kill me.' Rouf's voice stops me before I step through the doorway. 'But either way, thanks.'

Something tugs in my chest, even as I find the marks of the tally. 'You're welcome.'

∞

I wake at noon to a sharp pain in my toe. Bolting upright, I reach for the scalpel… until I see one of the mechanical dogs lumbering away, jaws clacking. I sag back onto the mattress pad, looking around at the unfamiliar room. I was too tired to notice much at dawn. Crinkled gold emergency blankets cover a window above an old control panel that has been gutted, little chilli plants growing from the holes where switches once protruded. A pilot's chair has been sewed with scraps of fabric and a mobile dangles from the ceiling, stars cut from rusted metal. A home, among Delos's grind.

Voices filter up the metal steps. I follow them down and find Gabi sitting at the kitchen table alongside one of the Harpies, a heavily muscled woman with the scars of a brawler, a range of ancient weapons before them. Song is propped on two chairs, talking with Silas, while old-fashioned music plays from an ancient radio. Rouf lies on a bench in the corner, smoking a buzz stick – pine-flavoured from the smell – and watching Gabi from beneath their lashes.

'Ten.' Silas smiles when I emerge, but I can't help noticing that the dark circles beneath his eyes are darker than ever, spreading down his cheeks. The few hours we spent in fitful sleep, holding each other, were not enough. 'Saved you breakfast.'

'Roufy here was going to eat it all,' Gabi mocks.

They flush. 'I was not.'

The Harpy at the table grunts. 'Don't listen to her, Roufy. You need your strength to weld those seams back together.'

I take the plate of what looks like protein grits, mixed with airtight cherries. 'Thanks.'

'The coffee is terrible,' Gabi says as she works, a buzz stick hanging from her lips. 'But it's alright if you mix it with enough syrup.'

The Harpy grunts in mock-affront. 'Not as bad as that slime you drink down on Factus.'

'Where's Falco?' I ask, spooning down the food.

'She and Eliska went to use the wire,' Silas answers, leaning against the wall. 'Try and reach home.'

Home.

I grip the mug, remembering Falco's face when I asked where Peg was. 'What happened while I was gone?'

Silas shakes his head. 'It's been bad. The G'hals got things under control at Angel Share, but you can bet it wasn't pretty. And anyway, with you gone any chance of alliance went up in smoke. If Hel herself could be captured…' He shrugs. 'Quan turned silver, the rest went back to their turf wars.'

'Peg's defending Angel Share,' Gabi says around her buzz stick. 'Falco didn't want to leave them, but they insisted. It's one of the last free ports. We lose it, we might as well surrender.'

'We can't surrender,' I say softly. 'I've seen what will happen if we do. A war that will cover Factus.'

'You could have stopped him,' she accuses. 'If you hadn't missed—'

I meet her gaze. 'I didn't miss.'

She blinks hard. 'Stupid. You could have ended all of this. One life for thousands. How does that sit with your tally?'

'Gabi—' Silas says.

'What? It's true. We might never have another chance to finish Xoon.'

I look up at Song. 'What will he do now?'

Song raises a shoulder. 'I don't know. Once, I could talk to him, but recently he has become unreachable. It began when he started reading his mother's research, a year ago. Whatever obsession took hold of her, the same is true of him. He's convinced he can succeed where she failed.'

'You sound almost sorry for him,' Silas accuses.

Song looks down at his bandaged wrist, where the implant once flashed. 'I am, in a way. Lutho's human, for all his mistakes. But he's single-minded. And right now, that makes him dangerous.'

The hairs on my neck stand up. 'What do you mean?'

'Lutho knows the Accord are overstretched and overcommitted. He thinks if he can gain control of Factus as well as Delos, he can force them to accede power to him.'

'No, they'd never grant it.' Gabi sounds like the official she once was. 'By giving up Delos and Factus they lose Brovos, then Prodor, then the whole of the Outer System. It would be the war, all over again.'

Song nods. 'And Lutho would have *them* to find a reality where he wins.'

Rouf snorts. 'That's *insane*.'

Wordlessly, I meet Gabi's eyes.

'No,' she says. 'It's not.'

Before I can reply, there's a cackle from outside and the parade of mismatched guard dogs start up their chorus of warnings, barking words in half a dozen different languages. The Harpy at the table grabs up a gun.

'Přestaň!' a voice hollers as Falco and Eliska shove through the door, swathed in huge oilskin dusters and heavy welding goggles. Everyone relaxes.

'Damn.' Eliska wipes her face. 'It's crazy out there.'

'Xoon Futures?' I ask, as Silas takes her coat.

'Silverfish crawling all over the districts like a rash. I need a drink.'

She pulls a bottle of liquor from the shelf, dumps out the coffee dregs from a mug and sloshes some in.

'Did you find a wire?' Gabi asks.

Falco nods. 'Scrap drogers owed me a favour so I used the station at their rest stop. Got on the tangle okay, for better or worse.'

Reaching into her vest, she pulls out a bulletin tab and tosses it down onto the table. It's still live.

Factan rebels attempt assassination

It has been reported that yesterday, Factan rebels made an attempt upon the life of the business premier and owner of Xoon Futures, Lutho Xoon.

The main perpetrator is believed to be wanted criminal gang leader "Hel the Converter", in a further retaliation against Xoon Futures for their recent land purchases on Factus.

Hel and her accomplices are thought to have been aided by an inside source, named as long-time Xoon Futures employee, Dr Yussef Ess.

A spokesperson for Xoon Futures commented: "Mx Xoon bears only minor injuries from this cowardly attempt upon his life. We will be working with the Accord's Factus-based military, alongside our private security forces, to find the group responsible and bring them to justice."

Gabi shoves the tab away. 'And I thought the Accord were the masters of spin.'

'I don't get it.' Rouf has limped to the table to peer down. 'Why wouldn't they take credit for capturing the Doc in the first place?'

'Because, *Roufy*, by blaming rebels for the attack, Xoon can justify whatever action he takes on Factus. Attacks, raids, increased paramilitary presence…'

'But now all the gangs will know that Hel the Converter slipped through his fingers,' Falco says slowly.

Silas snorts. 'Right. The same gangs that tried to kill you for her bounty?'

'We nearly had them, I know it. If it wasn't for that snake Valdosta…' She taps the bulletin. 'But this is proof Xoon Futures can be beaten.' Her eye shines. 'How soon can we leave?'

Silas grunts and jumps up, loose shirt flapping. 'Sooner we get off this ball-bearing of a moon, the better.'

'Your flyboy's right,' Eliska says. 'It will only get more dangerous here. Besides, you're drinking all my good coffee.'

'What's the bad coffee?' Gabi mutters.

'I'll pack you a hamper, Roufy,' the large Harpy says, heading for the kitchen. 'I think we've got some bread, and a bit of lard.'

Silas makes for the front door. 'Getting out of atmos might be sketchy—'

'What was that?' Rouf asks.

'—but if we get into low orbit, we can head for the drogers' lanes and use jammers to mask our call sign among theirs.'

'What was what?' Gabi says impatiently.

Rouf stands near the window, head tilted towards the yard. 'That?'

I hear a shout and a faint bleat of warning from one of the mechanical dogs, followed by another, then another, all of them starting up. Eliska strides forwards and flings open the door.

'Crawlers!' someone yells. 'Incoming!'

Eliska spins on her boot heel and grabs a handle on the wall, cranking it hard. An alarm starts to whine through the compound, followed seconds later by feet running, doors banging.

'You gutswill,' Gabi says, rounding on Rouf. 'If this was you—'

'I haven't even moved!'

'Then how did they find out?'

Eliska steps into her path, drawing her pistol. 'Because this is Delos. Go,' she orders Falco. 'We'll cover.'

'No, auntie.' Rouf grabs for her arm.

'Get off me, grub. Go with them.'

I step back. It's happening, just as I knew it would. Trouble and danger and death following on my heels and nothing I can do but flee. Outside, Harpies are mounting their skeletal buzzards, roaring into the sky as the sound of rumbling engines rushes closer.

'Flyboy,' Falco orders, 'get that bird in the air. Gabi, take the flank. Low, with me.'

I am almost out the door when I realise: Song. I turn back and find myself face to face with him as he stands bracing himself against the wall, one hand on his injured leg.

'Yussef.' I take his arm but instead he snatches up his medical bag and slings it awkwardly around my neck.

'It's alright,' he says, lips pale. 'I know this moment. I've seen it.'

There's a scream from the rear of the compound as trucks come crashing through the rusted metal walls, spitting fire. The mechanical guard dogs attack, firing bullets from their metal jaws, but it does nothing to slow the Xoon vehicles.

Song grabs a semi-automatic gun from the table. 'Go,' he tells me, arming the weapon. 'This is not your death. Go!'

I have no choice but to sprint through the front door as trucks drive full speed towards the house. Everywhere, Harpies are scrambling onto their birds, taking to the skies, trailing tethers. There's a deafening crash and a yell of challenge as Song opens fire, bullets flying, before his voice is cut off.

Choking, I run. The *Charis* is already aloft, Silas barely keeping her above the ground as the engines roar.

Gabi crouches on one side of the hold, sniping Xoon mercenaries with deadly accuracy, Falco tears the pin from a smoke grenade and hurls it into the path of an oncoming truck. Rouf scrambles up into the ship, hands pressed to the blood-stained bandages.

'Auntie!' they yell.

I turn to see Eliska facing down an oncoming truck, pistols in either hand, firing madly, metal teeth clenched. A red fly lands on her cheek and before I know what I'm doing I'm hurling myself forwards, shoving her out of the way of the sniper's bullet.

A zip, and something slams into my back, as hard as fist to the spine. I see Falco's mouth open in a scream, but all of a sudden there is no noise, no air. The breath has gone from my lungs like a burst balloon. I collapse into the dust.

This is not your death.

Strong hands seize my jacket, hauling me back to my feet. Eliska meets my gaze and nods once, before shoving me bodily towards the ship and drawing her pistols to cover my flight.

Forcing air back into my aching lungs, I put all of my strength into a leap towards the *Charis*, already six feet above the ground. Metal fingers lock around my wrist and I look up into Rouf's face as, with a grimace in pain, they drag me aboard.

∞

High above Delos, I stare at Song's medical bag.

The leather is blackened, a hole in the centre from the sniper's bullet that almost ended my life. I run my fingers over it, remembering how Song slung it over my neck, how he held my eyes as he told me *I know this moment, I've seen it*.

Their curse. Seeing what might happen, but not how it will come to pass. How long did Song live with that jumble of images – my face, the medical bag, silver mercenaries, his death? Since he first set foot on Factus? Since the other prisoners died, and he and Esterházy and those few others lived?

The door of the storeroom opens and Silas looks in. 'Here you are.'

All through the ship, the mood is shaken, sombre. I left Falco in the hold, checking our supplies, Rouf sweating and sick from the gut-twisting flight into orbit, Gabi hunched over the nav panel scanning obsessively for any sign of pursuit. But for now, we are safe. The *Charis* floats hidden among the huge, ponderous scrap drogers who drift between moons, jaws open like the lost whales of old Earth, living on the flotsam that washes up here, at the forgotten end of the system.

'I was just checking the damage,' I tell Silas, opening the bag. 'It's mostly still in one piece.'

His hand rests on mine and the words die in my throat.

'I thought I was about to lose you again.'

I cannot look at my hands, scarred with the tally, against his, so I close my eyes. 'I'm not sure what there is of me to lose.'

'There's you.' He draws closer. 'Not the woman they are hunting. Not Hel. You.'

I have no answer to give, so I lean my head on his chest, breathing in his scent of century smoke and spice and the faint tang of liquor. 'When this is over,' he says. 'Let's fly the stars together.'

If it's never over? I want to ask. But he knows that, and I know enough to realise that what we need in this moment is not truth, it's hope. And so I lean in, and tell him *yes*.

And for two days, all is held in stasis, as if outside the walls of the *Charis*, the worlds have stopped turning. With the ship's comms dark, there is nothing for us to do but wait out the journey to Factus and hope no Accord or Xoon patrols pass us by.

Gabi and Falco pass the time in the hold, sparring and practising fighting moves while Rouf pretends to doze, watching them from under their eyelashes. For all her hostility, Gabi seems to be warming to them. She even forgets herself once and pats them on the shoulder when they wonder aloud about Eliska and the Harpies.

Falco is less forgiving.

'How do we know they aren't still working for Xoon?' she asks, sorting through the kitchen cupboards. 'Someone knew where to look for us.'

'You could have been followed back. Or maybe we were tracked.' I wince at the vast bruise that spreads across my back. 'We won't know until we can get to a wire.'

'Why are you defending that silverfish? They sold you out.'

'So did Gabi, once. So did Silas. Admit it, you might too, in a different situation.'

She grunts. 'Does the hophead have *anything* that resembles soap on this junk heap?'

I hand her an almost-empty can of hygiene powder. 'We'll be home soon.'

'Thank god.' She squints at the can. 'Can't take much more of "Hibiscus Fresh".'

'Better than "Charis Stench",' Gabi says from the doorway, wiping her face. 'When's dinner? I'm starving.'

I smile at them, and for a few moments I wish absurdly that we won't reach Factus, that we can carry on drifting in the protective lee of the drogers forever.

But after three days our food is low, and our fuel is almost gone, and the real world waits in the form of Factus's shadow-haunted face. From this vantage in orbit, the Void yawns, a blanket of darkness so pure that the longer I stare, the more I think I see shapes moving and swirling, vaster than worlds…

'Everyone ready?' Silas asks.

I look at the moon where I know I'll meet my death. 'No. But take us down.'

The Personal Notes of Pec "Eight" Esterházy
Lunar Body XB11A – now "Factus"
Lutho-Plex Outpost

I woke to ringing silence in the heart of the storm. My mouth was full of sand; I choked, retching it free. My eyes were full of it too. I blinked them open and saw pitch darkness, except for the torch lying on its side. It showed me a strip of dark sand, and nothing else.

From somewhere to my right I heard coughing. I grabbed the torch and shone it until it caught on a faded blue scalp. Lon, on her knees, vomiting.

Relief flooded through me at the sight of her. I crawled over as she finished being sick, before slumping back and staring up at the sky.

'Pec,' she croaked. 'Where are the stars?'

I looked up and saw nothing, only darkness. Dead? The thought crept upon me from somewhere. Was this death?

Taking Lon's hand, I placed it on the back of my jacket. 'Keep hold of me and don't let go.'

She struggled to her feet and we took two hesitant steps, then four, the torchlight sliding over that fine, dark sand, so different from the pale dust that covered the rest of Factus. The feel of it beneath my boots made me shudder. It was like the skin of a snake, loose over flesh beneath.

Don't know how long we walked before the torch caught a scrap of yellow, protruding from a dune. I didn't hesitate. Whatever it was, it was something; proof of life. Lon and I fell to our knees beside it. A leg — someone wearing a prison jumpsuit. We dug frantically with our hands and dragged the body out.

It was Scratch. My breath stopped when I saw him, because it was just like *they* had shown: blood from a head wound painted his cheeks, the tattoos still writhing beneath dead, grey skin. I reached to find his pulse, only for Lon to knock my hand away.

'No.' Her eyes were wide to the whites. 'Put them back in the ground. Put them back.'

'He might still be alive.'

'They aren't. They're dead. Why are they here?' She started shovelling at the sand, tears and mucus running down her face. 'We buried them all in space. I never meant to kill them, I swear it.'

One of Scratch's eyes flicked open. Lon shrieked in terror, scrambling backwards.

'Stay away,' she babbled, staggering to her feet, 'don't touch me!'

Do not run.

'Lon,' I called. 'Don't—'

Too late; the darkness swallowed her broad, yellow back, cutting off the sound of her cries. I stepped to follow her, and stopped. Something told me she was no longer there.

'Wise. You'll never find her.'

290

In the torchlight, Scratch met my eyes, and smiled. His teeth were full of sand.

'Where are the others?' I asked. 'Where are we?'

'Gone.'

'That's not an answer.'

He lolled his head towards me. 'Seen you, you know. In the dark. But not you. Sometimes you're her. You have a knife. You take my heart.'

A shudder raked my back. No. Do not run. They are everywhere.

'What are you talking about?' I whispered.

'Help me up.'

I found myself hauling him from the sand, steadying him when he stumbled.

'Thanks,' he said, wiping the blood that dripped from the gaping skull wound into his eyes.

'You're dead,' I told him.

He shrugged. 'Doesn't seem to mean much here.'

'Here?'

He waved his hands vaguely before setting out, boots sliding. 'Come on.'

We walked for what felt like hours, or days, I couldn't tell. At first I tried counting steps, but the count became muddled in my head, turning into tallies, into thousands, and they merged with an old song, half-remembered from another world.

'Madárka, madárka ne zavard a vizet...' I sang under my breath.

'What's that?' Scratch asked.

'I don't know. A song. About a bird.'

My boot hit something. I stopped, swaying as I shone the torch. Bone shone pale through the dark sand.

Holding the torch between my teeth, I knelt and started to dig, uncovering what was unmistakably an elbow, then a femur, and finally a skull. A woman's body, I thought, stripped of all flesh by the sand, leaving clean, dry bones. One was outstretched, the other folded in to her chest. I started to brush at the ribs, dug and scraped until I had revealed all of her.

'This is wrong,' I heard myself croak. 'She shouldn't be here.'

Scratch leaned forwards and poked the woman's toe. I could smell the steady ooze of his blood. 'Sure she'd agree.'

'No, I mean she *can't* be here. These bones are too old. The first human only set foot on this moon a few years ago. Where did she come from?'

Scratch withdrew his hand. 'Or when.'

Something gleamed through the skeleton's ribs, silver in the torchlight. A coin? Gently, I worked my fingers into the skeleton's chest cavity, reaching for it...

Sharp metal sliced my skin and I hissed, snatching my hand back. There, where a heart would have been, a scalpel gleamed dully. It looked worn. Older than anything else I'd seen on this moon.

As I reached in and picked it up, my blood smeared the bones of the woman's skeletal hand, shining in the torchlight until it looked like she wore gloves of red. And when my sticky fingers rested on the worn handle, it was as if I had held that blade a million times before.

'I don't understand,' I murmured. 'What does this mean?'

'It means that life has a price.' Then whatever wore Scratch's skin asked me, 'Will you pay it?'

I closed my eyes. 'Yes.'

FOUR

THE
BOOK
OF
THE
SEEKER

I **T IS DUSK** when we burn through atmos above Angel Share. The *Charis* protests the whole way, rattling and squealing and shaking in a manner that makes even Falco break out in a sweat. But finally, the haze clears, bruised gold light streams across the flight deck and the sight of endless, bone-grey sand fills the windows. I thought I hated this place, but my chest aches at the sight of it, like a dislocated bone, pushed back into place. I place a hand to the window, almost laughing that a forbidding, desolate rock that once served as the Accord's dumping ground for the scum of the system should feel like home.

'I cannot *wait* for a shower,' Gabi says, scraping at her hair. 'I swear, I still smell like that Xoon Futures uniform.'

'Get in line, General,' Falco drawls. 'There's no way Peg's going to get near me smelling like this.'

'What about me?' Silas asks, as we break through sand-thick clouds.

'You always smell terrible.' Gabi sniffs.

I can't help but smile as we descend across the plains towards Angel Share. As soon as it comes into view on the horizon, Falco grabs the comms.

'Angel Share this is *Charis*, do you copy?'

Static crackles.

'Angel Share this is *Charis*,' she tries again, to no response.

'Their comms are probably down,' Silas says, but already I can feel a heaviness in my belly, as if it's filling up with sand.

'Something's wrong.' I lean over to scan the radar. 'Where are all the ships?'

'Binoculars,' Gabi barks at Silas, and he reaches into a compartment filled with trash before pulling a pair out.

'What is it?' Falco demands. 'What can you see?'

Her jaw tightens. 'Smoke. Too much smoke.'

'Flyboy,' Falco orders. 'Hit air.'

Grim-faced, Silas sends us roaring down.

'No,' he breathes as we draw closer. 'Oh, no.'

Angel Share smoulders, the dock gone, just a charred skeleton remaining, the twisted shapes of ruined birds at its base. Thick smoke obscures the rest of the settlement, but even from a distance I can see that the shantytown of tents and habitats has been torn apart, scattered across the barren sand.

Falco runs for the hold. Before the *Charis*'s engines have died, I hear her open the doors, letting in a blast of dust-filled air.

'Peg?' she screams into the swirling air. 'Bui?' She puts her fingers in her mouth and lets out a shrill whistle and a raw G'hal cry before leaping down to the ground.

I scramble after her. The second my boots touch the sand my head spins, my vision blurs and I feel *their* presence engulfing me, here, forty years ago, forty years from now, realities stretching across this moon like a vast web of light. I have to steady myself on the side of the ship.

'Doc?' Rouf asks. 'You alright?'

I nod and stumble into the pall of smoke, the thin air almost unbreathable. Before I've taken a dozen steps I see the first bodies; some face down, shot in the back as they tried to run, others crushed within their homes, or beneath the wheels of trucks, the dirt around them a churned mess of blood and fuel. There are wrecked vehicles among the carnage, mules and mares belonging to Barrens folk, but also Metaldogs' colts, their spikes blackened, their silver paint bubbled like blistered skin. I push on, towards the heart of the place.

Angel Share has been utterly destroyed, the cramped stores gutted, doors wrenched from hinges, some buildings still smouldering. There are more bodies here: signs of a vicious fight in the dead who hang over windowsills and sprawl in doorways. None of them have been plundered and the waste of life, the utter devastation of it closes around my chest until I can barely breathe. My eyes burn at the vision from the Edge made reality.

You could have stopped it, a vicious voice says. *You made your choice, Deathbringer.*

'Peg?' I hear Falco scream again, and a few seconds later there's an answering cry, weak and ragged.

It's coming from the direction of the tribute post. Falco races through the debris and the smoke and I follow, nausea thick in my throat.

'Bui!' Falco chokes.

The G'hal has been lashed to the post with cables and chains, her jacket and the flesh beneath torn to shreds. She struggles to lift her head, the floral scarf she always wears dark with dried blood.

No question about who did this; someone has spray-painted a silver infinity sign across her beaten face, the metallic paint mingling with blood.

'Help me,' Falco orders, and I try to untie the cords and chains with shaking fingers as Bui's breath rattles in and out.

'Fought,' she slurs. 'But there were so many. Mercs and Metaldogs, too much shine...' She chokes and dark blood sputters from her lips.

As she slumps into Falco's arms I suppress a cry of horror. The skin of her back has been flayed, hanging down in ribbons of flesh.

'Bui,' Gabi bursts, running to grab her.

Gently, we ease her to the sand, Falco holding the G'hal on her lap. I tumble open the medkit, searching out bandages, sealant. Bui heaves a breath as I shoot a dose of painkiller into her arm.

'The others?' Falco's eye is bright with tears. 'Peg?'

'Took them. Said Xoon would be waiting at Sagacity. Said... said they were the price.' Her eyes flicker. 'I'm sorry, Mala.'

She sags, head lolling.

'Doc, you have to stop the bleeding,' Falco orders. 'Find Silas, we need to fly for a surgeon...'

If this were Prosper, with their well-equipped, technological hospitals then perhaps we could save her. But it isn't. This is Factus, the place they made not in their own image but in their greed. I reach out and feel for Bui's pulse and find only stillness.

Falco's face is stained with tears as she presses her forehead to the G'hal's. 'Blood for blood, they'll pay,' she promises Bui. 'Blood for blood.'

∞

Bui lies in the dirt outside Esterházy's bar, among the broken glass and shattered furniture. Falco kneels beside her, holding her limp hand.

I turn away, grief crashing through me. Bui, with her sly smile and wicked humour, the way she'd tease Silas and Gabi as no one else would. Beside me, Silas wipes at his eyes, tears mingling with the pale dust from searching among the rubble.

'They're not here,' he croaks, 'Peg, Bebe, Franzi, I can't find any of them.'

'So they might still be alive?' Rouf asks.

Gabi nods, her face grimmer than ever. 'There are tracks heading in the direction of Sagacity.'

'Then what are we waiting for?' Silas asks. 'Let's go after them—'

'And get them back how?' Gabi snaps. 'Storm Sagacity, five against five hundred?'

For a while no one speaks. Falco shakes her head slowly. 'You heard Bui. She said the hostages they took were the price.'

'The price for what?' Silas demands.

My insides feel like lead as I raise my chin. 'Me.'

Falco returns my gaze, her eye red-rimmed and blazing and I know that Xoon was right. Everyone can be bought.

'No.' Silas holds up a hand. 'No, we're not handing you over. There's another way, there has to be.'

'There was another way when we had allies, weapons,' Gabi says. 'Not just a junkheap of a ship.'

'We could still have allies.' My voice trembles with shock and the fear of what is to come. I look around at them. 'Give me twenty-four hours.'

'To do what?'

I draw the scalpel from my belt. 'What I promised.'

∞

While the others begin the work of laying out the dead for the wind to bury, I stand outside the *Charis* and turn to face the Void.

'I feel you in hollows of the air,' I murmur, letting a handful of sand trickle through my fingers. 'Between the breaths that fill my lungs, you are here between bones, among atoms, everywhere and in all things.'

The prayer is from my childhood. Meant for comfort. Written by the first Congregation pilgrims in their loneliness as they stood in a bubble on an asteroid looking back at everything they had left behind. How long since I held a page that contained God between the lines? How long since I stopped believing what my fathers told me?

As the sand whisks away I think I see another figure watching from the shadow of a burned-out building, one with threadbare grey hair and eyes as dark as the sky. The mark on my chest prickles as I think about Esterházy's words, about a group of people deemed expendable. Gabi is right. This is about all of us.

I turn back into the *Charis*, to gather what I need.

It doesn't take long. The medkit. Esterházy's journal. The beacon that once saved her life. The scalpel.

The coin.

I unwind the scarf from my neck and place it on Silas's bunk, letting myself linger there for a moment, stroking the faded blanket and walls plastered with souvenirs of his colourful life across the system. One I might have shared, in another world.

'You're really doing this?' Rouf stands in the doorway, a sack-wrapped bundle in their arms. 'You're going back into that place?'

I push myself up. 'It's the only way.'

They nod. 'Found this, in the wreckage.' They pull back the sacking, and my heart contracts when I see that it is Rowdy. 'His legs are busted,' Rouf says, stroking the dog with his metal fingers. 'But he still works. Thought you might like to see him before…'

Smiling, I go to Rowdy and put a hand to his old, dented head. He thrums at my touch, his eyes flickering weakly, jaws clacking as he lets out a quiet *Doc*.

'You'll look after him?' I ask, tears in my eyes.

Rouf nods. 'If he'll let me.'

Swiping at my eyes, I step out into the hold.

'Doc?' Rouf calls. 'I know it's a dangerous word here but…' They give me a twisted smile. 'Good luck.'

At dusk, I stand by the loaded mare.

'You'll send the message out, about Sagacity?' I ask.

Falco nods. 'We'll be there. In twenty-four hours. If you aren't...'
She doesn't finish, just grabs me into a hug, her arm like a vice
around my throat. 'Don't come back without them,' she hisses and
lets me go, striding back towards Angel Share.

Gabi extends her hand and I take it in mine, feeling the scars
and calluses. She attempts a smirk. 'Try not to die, traitor.'

'You too.'

She squeezes my hand, once, before letting go and walking
away.

I turn to the *Charis*, where Silas waits to fold me into his arms.
I rest my head against his, breathing in his scent, wishing I could
rip myself in two, leave the tired, battle-scarred medic here with
him and send the woman with a curse on her chest into the desert.

But I cannot. I am her.

'I can't fly you there?' His voice is raw.

I shake my head. 'I have to go alone.'

'Will you come back?'

I hold him, knowing the answer in my heart, wishing it were
different. 'I hope so.'

'There has to be another way. We need you, Ten—'

I stop him. 'It's not Ten you need. It's Hel.'

He pulls away. His eyes are reddened, his black hair raked by
the winds.

'Wish me luck,' I say, voice breaking.

'Good luck…'

I turn into that gap where my name should be, climb onto the mare and ride into the darkness.

No compass, no map. I follow the prickling of my skin out across the badlands towards the Edge. Night falls and the wind starts up, dragging me along, throwing grit into my face, growing stronger every hour until I can barely raise my head. The mare's compass shudders and cracks and finally I see those vast walls of sand, towering in the distance like the gates of a ruined city.

No one who goes in comes out the same.

Lowering my head, I rev the mare into the storm.

After one klik, the vehicle starts to founder. *You thought this would be easy?* the wind seems to hiss. I abandon it, staggering into the sand, Song's medical bag heavy on my back.

After two kliks, I can barely move, the wind tearing at my clothes like a thief stripping a corpse, stealing the moisture from my tongue, the flecks of dried blood from my hands, fragments of my skin. After three, sand starts to fill my body, like fingers working their way into my nostrils and ears and lips, trying to drag me down beneath the surface.

There are no footprints in oblivion. Even before my cracked boot lands, the sand rushes to fill the hollows I leave behind.

Ten.

Doc.

Traitor.

Life.

Exhausted, I stumble and fall, crashing into cold sand and dragging the medical bag to me. The wind takes what it finds within, whirling bandages and dressings away to places unknown, but I pull out the beacon, unfold the legs and plunge them into the sand, cranking the handle with numb fingers until, at last, an orange glow flickers into existence, pulsing like the slow beat of a heart.

Taking Esterházy's coin from my pocket, I hold it tight.

I am here.

The light goes out, plunging me into utter darkness.

All around me, I feel *them*, beings outside any human concept of being. I feel *their* attention on me and instead of fighting to keep my mind from unravelling, I let myself fall into *them*, into the Void.

The touch of a hand brings me to. A human hand, not sand or shadow but flesh and blood, roughened by chemicals. I look up into a lean, wrinkled face, tangled white hair backlit by the unchanging yellow light.

With a smile, the Seeker pulls me up to sitting. All around, others wait. Some wear night-vision goggles pushed up on their ragged hair, others hold their belts, hung with knives and instruments. Their faces are marked with tallies of their own devising, and for the first time I understand the significance of those marks. I thought *my* reckoning of lost lives was vast, but the Seekers carry one far greater. Their reckonings are of realities, of countless lives saved across this and other moons, a vast sum of chance on which *they* can feed.

'Alive?' the Seeker asks me.

I nod. 'I need your help.' My voice is raw as rusted metal.

They frown. 'There is a price. One you haven't paid.'

'For your help, I will.' None of them answer. 'Please. *They* showed me what will happen, to this moon, to my friends.'

The Seeker's pale eyes crease. '*They* don't control the future. *They* only allow us to see what has the potential to exist. Every choice we could have made.'

'I choose to fight.'

'In this world.'

'Will you fight too?'

They lean forwards. In their hand is a scalpel, as worn as time. 'Hel wants to wear your name.'

I swallow. 'Hel can have it.'

The last thing I feel is the bite of the blade as they open my chest and cut me free.

The Personal Notes of Pec "Eight" Esterházy
Lunar Body XB11A – now "Factus"
Lutho-Plex Outpost

Don't remember how I got out of that place; I only remember darkness and bone and blood, and then, abruptly, light.

I was lying in the dust, alone, feeling every single day of my five decades. Around me, the ground was undisturbed. No footprints, no sign that anyone else had ever walked there. Not even me. Any trace of the ox or the dead inmates and the bones of the woman were gone, swallowed by the dark sand of whatever no-place I had walked.

But when I moved, something fell from my chest. The scalpel, impossibly old on this new moon, its blade still rusty with my blood. Tucking it into my belt, I looked around.

A single mule stood nearby, covered in a thick layer of dust, its saddle cracked by the sun. I staggered towards it and found the packs full – just as we had loaded them the night before. I drank the stale water I found like a woman dying of thirst, ate a protein bar as if I had never tasted food before. Then, I sat in its shadow and waited as the sun climbed high, until I was sure that no one was coming.

I set off, back towards the base, not knowing whether I was the only person still alive on the entire moon.

When I got there, the gates were hanging open, drifting gently in the breeze. The parade ground was deserted. I stopped the mule and climbed off, every joint stiff.

'Hello?' I croaked.

No reply, just the flapping of the flag above, that eyeless infinity. Sand had drifted against the walls of the buildings, filled the gaps around the windows.

The bunkroom was empty. Sheets and blankets lay scattered, as if torn off in a hurry. A few possessions lay among them – a page from an almanac, a colourful sweet wrapper, a pot of bright red lip paint, used up to the dregs. I turned my back and made my way towards the staff building.

In the corridor, small sheets of paper scudded, brushing up against my boots like creatures waiting to be let outside. Bulletin sheets from the wire. I caught one before it escaped.

```
FAO: MACOBOY (≠45182)
EVACUATION REQUEST: DENIED.
REMAIN IN SITU FOR FURTHER MONITORING.
FRIDA XOON: LUTHO-PLEX
```

Dated the day after we arrived. I let it fall. There were dozens of the things, all identical. I followed that trail of littered pleas towards MacOboy's office and found the door ajar. Beyond, the room was dim, shutters fastened tightly over the plastic windows.

It was empty, but signs remained to tell me what had happened. It smelled of old blood; the map and the wall behind MacOboy's

desk were covered in dark spatters, all the way up to the ceiling.
Crumpled on the floor, another bulletin. I picked it up.

```
FAO: MACOBOY (≠45182)
EVACUATION REQUEST: DENIED.
FURTHER REQUESTS WILL BE DISREGARDED.
FRIDA XOON: LUTHO-PLEX
```

Enough to send an already desperate man insane.

There was no one and nothing to stop me from looking through
MacOboy's desk. The top was a mess of strange objects. I recognised
Prosperian playing cards, a pair of polished metal dice, bits of plant
fibre, some short, some long. All games of chance. What was he
doing, at the end? Trying to call *them*? Trying to find a way out?

In the top drawer was a file. A dossier: information sheets on every
inmate who had arrived, bad carbon mugshots of us in each upper
corner. Almost all were crossed through in red. All except four: mine,
Harri's, Moll's and Song's. I pulled the last one free.

```
Name: Doctor Yussef Song
Inmate: ≠560221
Crime: Patient death resulting from intoxication
on duty. Theft of medical supplies for the
purpose of recreational drug use. Perjury.
Dereliction of duty.
Sentence: Nine Years
```

I let the page fall. On the top of the file was a letter, faded at the creases, as if it had been unfolded and read again and again. Topped with that same, haunting symbol of infinity.

FROM THE OFFICE OF FRIDA XOON
LUTHO-PLEX, DELOS
PRIVATE AND CONFIDENTIAL

FAO: Donald "Five" MacOboy,

I am delighted you have accepted the offer to be part of our research cohort on XB11A: the moon now termed "Factus". As per the terms of the agreement, upon arrival your inmate status will be divulged only to upper management, your collar removed and once on-moon you will hold the position of Commander.

Your first cohort of inmates will arrive in several days. We have requested a cross-section of felons from across ages, criminal backgrounds and experiences to maximise potential susceptibility to Factus's fauna and increase the likelihood of possible contact.

Any and all unexplained or unusual events must be reported directly to this address without delay.

In expectation,
Frida Xoon

The bulletin recorder sat on the desk. I imagined a woman somewhere – who knew what she looked like – sitting in a cool office on Delos, listening with bright, rapt eyes to my words, feeding them back to scientists, denying every single one of MacOboy's requests, even as he went insane, even as we disappeared one by one.

I threw the file back onto the desk, and something slipped to the floor with a clatter. Another coin. Didn't wait to see how it landed.

The infirmary door was open, a figure in a white jacket slumped over a workbench. When I stepped forwards, they raised their head.

Song looked terrible, his face drained, creased with lines that weren't there before. 'Pec?' He pushed himself to his feet. 'You're alive?'

I remembered the place of dark sand, Scratch's corpse walking beside me. Death. Or something like it. 'I think so.'

The doctor swayed as he stood. 'I knew it. I sensed it. Here.' He thrust an almost-empty bottle of arak at me. 'To life.'

I took it. 'Egészségedre.'

'We have to tell the others—'

'Others?' I grabbed him, lips still wet with the arak. 'Who made it out?'

'Harri did. And Moll. They said there was some kind of storm, but they managed to get into the ox before it hit. By the time it passed...' He shook his head.

A slow shiver crossed my skin. 'How long have I been gone?'

'Eight days.' I felt him staring at me, taking in the fact that I stood and walked and talked when I should be a wind-dried corpse. 'Where were you, Pec?'

No roads, no sky. No time, even. I reached for the scalpel at my

THE BOOK OF THE SEEKER

belt, taken from a dead woman who might not even have been born yet. 'I think I was with *them*.'

Song was silent for a long moment before striding into the corridor. 'We have to report this to Lutho-Plex.'

'What?'

'When Frida Xoon hears you survived eight days with *them* and emerged with barely a mark on you?' Song laughed wildly as he strode towards MacOboy's office. 'She'll probably come down here herself. Or take you to Delos. We could finally get off this rock.' He went to the wire receiver, started to wind it. 'She's already interested in you, Pec – a directive came through, right after MacOboy sent you out. He was meant to keep you here, conduct a series of tests.' He jerked his chin at the desk, littered with all those artefacts of chance. 'Think the fact he lost you sent him over the edge, he realised there'd never be any hope for him after that. Ah!'

The wire receiver began to fuzz, the screen flickering grey. Song pulled the keyboard to him, tapped in an authorisation code and started to hack out the message.

```
FAO F. XOON
INMATE P. ESTERHAZY RETURNED
CONFIRMED CONTACT WITH LIFEFORMS
REQUEST IMMEDIATE EXTRACTION
```

I closed my eyes as he typed, trying to see the future he described; all of us scooped up in a private shuttle, flown to Delos – a moon so different to this one with its rich resources – already burgeoning with factories and mineral mines. But the only image that came to me, time and again, was silver infinity washed with blood and a woman with a blade in her hand. Offering or taking, I wasn't sure.

Before Song could hit send, I took out the scalpel, walked to the wire receiver and severed its umbilical.

The screen died.

Song stood frozen. 'What are you doing?'

I tucked the scalpel back into my belt. 'We don't belong to Lutho-Plex. Neither does this moon. Neither do *they*.'

'Pec.' Song's face was ashen beneath the windburn and the grime. 'We have to get out. Or we're all going to die here.'

I smiled at him, that young doctor-criminal who held the key to my future. 'No, Song. We're not.'

Hours later, after an emotional reunion with Harri and Moll, I walked out alone beyond the base's walls, until the single floodlight dwindled to a sharp-toothed star in the distance.

There I sat and faced the Void. Before me, two objects: the coin and the scalpel. Above me, a whole system, living and dying. Abruptly, I understood why a rich woman like Frida Xoon might turn her eyes here, bewitched by thoughts of what might wait beyond the border of the known universe, for those determined enough to push through.

'I'm here,' I said.

And *they* were there too, as if they always had been, but I'd only just sensed *them*. *Their* presence threatened to strain my mind to breaking as I tried to comprehend what *they* were, beyond space and time and size...

Esterházy, someone said.

You stood in the darkness, bloodied and tired and wind-bitten, with the eyes of someone who has seen the raw edges of worlds. But you were not alone; the air around you was a web of lives – every choice a road, every road a world. I saw you as a woman with a shorn head and a prison scar, I saw blood and ships and organs hot and slippery in my hands, I saw gunfire and the dark sand of the place on the edge of reality. I saw people, living thanks to stolen blood, their lives spawning countless new realities. I saw Factus lit up in a sprawling tangle of a million choices.

And I thought: how long have *they* been starving, here at the edge of the system? A hunger that is life itself. A hunger we can feed.

I reached out, and chose the blade.

T HE ALKALINE FLATS glow in the light of a new day. The surface cracks under me as I stagger the wastes towards the foothills, eyes fixed on the shape of a familiar ship hunkered in the lee of the rock. My head feels strange and full of light, but I keep walking, I keep one hand pressed to my bloodied chest, Ess's medical bag thumping against my back. At last, I see a flash of binoculars and silhouetted figures start to run towards me.

'It's her!' Rouf's voice screams. 'She's back!'

I stumble, falling to my knees in the dirt but then strong hands are lifting me, someone is slinging my free arm about their shoulder to half carry me the remaining distance to the *Charis*.

'Ten?' Silas stumbles from the ship, a bulletproof vest slung over his floral shirt. 'Ten, thank god!'

They ease me down onto the edge of the hold and I slump, my body thrilling with exhaustion. Someone pushes a canteen into my hand and I gulp down chemical-treated water.

'Did you do it?' Falco grabs my arm, her face tense. 'Did the Seekers agree?'

Pain stabs through my chest and I gasp, pressing the flesh there. 'I think so.' Carefully, I peel away my bloodied shirt. The Seekers' scar – that before had healed to white – has been cut into afresh, and deeper. Dark stitches close the skin, as if something inside has been taken out. 'There was a price,' I tell them. 'I paid.'

Rouf looks sick. 'With what?'

I don't answer.

Gabi's voice breaks the silence as she kneels before me. 'It's nearly time. Can you ride?'

No pitying in her gaze, no doubt or fear, just conviction. A torch, blazing a path into the future. I nod. 'My medical kit.'

She jerks her head and Rouf scrambles towards me, pushing the kit into my hands. Mechanically, I slot ampules of amphetamine and painkiller into the injector gun and fire them into my system.

Falco hands me a protein pouch. 'Don't complain about the flavour.'

As I push myself to my feet, Silas steps from the *Charis*, holding his bottle of Super Green liquor. 'For the road,' he says, looking into my eyes. I take it and drink. One by one, the others follow suit, Gabi pouring out a libation to the dead before draining the bottle to its dregs.

'Alright,' she says, tossing it aside. 'Let's ride.'

∞

Noon, and we cast no shadows. I stand in the dust outside the walls of Sagacity with the collar loose about my neck and my jacket hanging open, the Seeker scar stark as ink. The others stand alongside me: Gabi and Falco, Rouf and Silas, all with pistols pointed at my back. And behind them stand the dead: Bui and Song and Esterházy and every person who lost their life to infinity on this moon.

Silver smacks back at us as the gates of Sagacity creak open and Metaldogs appear, engines snarling through the dust, chains clanking, the spikes and bull bars of their colts still stained with the blood of those they ran down. If Baba Guelo is Xoon's mouth, then here are his teeth. Behind them I see deputised Peacekeepers and marshals, drunk on scrip and new weapons, mercs in their imported Delos armour, shining with the promise of a new gun not yet fired.

Just out of range, we wait. Suicide, some might say, but so long as the man who controls those forces still believes my mind has a value, they won't attack us. Yet.

Baba Guelo's truck rolls out. She sits on the back in wet silk and armour, hair dripping luxuriously down her back, knives at her waist. Her augmentations have been fixed, gleaming dark as insect eyes on her brow.

'Malady Falco,' she calls, her voice magnified by some device I cannot see. 'What do you have for us?'

Falco raises her head. 'Where the fuck are they, Baba?'

Baba waves a hand and a group of Metaldogs roar forwards. There are figures tied to their bonnets, I see in horror, some lashed to posts, others chained like beaten figureheads. Among them, I see the wild thatch of Peg's pale hair, full of dust and dried blood. They raise their head, and their face is a swollen mess, but they are alive. Frantically, I scan the other hostages and see an unconscious figure in a rusted cage who might be Franzi, G'hals dragged by chains, their flesh raw and covered with road dust.

I can feel Falco's fury. 'Let them go.'

'When you hand over the Converter.'

'She's here.' Falco shoves me forwards with the pistol. 'Where's Xoon?'

Baba Guelo laughs. 'You didn't expect him to deal with a dirtrat rebel in *person*, did you?' She waves a hand to the gleaming jet lenses in her forehead. 'He's nearby. Watching. Let that satisfy you. As for the exchange, you have his word and mine.'

Curtly, Falco shoves me forwards. I walk, keeping my head down, even as my heart threatens to kick through my ribs, knowing they will gun the others down the moment I am out of the line of fire, knowing Baba Guelo's augmentations are recording my every move. I stop and open my hand. A silver coin glints on my palm. I look up into Guelo's lenses and smile.

'Now!' Falco screams as I hurl the coin into the air.

The air explodes, Baba Guelo's guards opening fire. I throw myself to the ground as something streaks over my head, followed by a G'hal war cry. A flash grenade, bright enough that it sears my vision even through closed lids. It buys time, maybe five seconds. I get to my feet and sprint back towards the mares that Falco and Rouf have pushed over on their sides, diving behind them just as the shooting starts again.

'Xoon's in Sagacity,' I gasp.

'How do you know?' Gabi asks, arming a blaster.

'He's watching through Baba's lenses, must be within range.'

Behind us, the *Charis* is already rising into the air, creating a churning dust cloud to cover us. Rouf grins at me as they pull goggles down over their eyes.

'Incoming!' Gabi yells, shouldering a blaster, and I hear the sound of raw-toothed engines: Metaldogs, racing through the smoke towards us.

'Falco,' I gasp. 'Where's Falco?'

Through the gap in the mares I see her, aiming at the spiked Metaldog colt where Peg is tied as it races back for the safety of Sagacity.

'Mala!' Gabi screams – too late. The Metaldogs smash into our barricades on their brutal machines, baying and hollering.

With a shriek of fury, Gabi fires her blaster at an approaching Metaldog, bursting them apart in a rain of blood and metal and flame. But others are roaring up, a dozen of them, two dozen and any second we'll be surrounded.

'Where are they?' she yells, reloading.

Rouf surges up, lobbing another grenade into the Metaldogs' path only to blanch. 'Oh shit,' they say, grabbing my jacket. 'Move, move, move…'

An explosion sends us flying into the dust, the mare we were sheltering behind tossed aside like debris. Choking, I look up to see a silver armoured tank bearing down on us.

With a shriek, a grease-black craft hurtles from the sky, peppering the tank with charges before veering recklessly away. In the Rook's wake fly others; Butcherbirds in their swift shrikes and the Dhūlanā śētānō on their smoke-trailing souped-up buzzards, earning their name of dust devils. Nearer Sagacity's gates, the ground explodes as the Sand Eels burst from their hidden foxholes among the

Metaldogs, firing cable-trailing harpoons through metal, armour, flesh until the ground is a mess of blood and fallen colts with spinning wheels. Factus's gangs streak towards the fight from every side of Sagacity, yelling war cries.

Gabi vaults into the carnage, turning wildly. 'Falco!'

A second later a riderless colt hurtles out of the smoke. In its wake strides Falco, covered in blood that something tells me isn't her own.

'They've taken them inside,' she yells, tossing a pistol and loading another. 'The hostages.'

I stare at Sagacity's gates. 'Then let's go get them.'

Crowded onto one mare, we hurtle through the chaos, the *Charis* providing covering fire as Falco veers and swerves through danger, Gabi stood in the saddle with blaster raised, Rouf holding onto her legs to steady her with a look of undisguised adoration. I hang on to the rear, Esterházy's coin clutched in my hand. There is something I need to do but I am afraid; afraid that once I open this door, there will be no way back.

Before I can flip the coin something dazzles in my eyes, leaving visions in its wake – *a charge flies, Gabi jerks backwards her throat torn open, Rouf's eyes roll in death* – and I act without thinking, grabbing Gabi's legs and dragging her down as a sniper charge streaks through the air where her neck had been a second before.

The mare crashes onto its side, sending us all flying as sniper shots from Sagacity's towers spit up the dust. 'There,' Rouf yells, pointing to Baba Guelo's abandoned, smouldering truck.

Frantically, Gabi drags Falco from under the mare and we stagger out of the line of fire.

'Mala?' I ask as she hisses, clutching her arm. From one glance I can see it's broken, the forearm jutting at a bad angle.

'Just give me a shot,' she orders, sweat running through the dust on her face. 'We have to get in there.'

I rip open a needle of painkiller and stab it into her arm. With her other hand she draws her pistol. Her eye is bright with adrenalin. 'Good job I can shoot with both hands.'

'G'hals?' Rouf's voice cuts across the din of battle.

They are staring at the sky. I follow their gaze and get one glimpse of silver birds flying in formation, slicing the air like blades. I don't even have time to cover my head before the ground explodes, sand fountaining up and crashing down.

Ears ringing, choking on dust I look around at Falco, bleeding from a shrapnel cut to her cheek, Rouf crawling dazedly to their knees.

'Gabi?' I call, voice muffled in my ears before I realise she is already on her feet, firing a blaster uselessly at the ships as they streak away and bank for another attack.

All around people are fighting and dying, lives being stolen that should have sparked a thousand connections, a million new realities. I see a Rook spiral to the ground and explode, Sand Eels lying dead, their bodies dragged behind Metaldogs. And Amir was right, there aren't nearly enough of us, not when mercs in armoured vehicles are streaming through Sagacity's gates.

We can end it. We have to end it.

The coin is still in my hand. I open my fingers and the infinity sign gleams back. I can feel the air changing around me, the light shifting from magnesium white to bone yellow as I grip the scalpel and reach out.

Here.

They flood into my perception and I realise *they* are already present – in every split-second decision and twitch of synapse, every moment of wordless terror on which worlds hang. *They* glut on all those possible realities, swallowing down the energy contained in a single second of human life.

'Low!' Gabi cries and I look around to see the Seekers hurtle from the wastes towards Sagacity, their remade ships pushed far past breaking. And I laugh because I know their wings will not break, their engines will not burst. They open fire on the Xoon ships, wheeling away a split-second before being hit, diving and pulling up, heartbeats from death until the air is full of phantoms; for each Seeker there are a dozen others, ghosts of probability tearing across the sky, sending the mercenaries scattering in mad terror.

I turn towards the others, bloodied and filthy and alive and don't need to say a word.

Together, we run through the gates and up the slope towards the streets of Sagacity. The air is a soup of toxic smoke and mica, shattered rock and gunfire, mercs shooting wildly at shadows. As we stumble into the streets I see that as we fought outside Sagacity's gates, Falco's spies attacked from within. Some passageways have collapsed, rubble strewing the ground, bodies lost beneath it. Xoon vehicles smoulder and above the settlement the dock is on fire, sending karburant flames of blue and purple and green shooting into the sky. But there is no sign of the Metaldogs and their hostages. Behind an overturned droger's ox, we stop to catch breath.

'Where will they have taken them?' Gabi asks, checking her blaster. 'The tunnels?'

'If they have we might never find them.' Rouf spits out dust. 'It's a warren.'

'Baba said Xoon was nearby,' I gasp. 'Somewhere close enough to receive her transmissions—'

Falco lurches to her feet, broken arm held against her chest, eye fixed. 'Why don't we ask her?'

One of Baba Guelo's personal trucks is speeding through the chaos, running people down as it makes for the dock. Sprinting forwards, Gabi aims the blaster up at the rock wall and fires.

Rubble cascades down into the truck's path and it screeches to a halt. As I race towards it, lungs burning, the back door flies open and four guards leap down, guns ready. I stride towards them.

'Hel!' one chokes and drops her gun, stumbling away. The other guards open fire – *the bullets strike me in the leg, the chest, the shoulder* – and I sidestep and twist, out of the path of those possible deaths, as Falco and Rouf let charges fly and Gabi scrambles towards the front of the truck.

Gripping the scalpel I tug open the side door.

Skin splits, blood on sand.

I lean back as a blade slices the air where my throat was a

moment before. With a yell Baba Guelo hurls herself at me, stabbing, slashing, a blade in each fist. Worlds blur as I spin and stumble. She gets behind me – *a blade drives into my liver* – and I duck. The tip of her knife scores my head as my knees meet the ground but it's enough. As I fall, Falco grabs Baba's shoulder with her good hand and spins her around.

'See this, Lutho?' she snarls before headbutting the woman in the face.

Baba stumbles, hands over the shards of the augmentation, straight into the barrel of Gabi's gun.

'Where are they?' she demands, jamming the weapon into Baba's side. 'Where's Xoon?'

Baba looks up, blood running down her face, and laughs.

A blast from somewhere shakes the rock, and in that second Baba dives, scrambling away under the truck.

'Don't let her go!' Falco yells.

'This way!' Rouf points to a path through the rocks.

Dimly I'm aware that I am hurt, my body aching, blood running down my neck from the scalp wound, but it all feels strangely unimportant. The closer we get to the centre of Sagacity, the more distant the fighting gets; some of the mercs driving out onto the plain to engage Factan forces, others fleeing in terror. Charge shots still streak through the smoke, shattering rock as we run, and within seconds I hear the guttural snarl of engines echoing like thunder from the canyon walls, coming from the direction of the stage. We run into the centre of the space, filled with dust and noise and smoke.

'The cells.' A noise like crushed metal cuts off my voice as a colt comes roaring backwards out of the rock passageway, a Metaldog within firing madly. Gabi raises the blaster.

'No!' I knock it aside as she fires and rock dust rains down. A G'hal is lashed to the colt's fender, choking weakly. Other vehicles are revving from the passageways and alcoves: a dozen Metaldogs, all rust and blood and charred metal teeth, with hostages chained to the fronts or tied to poles over their back wheels.

One of the Metaldogs lets out a howl over the din and the others take it up, baying, snarling as they encircle us, pushing us into a tight group.

'Peg!' Falco yells, her broken arm clutched to her chest. 'Don't shoot,' she orders, coughing in the dust, 'not until we can see.'

'We'll be dead before that,' Rouf shrieks.

Gabi thrusts a pistol into my hands, her eyes fixed on the vehicles. 'Aim for the heads.'

I stare at the greasy black metal and plastic in my grip, an instrument of destruction that makes my flesh recoil. *They only allow us to see what has the potential to exist. Every choice we could have made.* But in that moment all I see is death; kill the Metaldogs and risk killing prisoners, don't and die.

With a howl, one of the Metaldogs shoots towards us, firing from behind their human shield, a woman in a bloodied floral dress. Bebe, I realise in horror, the head of Angel Share. Taking aim, Gabi fires, hitting the Metaldog square in the eye. They collapse forwards over the handlebars, sending the colt hurtling towards the rock wall.

'No—!'

Too late, other Metaldogs are attacking and there are too many, too few worlds where we live…

A shadow slides overhead, blotting out the light and I look up, into the belly of a ship, rusted and scarred and remade many times, emblazoned with the symbol that marks my chest.

'Seekers!' someone screams.

Some of the Metaldogs break from the circle and flee for the passageways, others aim upwards as cables come coiling down from the ships' bellies, followed by bodies sliding to the ground in their bloodied leather and stolen armour and night-vision goggles. They do not even pause when they hit the ground; pistols and knives out, they stride into the chaos, flanked by the red beams of gun-sights.

They have no fear. I see one snatch a Metaldog from their colt as they drive past and plunge a knife into their spine, see another leap onto the back of a vehicle and plant a bullet in the driver's skull, the knives and saws on their belt clanking.

Dropping the gun, I pull the scalpel from my belt and lunge to help them, aiming for flesh rather than damaging organs that will become a harvest of life.

Someone screams and I spin around to see a Metaldog bearing down on Falco, Peg's bloodied form lashed to the front. Falco aims but it's no good; she'll be crushed beneath the wheels.

Gabi hears Falco's cry and turns to take aim at the cables tying Peg, a Seeker leaps onto the back of the colt and cuts the Metaldog's throat… Different realities, branching worlds. With a surge of effort I cry out to *them*.

Gabi's shot snaps the cables. Falco stumbles aside, catching Peg with her good arm just as the Seeker slashes the Metaldog's throat and jumps clear, sending the colt careering into the rock with a sickening crash.

Shaking, I stumble forwards.

'Peg,' Falco says, pushing at the G'hal's bloodied hair.

'Mala?' Pegeen's face is so swollen and beaten they can barely open their eyes.

'It's alright, I'm here.'

There's a cry and I look up to see Rouf pointing towards the walkway where we once stood to watch the tribunal. I catch a flash of torn silk disappearing around a corner. Baba Guelo. I meet Falco's eye.

'Go,' she says.

∞

The metal walkway shudders after me as I run, leaving the rapidly turning fight between the Metaldogs and Seekers behind me. I hear footsteps and look back to see Gabi, arming a pistol and Rouf behind her, knuckles pressed to their wounded chest.

We round the corner and I catch a glimpse of Baba Guelo disappearing through a silver door in the rock.

'No!'

Gabi opens fire, too late. The charges bounce harmlessly from the door as it clangs shut.

Heaving in a breath, I run forwards, searching for a handle, a panel but there's nothing, just blank metal emblazoned with infinity. With a cry Gabi slams her boot into the surface but manages nothing more than a faint dent.

'Wait.' Rouf shoves their pistol into their waistband, running their hands over the central seam of the doors. 'Help,' they ask.

Using fingertips we haul at the metal, heaving it back until it opens the smallest amount. Immediately, Rouf jams their metal fingers into the gap and starts to lever it open, veins standing out on their forehead, blood seeping through the bandages on their chest. With a cry, they twist their arm and the door opens a hand's breadth, just enough to squeeze through.

'Quick,' they choke. Gabi scrambles in first, and I squeeze through the gap after her, leaving smears of blood on the door as I go. It's only when I turn that I realise Rouf's fingers are sundering, the metal crumpling under the weight of the door's mechanism.

'No!' Gabi grabs for the door, and Rouf looks into her face in wonder for the space of a heartbeat before sparks fly and their hand breaks open with a *crack*, sending the door crashing closed.

'Idiot,' Gabi swears.

I look around the dim corridor, abruptly quiet after the chaos outside. My throat is raw from running, mica powdery on my tongue as I try to catch my breath. A few feet away, an elevator gleams: the same we once took down to Baba Guelo's private quarters.

'This way.'

No sensors here thankfully; Gabi thumps a button with her

fist and glass doors slide open, letting out a swirl of oxygen-rich air. I step inside and for just a moment, slump against the wall.

'Hey.'

I look down at Gabi, her hair dishevelled, her face streaked with dust and blood, her eyes holding more weariness and rage than any teenager's should. 'If anything happens… I've been glad to fight with you, traitor.'

Has she seen it too, the death that Esterházy foretold? I don't ask, I just smile. 'You too, General.'

She lets out a sort of choked laugh as the lift slows.

'Never thought I'd say that to a Limiter—' She breaks off as the corridor beyond the elevator slides into view. 'Oh shit.'

It's crowded with armoured Xoon mercenaries, Baba Guelo sheltering behind them.

In the moment before the doors open Gabi grips my arm. 'Find Xoon,' she says. 'Hell, go!'

Gunfire explodes around us, ricocheting inside the elevator. I hurl myself to the ground as Gabi strides straight towards the guards, firing with one hand, pulling a smoke grenade from her pack with the other. And there is nothing I can do but follow, screaming silently for *them*. Gripping the scalpel, I get to my feet and plunge into the smoke, the blade in my hand carving a path towards the door at the far end, where Baba Guelo disappears, where I know Xoon must wait.

I falter, turning to look for Gabi, and for a heartbeat I see her as *they* must see her: searing through realities like a bullet with her more-than-human mind and body. In her presence mercenaries hesitate, seeing a slight young woman when they should see death. Smoke explodes and the last thing I see is her pistol-whipping a guard with her dead gun before she's lost to a tide of silver bodies.

Alone, I fight on with blood and blade until I find myself in front of a familiar door. Chest heaving, I use a fallen mercenary's wrist implant to open the lock, and slip inside.

The door clangs shut behind me, echoing through the dripping space. Steam swirls just as before, pumped from somewhere at vast expense, in this place where control of water is control of life. I take one step forwards, onto the slick tiles, then another, towards a dim light at the other end of the room. Flickering screens show scenes of Sagacity, the battle captured by Baba's hidden cameras.

'Xoon,' I call, and my voice is that of the dead, echoing from beneath the sand, from the inside of a cave.

'Hel,' his voice echoes. 'Stop this. I'm offering you the chance to change the world with me.'

I grip the scalpel. 'It's not yours to change.'

A click and I spin: too late. The bullet thuds into my shoulder, sending me staggering backwards.

Shaking, I look up as Baba Guelo steps from the steam, holding Xoon's silver pistol. With a surge of effort, I get to my feet and she fires again, hitting me in the gut. I double over, feeling blood pulse hot through my fingers but there is no pain, just pressure and white-hot anger. I force my body upright, holding the scalpel tight, and take another step towards her.

She retreats, firing three times and though she is aiming for my head I step through those worlds, into ones where the bullets strike my chest, my arm, my leg instead.

'Don't damage her brain,' I hear Xoon shout. 'We need it intact!'

But Baba isn't listening; sweat trickles between her augmentations, her eyes glossy with fear as she backs up through the steam. I follow her towards a desk covered in control panels and find myself face to face with Lutho Xoon.

His image flickers from the screen above, mirrored eyes holding the ghosts of what he is seeing. Too much of a coward to face us, in the end.

'Who are you?' his voice demands from some hidden speaker. 'What are you?'

I raise the blade.

'I'm Peccable Esterházy.'

'Get away!' Baba fires, the slug grazing the flesh of my cheek.

'I'm Bui Anderson. I'm Yussef Song—' She fires again and again, the seventh bullet striking my ribs, the eighth scoring a path across my hand.

I look into her eyes as she levels the pistol at my forehead.

'I'm Life Without Parole. I'm Ten Low.'

She pulls the trigger. The gun clicks on empty.

I look into the dark lenses in her forehead, straight at Xoon and I see myself reflected there, my eyes as featureless as the Void.

'I'm Hel,' I say and plunge the blade into her heart.

The Personal Notes of Pec "Eight" Esterházy
Lunar Body XB11A – now "Factus"
Lutho-Plex Outpost

This will be the last entry I write. In an hour from now, a new prison transport ship will start its descent. Not long after, the doors will clank open and a new cohort will stumble – air-sick and weak like we were – onto this moon.

I can see Yussef through the window, tugging at his new, silver uniform. It was MacOboy's and is too big, but Moll altered it for him as best they could, and the infinity badge on his chest does look impressive. He has been given his freedom, in a way – if continued service to Lutho-Plex can be called freedom – for being the sole survivor of Cohort Two. And for his silence.

The scabs from the prison collar itch like hellfire. Every time I scratch them I remember that I'm a dead woman, according to company records, at least. Thought about reclaiming my name, the one I wore before I was sentenced, but that woman is dead too. I think the others feel the same. Factus-names, Harri calls them. They suit this place, and will suit our purposes.

'What happens when it begins again?' Song asked me earlier, as Harri stowed the final box of supplies onto the mule. 'When the inmates escape or disappear?'

I smiled at Moll as they appeared from the bunkroom dressed for the road, in goggles and a duster fashioned from a blanket. 'Leave them to us.'

Song nodded. It's the deal we agreed. What we search for, we'll find, and what we find, we'll keep. On his forearm, the incised marks are healing. Two sloping lines and a single line across. Don't know how I thought of it, but it just seemed right. A symbol to represent human and non-human, past and future. *Them.* Us. This place where we meet. This promise.

In the sky, a flaming point of light is just beginning its descent.

I don't know what my future holds. *They* show the what but not the how. I only know that one day, you'll read these words, you with the scarred throat and sadness in your brown eyes, you with the dead at your heels and a debt that can never be paid. You'll read this and think — that mad old woman — and you'll make a choice. I can't make it for you.

All I can say is that, whichever way you choose, you won't be alone. We'll be there, in the wind and the sand, waiting.

IN THE DRIPPING silence of the baths, I stare at the dead woman until I realise *they* are gone. Just me, alone, a blade in my hand and a screen fuzzing with static. Above, other screens show the battle across Sagacity, mercenaries fleeing into the desert, Factan rebels plundering Xoon crates for loot, the Seekers taking their tribute from the dead.

Liquid spatters onto the floor. When I touch fingers to my torso, they come away red. Of course. *They* are intangible but I am made of flesh and blood.

Step by staggering step, I make my way towards the exit. There is no shooting outside now, no violence. Perhaps we are all dead, moving mechanically through our final moments. My feet leave bloody prints on the tiles.

The pain arrives as I reach the door, first as a distant knowledge, then a rush that threatens to send me under. One of my hands won't work. With the other, I fumble in my pocket for the breath beads and push one into my mouth, fingers sticky on my lips.

Enough fuel to let me push the handle, and stumble outside.

The corridor beyond is a wasteland of smoke and shattered rock and broken bodies, some groaning softly, others unconscious, more dead. I move among them a step at a time, but none of the corpses reach to stop me and for that I'm grateful.

I find her in the elevator, her legs out in front of her, slumped beneath a huge smear of blood upon the glass. The doors open and close repeatedly upon a dead mercenary's foot. Her head lolls, chest glistening with what look like a dozen gunshot wounds, but when I let out a choke, she opens one dark eye and laughs through red teeth.

'Xoon?'

I shake my head. 'Gone.'

I stagger into the lift and slide down beside her, feeling the wrongness of the bullets within me, the lightness in my head from too little blood. After three attempts I manage to push the mercenary's foot clear. The doors slide shut and the elevator begins to drift upwards.

'Think we'll manage it, this time?' Gabi wheezes. 'Think we'll die?'

I breathe a laugh. Lying here, the pain doesn't feel so bad anymore.

My injured hand twitches towards my pocket. With effort I reach in and pull out Esterházy's coin. 'Flip for it?'

'Sure. I know this one.' Her eyes drift closed. 'Snake eats all.'

Weakly, I toss the coin, sending it belly-flopping into the air. Lives spool out across my vision – a tangled web – all of them leading back to her.

Soldier, smuggler, fighter, convict, spy, hero, lover, killer.

The coin hits the metal floor, clattering to a stop on infinity.

'Eight.' My voice is thick. 'You live.'

'Just my luck,' she slurs, rolling her head to look at me. 'What about you?'

I feel my lips crack in a smile. 'Haven't you heard? Hel can't die.'

'They're here!' a muffled voice shouts. The glass doors slide open to reveal Rouf, his metal hand shattered to pieces.

'Oh my god.' They turn over their shoulder. 'Medic! Someone, help!'

The next minutes are a blur of hands lifting me, the sensation of being carried outside. I catch glimpses through the haze; Falco helping Peg along, other G'hals and hostages slumped or limping through the aftermath of battle, injured and bloodied but alive.

'Ten,' Silas cries, and I smile to see his wild black hair, his dark eyes creased in fear. 'We need to get you to a hospital —'

I manage to shake my head once, before everything goes dark.

∞

I wake to the sound of machines, the smell of dried blood and sealant and antiseptic. My eyelids are steel doors that I have to heave open. A tarpaulin ceiling swims into view, lit by a flickering solar lantern. Night. I can tell it by the smell of the desert, the brush of the night wind that coils over my chest and around my neck like a cat, whispering for me to come away…

With effort, I raise my head. I'm in what looks like a makeshift hospital tent, beds made from tables and crates holding huddled figures in the gloom. One hand won't move, but when I shift the other, a line comes with it, red as life: a tube, feeding blood into my system from a bag that sways above.

The emergency blanket crinkles as I try to push myself to an elbow. A tangle of black hair comes into view. Silas, stretched across two metal chairs, his flight jacket hunched around him, sound asleep with exhaustion. I look at him, taking in every last inch of his face, before rolling onto my side.

I should not be moving. I can feel it, how close my body is to sundering as I set my bare feet on the cold night sand. Blue and yellow stars fill my vision. When they clear I see familiar figures. Rouf is slumped on a chair, snoring softly. Their ruined metal hand rests on the edge of the bed where Gabi lies asleep, her chest swathed in bandages. Across the room I see Falco and Peg, curled together on a single bunk.

With one hand I work the cannula free, wondering whose blood is filling my veins. A gift, a tribute. My clothes are stiff with stains. No matter. But at the foot of the bed, someone has placed my medkit, my hat. My belt that still holds the scalpel. Taking them up, I hobble like an old woman towards the opening in the tent.

As soon as I step outside, the night wind engulfs me and I sigh in relief, closing my eyes to hear its endless song. When I open my eyes again, they are there.

Six Seekers stand at the edge of the light, their boots and hands stained red from the day's harvest. I stand still as the leader walks towards me, the instruments at their belt clanking, their hand outstretched.

'Now?' they ask.

I look back over my shoulder into the tent, at Rouf and Gabi, Falco and Peg and Silas. Whatever happens, this fight will go on. And I will be what they need me to be. I will keep my promise.

I turn back to the Seeker. 'Now,' I answer.

Behind them, in the shadows, a figure with threadbare grey hair smiles.

And *they* are with me as I follow the Seekers into the darkness, a scalpel in my belt and a medical kit upon my back.

They are with me as I step onto the flight deck of a strange ship and collapse into the co-pilot's chair.

They are with me as I give the signal and we set off, unbound, into the future.

ACKNOWLEDGEMENTS

WRITING IS AN adventure, but there are times when it feels like a long road full of potholes and pit stops – so I'd like to thank the people who show up when the going is slow.

Firstly, to Nick, for helping me back to my feet more times than I can count. To George Sandison, legendary editor with the patience of a saint (unless you're a semicolon). To Michael, Katharine and everyone at Titan – for making these books a reality – and to Hélène for sending them out across the world. To my readers for showing up: there'd be no Factus without you. To my generous Patrons, especially Lee and David; I truly appreciate your support. To Becky, Charlie, E, M and A: *my* G'hals. To my family, and lastly to Lucy: sister-in-arms.

ABOUT THE AUTHOR

S TARK HOLBORN IS a novelist, games writer, film reviewer and the author of *Nunslinger*, the British Fantasy Award nominated Triggernometry series, and *Ten Low*. Stark lives in Bristol, UK.

Want more *Hel's Eight*?

To read an exclusive story visit starkholborn.com/factus

EMBERS OF WAR
by Gareth L. Powell

The sentient warship *Trouble Dog* was built for violence, yet following a brutal war, she is disgusted by her role in a genocide. Stripped of her weaponry and seeking to atone, she joins the House of Reclamation, an organisation dedicated to rescuing ships in distress. When a civilian ship goes missing in a disputed system, *Trouble Dog* and her new crew of loners, captained by Sal Konstanz, are sent on a rescue mission.

Meanwhile, light years away, intelligence officer Ashton Childe is tasked with locating the poet, Ona Sudak, who was aboard the missing spaceship. What Childe doesn't know is that Sudak is not the person she appears to be. A straightforward rescue turns into something far more dangerous, as *Trouble Dog*, Konstanz and Childe find themselves at the centre of a conflict that could engulf the entire galaxy. If she is to save her crew, *Trouble Dog* is going to have to remember how to fight…

"It's a smart, funny, tragic, galloping space opera that showcases Powell's wit, affection for his characters, world-building skills and unpredictable narrative inventions" – *Locus*

"This is fast, exhilarating space opera, imaginative and full of life" – Adrian Tchaikovsky, author of *Children of Time* and many more

"Powerful, classy and mind-expanding SF, in the tradition of Ann Leckie and Iain M. Banks." – Paul Cornell author the *Shadow Police* and *Witches of Lychford* series

TITANBOOKS.COM

For more fantastic fiction, author events,
exclusive excerpts, competitions, limited editions and more

VISIT OUR WEBSITE
titanbooks.com

LIKE US ON FACEBOOK
facebook.com/titanbooks

FOLLOW US ON TWITTER AND INSTAGRAM
@TitanBooks

EMAIL US
readerfeedback@titanemail.com